HEART'S EASE

HEART'S EASE

Sarah Harrison

This first world edition published 2019
in Great Britain and the USA by
SEVERN HOUSE PUBLISHERS LTD of
Eardley House, 4 Uxbridge Street, London W8 7SY.
Trade paperback edition first published
in Great Britain and the USA 2020 by
SEVERN HOUSE PUBLISHERS LTD.

British Library Cataloguing in Publication Data
A CIP catalogue record for this title is available from the British Library.

ISBN-13: 978-0-7278-8895-2 (cased)
ISBN-13: 978-1-78029-628-9 (trade paper)
ISBN-13: 978-1-4483-0321-2 (e-book)

All Severn House titles are printed on acid-free paper.

Severn House Publishers support the Forest Stewardship Council™ [FSC™],
the leading international forest certification organisation.
All our titles that are printed on FSC certified paper carry the FSC logo.

MIX
Paper from
responsible sources
FSC
www.fsc.org   FSC® C013056

Typeset by Palimpsest Book Production Ltd.,
Falkirk, Stirlingshire, Scotland.
Printed and bound in Great Britain by
TJ International, Padstow, Cornwall.

For those who lived there

London Borough of Hackney	
91300001074034	
Askews & Holts	
AF	£20.99
	6074153

One

The family set out at eleven thirty on the eve of the Queen's Jubilee. This, as Charity pointed out, would have them hanging around at the beacon for a good twenty minutes before anything started, but their mother decreed that it was vital to arrive in plenty of time, not only to secure a good place, but to soak up the atmosphere.

Soak was about right, observed Felicity, it was forecast to rain.

What did that matter? said Marguerite, it was practically midsummer!

Their father commented affably that it was theirs not to reason why.

Which was what Hugh usually said, give or take. His preferred line was that of least resistance, and it had stood him in good stead over nearly twenty years of marriage to Marguerite, being both emollient and a way of keeping his powder dry. Given any real objection on his part, he liked to think he was no pushover. But since real objections were vanishingly rare, there was little discord.

There were five Blyths leaving the house that night, the full complement so far: Hugh and Marguerite, and their daughters eighteen-year-old Felicity, Charity, rising sixteen, and Honor, eleven. They left just one lamp on in the house, to welcome them back later. As they crossed the wide grey pool of the lawn, the soft night gave up what small residual light it had, and they could see their way without the use of Hugh's torch. They passed with a 'clink' through the small metal gate between the rhododendrons, over the narrow lane, passing the sixth tee on their left, and on to the path that led up to the cliffs.

The route was a well-trodden one, the scene of so many family walks at all times and in all weathers that they could have negotiated it blindfold. On either side of the path was a bank, with trees growing out of it, the exposed roots twining and twisting down so it was hard to say whether the trees were clutching desperately at the earth, or the earth being held together by the trees. In daytime on the sunny side of the bank, the side that flanked the golf course, the girls used to hunt for adders. Felicity had even caught one once, using a forked stick, but when it slithered free quick as a whip they'd fled for all they were worth, shrieking in an ecstasy of fear.

Now it was Charity who walked ahead, at a brisk pace; Felicity followed, affecting to go at her own speed, but actually maintaining a safe distance from her younger sister. Bringing up the rear were Hugh and Marguerite with Honor. The three of them moved a little slower because Marguerite's due date was only three weeks away.

The sisters had reacted characteristically to their mother's pregnancy. Felicity, with a string of admirers and a prospective flat-share in Fulham, found it faintly disgusting, as if her parents at their advanced age should have known better than to cling on to normal sexual function, let alone flaunt it in the all-too-noticeable form of a late pregnancy. She was just glad that she wasn't going to be around much.

Charity was not censorious, but drily amused. 'Don't tell me that was an accident – after all this time they must know how it works!'

Only Honor was unashamedly thrilled. She walked protectively next to her mother, keeping in step, imagining the baby bobbing along next to her in its safe bubble, wondering about its hair colour, its weight, its sex . . .

Whenever she asked, 'What do you think it is?' her father always said, 'A baby I sincerely hope', and her mother, 'A surprise', which got her no further forward.

Charity had reached the place on their walk where during the day you had to stop to look out for golfers teeing up or driving off. Now she strode straight across the fairway to where the path in a narrower form plunged between the black ramparts of gorse and scurried on its way to the cliff top.

Despite being a little impatient with her family, which was nothing new, she was enjoying the expedition. The Silver Jubilee was history, of a sort, and she was secretly excited by the idea of the message leaping from beacon to beacon as the flames were lit. And she was prepared to concede, as she led the way, that her mother had been right to make them come early. You wanted to be able to see everything! It was pitch dark on this stretch, but the prickly fingers of gorse on either side kept her on track, and soon she could make out the paler grey of the skyline – nearly there.

Felicity slowed down a little on the fairway, still susceptible to this first sight of the sea. Salting Bay was invisible from here, but to the right you could make out the long wavering arm of the coastline reaching westward, broken only by the river estuary a few miles away. Between here and the estuary a single set of gliding car lights marked the ribbon of road that led to the cove they used to like going to as children. Not many people bothered to go down to the beach, there were no 'facilities' and the access was via a rickety wooden staircase, but once you were down it was like being in your own kingdom, with the sweep of sand guarded at either end by buttresses of rock. Felicity hadn't been there for at least a couple of years but in private moments she imagined taking her own children there, dipping baby toes in the waves, making a castle with a moat and pebbles, eating egg mayonnaise sandwiches with a tiny crunch of grit . . .

Marguerite marched at a steady pace between her husband and youngest daughter. This simple exercise was good for the baby, she could feel the well-oxygenated blood coursing round her system, her muscles strengthening for what they would soon have to do. At the cottage hospital they said things like, 'Number four? Oh well, you're a practised hand then!', but all experience had taught her was that each birth, like each baby, was unique, and anything could happen. You needed to be strong and healthy – they didn't call it labour for nothing.

Hugh touched her arm. 'OK, Daisy?'

'Fine!'

'You, my girl?'

'Yes thanks.' Honor was glad of the soft darkness that hid her blushing squirm of pleasure. Though he had three daughters, her father reserved 'my girl' for her, perhaps because she was the youngest. She hoped if the baby was a girl he wouldn't simply transfer it to her. Honor's was not a jealous nature, but

she would find that hard to bear. Not that she considered herself
a favourite, parents had no favourites as her mother always
said, and anyway she wasn't favourite material, being plump,
plain and neither brainy nor sporty. Sometimes she suspected
that those were the very reasons he called her his girl – because
she needed a bit of a boost. But if so she wasn't complaining. It
was nice.

Hugh was a happy man, walking through the midsummer night
with his trio of daughters and his lovely, fecund wife. He was
aware that nowadays such thoughts might be construed by some
as unregenerate male chauvinism, but that didn't tarnish his
pleasure. He was proud of his ladies, even when male friends and
colleagues made wry remarks about the escalating cost of weddings.
Indeed he half hoped that this fourth one would be a girl too,
so the picture would remain complete, and he the only man in it.
But this was a kind of private joke with himself, and he knew that
whatever happened he would be absolutely delighted.

The family were all at the beacon by a quarter to twelve. Over a
hundred people had already foregathered, and more were still
arriving via the Salting cliff path, and from the direction of the
golf club which had judiciously laid on a late licence and buffet
supper for members who might want to attend. There were
plenty there who knew the Blyths and Charity, who along with
a conspicuously pregnant mother had a brisk manner and sharp
elbows, got them a place near the front. Hugh, being extremely tall,
remained politely at the rear.

The beacon stood on a smooth patch of rising ground
amongst the gorse bushes between the cliff edge and the seventh
fairway. The path itself, in a continual state of erosion, was not
considered safe for large numbers so the golf club had taped off
a generous corral for the crowd. There were plenty of torches,
and the small group of dignitaries near the beacon carried lanterns
provided for the occasion. The official lighter was to be Mrs
Drake, a young widow who as well as a very suitable name had
the same birthday as the queen. Her two teenage boys, a touch
awkward in attendance, wore anoraks over their collar-and-ties.
As the moment approached the mayor announced that they
should all look out for the beacon ten miles to the east – the

signal for theirs to be lit. Mrs Drake mounted the small wooden dais and the younger of her two boys jumped up and down to try and get a look over people's heads.

'Yes!'

'There!'

'There it is!'

'Look – can you see?'

And there it was, a distant, flickering yellow flower and a pale ribbon of smoke unspooling into the dark sky. Those at the front stood aside and pointed, children were lifted up, people stood on tiptoe, oohing and aahing. And then it was time to light theirs, and Mrs Drake was handed the taper and applied it to the sticks and logs piled in the metal basket. There was some nervous laughter when at first it didn't catch, but then the flames took hold, and all their faces were warmed and illuminated by the crackling brightness. Just as it did on bonfire night, the fire drew them together in a simple, primitive way. Mrs Drake was helped down and people clinked cups of coffee and beakers of wine. The mayor said, 'God bless her Majesty!' and that became the general toast.

Felicity had bumped into people she knew, so for her this had become a social occasion. Charity had brought her camera to obviate the need for small talk, and was taking photographs, though the likelihood of the flash working was remote with so much competition from the beacon.

Honor remained by her mother, but an old gentleman next to her needed to sit down, and she carried his cup of soup while he was helped to one of the two benches which in the daytime afforded a sweeping view. Having parked him she returned.

'There's room if you want to sit down, Ma.'

'Do you know, I think I'm alright.'

'OK.'

'You don't have to keep an eye on me, as long as you don't go too far.'

Given leave to wander, Honor wasn't sure where to, or even if she wanted to. Charity was sidling around the edge of the crowd lining up potential shots on her camera and Felicity was at the centre of a small group of vivacious friends.

'We don't want to lose you in the dark,' added Marguerite.

Honor thought that the best way to avoid such a thing would
be to stay where she was, but not wanting to seem either un-
adventurous or, more importantly, over-protective of her mother,
she moved away a little and gazed up admiringly at the beacon
which was now blazing merrily. Somewhere in the crowd behind
her she could discern Felicity's clear, teasing voice. She and the
others were discussing a barbecue on the beach.

'Exton Point, right . . .? There won't be many people, they'll
all be watching the queen on the box . . . I know, but it doesn't
matter about the weather, does it? Does it? I'll bring a bottle
of plonk . . .'

Felicity was enviably lively and attractive. Everyone knew it,
everyone said so. She was 'a delightful girl', as well as being slim
and tawny-blonde. Honor didn't grudge or envy her any of these
attributes. If she, Honor, had looked like that, she might have
felt obliged to organize beach barbecues, tennis, trips to pop
concerts and so on, when there was nothing she'd have hated
more. Honor liked to be at home, or when occasion demanded
in other people's homes. In her limited experience there was
quite enough drama and entertainment to be had from domestic
life. People like her parents and her older sister Felicity talked about
'Fun' as if it were something one was supposed to be having,
but the sort of things they meant didn't interest her. For now
that didn't matter much, but she worried there would soon
come a time when she would be exhorted to go out and have the
dreaded Fun, and she didn't look forward to it.

She went and sat down on the bench next to old Mr Jessop.
'Was the soup nice?'

He peered into the mug as if to remind himself. 'Very nice. Very
tasty. My thanks to whoever made it.'

Honor was pretty sure that was Mr Heinz, but she didn't say
so, and took the empty mug.

'Who did you come with?' she asked, and then hoped that
didn't sound rude, as though he were incapable of getting here
under his own steam. But Mr Jessop was gentleman enough always
to be appreciative and not touchy.

'My kind neighbours gave me a hand. Do you know the
Collingses, Geoffry and Iris?' Honor shook her head. 'They're
very good to me, I'm very lucky.'

'That's nice.' Honor liked to think of these good neighbours. She hoped someone would say the same of her one day.

'We parked at the golf club and they towed me up the fairway.'

'We're lucky, we live quite close.'

'I know.' Mr Jessop gave her the sort of smile in which a wink was implicit. 'Heart's Ease, am I right?'

'Yes.'

'A lovely house.'

'It is.'

Honor would have been happy to continue this conversation with Mr Jessop but just then Charity arrived, camera over her shoulder, with an air of brisk urgency.

'Honor – sorry to interrupt – Honor, we need to go. Ma's started.'

Honor looked blank. 'What?'

Charity puffed an impatient sigh. 'What do you *think*?'

Marguerite's first reaction was, 'Oh no, for heaven's sake, not here, not now!' But at least this time no one else could see. When her waters had broken with Felicity she'd been standing in Gents' Clothing in Marks and Sparks, and it had caused not just a mess, but a considerable stir as well-meaning staff rushed to mop up and get her out of the way of the lambswool jumpers. Now she felt the pop and gush, and there was the familiar warm, salty smell as the liquid coursed down her legs, soaking her shoes and stockings. Everyone around her was chatting, drinking, gazing up at the blazing beacon. She cast round for Hugh and saw him a little further back, deep in conversation. She waved vigorously and began making her way back to him, but he'd seen the wave and came to meet her.

'All well? Something happening?'

'Yes, I need to go.'

'You mean go as in *go*?'

'Back to the phone, the hospital.' She stretched her eyes. 'Urgently!'

Realization dawned. 'Right – OK. Wait there and I'll round up the girls—'

'Felicity can stay longer if she wants to, as long as she walks back with someone.'

'Alright, the other two – hang on, don't go anywhere.'

Hugh disappeared. Marguerite told herself to remain calm, there was time in hand. Wendy Waller hove alongside.

'Hello! I didn't expect to find you here.'

'We wouldn't have missed it for anything,' said Marguerite. 'But actually we'll be off soon.'

'Ditto,' Wendy agreed. 'Beacon duly lit, fizz duly drunk, and it's not that warm for June, is it? Here's Hugh, evening!'

Hugh took his wife's arm. 'Charity's fetching Honor and they'll be hard on our heels – hi there, Wendy – so let's get going.'

'Are you quite sure they're—?'

'Charity's on the case. Trust me, they'll be on their way. Bye.'

Seconds later, the two daughters appeared.

'Hello girls, your parents have just—'

The younger one, Honor, blurted out a 'Hello' but the teenager simply stalked on without a glance and Wendy went to find someone else with whom to share the potential news.

Felicity stayed another half an hour, but it wasn't quite the same. Family matters had taken over as they so often did. She'd been through this particular one twice before and it was always a bloody upheaval, she might as well go home. Pete Spurling was all too keen to walk back with her but following her father's advice would mean dealing with Pete's enthusiasm en route, so she fudged it by saying she had another offer and would be fine. Only the first was a lie. The path home held no terrors for her, the beacon was still burning and there was the planned barbecue to look forward to in a few days' time.

A friend of her mother's lent her a torch, and the quiet walk home did her good. As she passed between the enclosing gorse bushes, over the soft, tranquil space of the fairway and down the avenue of twisty trees towards Heart's Ease, she reminded herself that the arrival of another sibling was supposed to be a happy event. Ma was healthy and strong, Pa was with her, and for a while following the birth, normal service would be suspended while they ate shop-bought food and takeaways, and the routine of domestic life was disrupted by feeds, and people taking naps, dropping off at funny times and stumbling about at night while the baby yelled.

Felicity herself definitely wanted to be in possession of three children of her own ten years from now, but when she pictured this it was usually in idealized form: herself presiding over the unwrapping of presents before the fire at Christmas; frolicking on a deserted beach in summer; or serving food at Sunday lunch at which her parents (the most benign of grandparents), but not her sisters, would be present. A little further down the road the picture was of herself at some school event – shiny-eyed at a play, modestly proud at prize-giving, breasting the tape with skirt flying in the mothers' race . . .

As she went through the back gate she saw there were several lights on in the house, and the door of the conservatory (for some reason always called the loggia) must have been open because the labrador Mavis came trundling out, tail wagging, carrying her soft toy in tribute.

They greeted one another and went in, Mavis leading the way. There was that unmistakable sense of something going on – the television in the family room at the end of the house, voices from behind a door upstairs, the sound of what might have been a chair being moved about. The door of the dining room was open and Felicity could see Charity with a newspaper spread out on the table in front of her.

She went in. 'What's going on? Are they still here? I thought they'd be gone.'

'No, they're here,' murmured Charity offhandedly without looking up.

'But why? Shouldn't Ma be in hospital?'

Charity turned a page. 'Probably.'

'What's that supposed to mean?'

'I mean it looks as though she'll be having it right here.'

'What? Now?'

'Well, not next week.'

'Sarcasm is the lowest form of wit.' If Felicity hoped to get a rise out of her sister, it didn't work. 'Where's Honor, then?'

'She was watching telly, but you know what she is. Probably up there' – Charity jerked her head upwards – 'getting involved.'

'Is anyone else coming?' Felicity was worried now. If their mother was actually going to have the baby under this roof, what might be required of the rest of them? Whatever it was, she didn't fancy it. 'They did call the hospital, I assume?'

'They did, but everything was moving a bit quickly.' Charity, quite gratified to be the one in the know, warmed to her theme and became more animated. 'I think some district nurse or other is due to show up.'

'I bloody well hope so!'

Charity smirked theatrically. 'Otherwise it'll be all hands to the pumps, or whatever's required.'

'Oh God!'

'Come on,' said Charity, 'where's your spirit of adventure?'

Just then a door opened upstairs. There was a keening sound, and their father's voice making encouraging noises, and Honor leaned over the banister. 'Hey, you two!'

Charity grimaced at Felicity. 'Told you . . . *What?*'

'The baby's arriving!'

'Glad to hear it!'

The keening rose in pitch, Honor flapped her arms. 'Do you want to come? Come on!'

'No thanks, keep us posted.'

Just then the doorbell rang, and Felicity took the opportunity to answer it. Mavis's friendly woofing almost drowning out Hugh's bellow of, 'It's a boy!'

So it was that Iris the community midwife stepped over the threshold of Heart's Ease, to find herself at the end of a chain of Blyths: Mavis round her legs; Felicity in the hall; Charity at the foot of the stairs; Honor halfway down; Hugh on the landing; and, somewhere in the upper reaches, mother and baby, the latter in good fettle if the screeching was anything to go by.

'Sounds as if I'm too late,' she said, hurrying in the direction of the noise, adding cheerfully, 'but all well.'

Felicity didn't reply. Charity turned a page. Honor led Iris in the direction of the main event.

Two

A boy! At speed, at home, in the early hours of the Queen's Silver Jubilee! The story of Bruno's precipitate arrival became part of Blyth family lore and Bruno lapped it up with his mother's milk.

No one gave him explicitly to understand that he was a golden child – as parents Marguerite and Hugh were far too wise for that – but they didn't have to. It was implicit in the circumstances of his birth. And then, of course, he was an enchanting boy, a real heartbreaker with dark hair, round grey eyes fringed with sooty lashes, and a winning manner. He wasn't always sweet and good, there was an impish streak in Bruno and he could be a little devil, but that was true of any boy worth his salt.

Honor loved him the most. She'd been there, after all, when he'd appeared, when her father, a surprised expression on his face, had caught him as he slithered out all sticky and new. She knew right away there could never, ever, be a moment in her life as exciting as this one. A whole person, with a loud, scratchy quavering voice and waving fists, who had been until a moment ago inside Ma! And Ma was fine, moaning and puffing (and swearing a bit) while it was going on, and then laughing with delight, and Pa the same, somehow astonished but tremendously pleased with themselves at having beaten the nurse to it. By the time her sisters arrived on the scene she, Honor, had been holding the baby, proud as punch. He didn't have a name then, or for a couple of weeks afterwards, he was just referred to as 'Boy' and that stuck for quite a while.

In spite of her carefully-assumed cool, Charity was interested in the events of that summer night. A purely scientific interest, she told herself. By her calculation the baby had arrived exactly one hour after their mother's waters had broken, which was rapid by any standard, and Marguerite had obviously delivered with something of a flourish – if not painlessly, then certainly not in agony. She deserved some respect for that. Honor, as Charity recalled, had been born in hospital with no complications that anyone knew of (Marguerite had been home in a couple of days) but this had taken place right there in what Felicity referred to rather prissily as 'peasant-style'. Charity was amused by both peasanty-ness and the prissiness, and the baby looked fine to her, especially compared with some you saw being wheeled around who were just plain plug-ugly, like mewling gargoyles. That it was a boy was neither here nor there, why should that be a big deal? She believed her parents when they said they didn't care as long as it was healthy. But all in all, in the back of Charity's mind the notion was forming that she herself would never want children.

Felicity, whose fantasy it was to be the graceful mother of a Bruno, found herself rather resentful of this single intruder. She recognized the reaction as undignified, but couldn't help herself. The baby's arrival had even upstaged the queen, for heaven's sake. She supposed he was sweet – prettier than the girls had been anyway – and she joined in the general cooing and passing round, but her heart wasn't in it. She wanted no part of this boy-centred household. The sooner she got back up to London the better. She had a job in the MG showroom in Piccadilly which suited her down to the ground, and though she quite liked the country stuff down here in Salting, she missed (even more now) the footloose hedonism of her London gang. The pungent domesticity of the perinatal period really got on her nerves. She swore she could actually smell the birth, a warm, sweetish aroma that hung about for hours, days, along with all that washing in the utility room like something from the Crimean War. It wasn't nice.

In London she had what her father called 'a swain'. The swain's name was Gerry. The boys down here, Pete among them, were referred to by Hugh as 'followers'. Old-fashioned terms, but expressing a crucial difference which she was pleased he recognized. Gerry's entire attention was devoted to her; Pete and co were, as the term implied, sheep wanting to bask in the reflected glow of her beauty and popularity. Felicity was not so much vain as a realist, who recognized her own social value, and it was worth more than either Gerry or the sheep. Before her dream of glammy motherhood could be realized, she'd have to meet someone worthy of her steel. She wanted to be challenged, before (naturally) carrying the day.

Anyway, here was Bruno, and she had another two days of the whole thing to endure before she was due to return to the Smoke – her father's word, he would never understand that to her London was the sunny uplands.

Bruno saved his first full assault on the Blyths' combined nerves for three a.m. Marguerite hauled herself out of bed, Hugh sat up with a snort and lay down again, but three hours later he was intoning, 'Macbeth hath murdered sleep . . .', as he paced and jiggled with the dawn breaking outside the window and his wife lying torpid and open-mouthed on top of the covers.

Charity woke only briefly before returning to the calm sleep of the supremely uninterested and uninvolved. Felicity lay awake throughout, vainly trying to drown out the racket with her transistor and vowing to exchange her return train ticket for an earlier one if humanly possible and at whatever cost.

Honor on the other hand was there in seconds.

'Is he alright?'

'Of course he is, he's just hungry,' said Marguerite. 'Now go back to bed.'

'But I can't sleep. Are you sure he's OK? He's crying so hard.'

'It's what little babies do, you'll soon get used to it.'

'Really . . .?' mumbled Hugh. 'Just like the rest of us? Get a tit out woman, do.'

'Hugh, *pas devant*—'

'OK, yes – come along my girl, to bed.'

'Please? Till he goes back to sleep?'

'That could be a long time.'

'*Please* . . .?'

Honor's eyes drifted towards her mother who was attempting a docking manoeuvre between her nipple and the baby's vibrating maw. Hugh pulled a helpless, shrugging sort of face.

'Any objections, Daisy?'

'Alright, come on.' Marguerite tweaked the duvet. 'Hop in.' She glanced up at Hugh as Honor leapt aboard. 'I could murder a cup of tea.'

'Good idea, I'll make that two—'

'Can I have one?' asked Honor.

'Or even three.'

For years thereafter Honor considered the next half an hour or so the happiest in her life. Sitting in her parents' big soft bed, with the baby's silky head next to her, her mother quietly, passively occupied, her father pottering about downstairs and then coming in with sweet tea – it was a memory of perfect contentment, a personal heaven.

Even when things became a lot less restful, she still loved every moment. Now that she'd been reassured that there was nothing seriously wrong, she didn't mind holding her screeching baby brother, and it was thrilling to realize as the day outside turned grey, and the birds began a first desultory cheeping, that they had been up all night!

That of course was Bruno's cue to fall asleep. Hugh lowered him into the bassinet as though handling a live bomb, and they all three collapsed on the bed and passed out.

Charity had switched on the television to watch the jubilee procession. She quirked an eyebrow as Felicity came in.

'So?'

'Out of it, all of them.' Felicity flopped down on the sofa. 'Think we should wake them – you know – for this?'

'Good God no.'

They sat side by side gazing dispassionately at the gold coach, the sea of people, the queen in pastel pink, the duke in uniform.

'That must be several pounds of gold braid he's got on there,' remarked Charity.

'She looks nice. So much better when she smiles.'

After another minute or so Felicity, her eyes still on the screen, remarked, 'I'm going back to London tomorrow.'

'Don't blame you.'

'I'll have to buy another pricey single, but frankly . . . You know?'

'Quite. Wish I had the option.' Charity and Honor were both at the local private girls' school and for Charity this royal day off came right in the middle of O Levels. She was expected by others, not to mention herself, to do well, but even so the timing wasn't brilliant.

Felicity asked cautiously, 'Everyone seems fine, don't they?'

'Yes. And anyway' – Charity jabbed a finger at the ceiling – 'Honor is on the case.'

'God, I know! She puts us to shame.'

'*I* don't feel shamed, she loves it. Not just the baby – the whole thing.'

'Actually she does, doesn't she?'

'Also, we've been through it before, especially you,' observed Charity carelessly. 'The novelty's worn off.'

There followed another silence during which the camera

picked out faces in the crowd, before cutting to other members of the royal family waiting in St Paul's.

'Princess Margaret's wearing pink too!' observed Felicity. 'Isn't that a bit strange?'

Charity said drily, 'I'm sure they've discussed it.'

'I still think it's odd. We've all read Margaret can be a bit tricky.'

'The question is more – why pink?'

'That too . . .'

They relapsed into silence.

Marguerite was the first to wake. She extricated herself from the heap on the bed, took a peep at Bruno, and padded downstairs and along the passage to the family room.

'Oh my goodness, it's that – of course – maybe I'll watch a bit of the queen.'

Felicity shunted up. 'Would you like some coffee?'

'Tea would be bliss, darling, two sugars.'

As her sister went to the kitchen, Charity asked, 'How are things?'

Marguerite sighed, with a smile. 'The night was a bit lively as you probably gathered. But he's sleeping it off now, and so are the others – good lord they're both wearing pink.'

'Felicity said that.'

'Queenie looks better in hers today, which is as it should be.'

Felicity came back with the tea. 'Actually I agree.'

Charity got up and went back into the hall and out through the loggia into the garden. In the dining room they had a framed photograph of the house as it used to be – it was an enlargement of the estate agent's shot – which showed what was now the conservatory as a sort of large open-fronted porch, with a low wall and wooden uprights bordering the garden. She'd always liked the look of that and half-wished it was still the same.

To the right of the lawn was the Fort (the origin of the name lost to memory), a miniature hill covered in tussocky grass and fringed by scots pines in which the wood pigeons crooned languidly in the early morning. Just now she could hear the distant seagulls – those and the pigeons were the background music of home. The sky was heavy with clouds, she felt the first large, soft drops as she crossed the lawn. Three energetic strides took Charity to the top of the Fort, where a broad flat stump provided a vantage point. She stood on this, and looked out over the top of the massed rhododendrons – now in all their pink, white and crimson glory – to the broad bay of Salting, two miles away at the foot of the hill. They all loved this place in their different ways even when they wanted to get away from it. She was a realist, she suspected she would never again live in a house like this – in such a beautiful location, with such pleasing proportions and so benign an atmosphere. She'd heard more than one person call it 'the nicest house in Salting' and she believed them. There were plenty of bigger, smarter, better appointed houses, but surely none with the magic of Heart's Ease.

The rain was pattering down now, blurring her view of the bay and making the fat, glorious rhododendron blooms shimmer and tremble. Looking towards the house Charity saw Honor looking out of their parents' bedroom window. She was holding the baby, gazing rapt into his face and Hugh was standing just behind her. When he saw Charity looking he gave her a wave over Honor's shoulder.

She had been going to go back in but now, rain notwithstanding, she went down the back of the mound, through the bracken, and out of the front gate for a walk. Her uncharacteristically sentimental mood turned more practical. Tomorrow was RE. Charity was no believer, but this was one of her strongest subjects and she fully expected to sail through and emerge with flying colours.

Hugh, with Honor carrying Bruno, trooped into the family room as the congregation was raising the roof with 'All creatures that on earth do dwell'.

'And here we all are, right on cue,' said Hugh. 'I sense the moment is approaching where none of the rest of us is likely to be much good.'

Marguerite remained where she was and held out her arms.

'I could give him a bottle,' suggested Honor. 'I changed him.'

'She did,' said Hugh. 'In fact she was rather more competent first time out than I'd have been with years of practice.'

'Well done, Honor. And you can give him a bottle in due course but just for now he needs me.'

Honor handed over Bruno who was already starting to stretch and make small explosive grunting noises. On the television, the royal family and the mighty congregation went about their majestic business. In the family room of Heart's Ease the Blyths gazed with a variety of emotions at Bruno, with fewer hours in his life than the queen had years in her reign.

Three

1984

'Coming, ready or not!'

In the silence, Sasha's own voice rang in her ears. Up here you were so far out of town and the garden was so massive, you couldn't hear anything – no traffic, no people (at the moment), even the seagulls were too far away. And she didn't trust Bruno further than she could throw him. He was one of those kids who was all smiles and cuteness on the surface, and a right sneaky little bugger underneath. He could easily be hiding really nearby, spying on her and having a laugh.

The rules were, no hiding in the house, or in any outbuildings. She turned round on the spot, scanning her immediate surroundings: the 'loggia' (she had no idea), the encircling green wall of giant bushes, the weird hilly thing . . . He'd been wearing a pale blue Smurfs T-shirt but she glimpsed nothing, and there wasn't the smallest movement or rustle. Sasha wouldn't have put it past him to cheat, or camouflage himself in some way.

It creeped her out, standing there. Time to get moving. Six o'clock in mid-September she didn't fancy still wandering about the garden in an hour when it would be dusk. There would be the usual shenanigans about no ice-cream, upstairs and bath, and then she'd have to endure the agony of reading aloud, something she didn't like and was no good at, but which was apparently indispensable.

As Sasha set off on a systematic sweep of the garden she reflected grumpily that this was a lot more than she'd normally expect to do for a babysit. On her card in the post office she billed herself as 'responsible, experienced babysitter, 16 yrs'. Her ideal was to show up at seven when her charge or charges were in bed, see the parents off on their night out and consume whatever had been left out in front of the TV (she wasn't fussy, chocolate, crisps, cake, biscuits, 'there's the breadbin'). She didn't mind a certain amount of toddler-soothing during the course of the evening, that made her feel useful, and if there was uncontrollable yelling she could always ring the parents.

This was different. She had to entertain the dreaded Bruno for an hour before bedtime. She never wanted to be a nanny, just a babysitter. On the other hand the Blyths were nice, Mrs B was kind and lovely and Mr B was funny, and they invariably added a couple of quid to her rate – 'danger money' Mr B called it – at the end of the evening. If only she didn't feel so nervous. The place was so big, and she couldn't help feeling that Bruno had the drop on her. He was a smart, spoiled kid on his own patch which gave him bully's rights. She felt it now, as she paced stealthily round the back of the hill and down the narrow green alleyway behind the bushes. She should never have agreed to hide-and-seek out of doors. Fuck's sake, she might never find him! And what if he had an accident, fell down the boiler room steps, out of a tree, broke his ankle . . . At that moment Sasha wished herself anywhere but at Heart's Ease.

After a good five minutes by her watch, she stopped and called.
'Bru-no, Bruno-oo, give us a cooee!'
Nothing.
'Bru-no! Give us a—'
This time she heard it, the faintest, most distant, '. . . ooo . . . eee . . .' like a late, far-off echo. It was difficult to tell what direction it came from, but since she was on the boundary of the garden, and had already been round the hill, she kept going anti-clockwise in the direction of the kitchen garden, the fruit cage, and the murky far corner which contained the compost and bonfire piles. This part of the garden was at the bottom of a slope, so the house loomed above her to her

left, like a ship riding at anchor on its surrounding wave of green. Sasha didn't care for the big bushes, the flowers were pretty in the summer, but the insides were like dark tents. She'd checked but Bruno wasn't in any of them, that would have been far too obvious.

Stupid game.

She advanced on the fruit cage. The call had sounded further away, but it'd be just like him to hide in there so he could fill his face with raspberries *and* give her the runaround. Bucked up by this possibility, she opened the wire door, but just as she did so she heard the distant summons of the phone in the house. She hesitated, but only briefly – if that was Mrs B calling to check and she didn't answer, what on earth would they think?

She ran along the track, up the steps, and through the loggia into the hall. The phone's ringing was loud and peremptory, she was sweating and out of breath as she answered.

'. . . Hello?'

A pause. 'Who is that?' A woman's voice she didn't recognize.

'It's Sasha. The babysitter?'

'Right, in that case I know the answer to my question.'

'Can I help?'

'I was going to ask to speak to Mrs Blyth.'

'Mr and Mrs Blyth are out.'

'Well, yes – I gathered,' said the stranger coolly. 'Since you're there.'

'Can I take a message?'

'Why not? Have you got something to write with?'

Sasha picked up the biro that was attached by string to a spiral-backed notebook. 'Yes.'

'Please can you tell them Felicity called?'

'Felicity . . .' Sasha wrote it down. 'Shall I put a number?'

'It's alright, they know that. I'm their daughter.'

'Oh! Sorry.' Sasha wasn't sure what to make of this. So the Blyths had this posh, grown-up daughter as well as the little terror. It was disconcerting.

'That's alright, you weren't to know.' There was a hint of a smile in the voice now. 'So how are you getting on?'

Relieved at the slightly warmer tone, Sasha said, 'We're playing hide-and-seek before bed.'

Felicity gave a little laugh. 'Good luck with that! Who's hiding at the moment?'

'He is – Bruno.'

'I bet he is. How long have you been looking?'

'I'm not sure . . . for a while.'

'Want a tip?'

'Yes please.' Sasha's reply was heartfelt.

'Don't knock yourself out searching.'

'Really . . .?' Easy for her to say, thought Sasha, what was she supposed to do, just leave him out there?

'Let him stew,' said Felicity, reading her mind. 'Once he thinks *you've* lost interest, he will.'

This made a certain sense, but Sasha was torn between the impulse to put Bruno in his place, and her responsibility to Mr and Mrs B.

'Are you sure?'

'Completely. I know the workings of his horrible tiny mind.'

Sasha couldn't deny it was a comfort to come across a person who appeared to take the same view as her. And his sister, no less.

Tentatively she asked, 'So, what, just stay in here and wait for him to show up?'

'That's right – sorry, I've forgotten your name?'

'Sasha.'

'Sasha. Believe me, he will. Nothing kills a prank stone dead quicker than being ignored.'

'OK.'

'Anyway, got to go. Just be sure to let them know I called.'

'I will. Thanks—'

But she was talking to herself. The handset gave off its blank, indifferent buzz, and she put it down. The house lay around her, deathly quiet. She felt a prickle of anxiety, but she had accepted the sister's advice so she might as well act on it, and sit tight.

There was a small half-landing on the turning point of the stairs, with a window affording a view of the front drive. Sasha sat on the end of the windowsill, from where she could also see part of the loggia. She reckoned she'd got the situation pretty well covered, but she still hoped Bruno wouldn't take too long to get the hump and come back. This was a risky strategy.

The silence seemed to take on a gloopy, tactile quality. When she changed position, however slightly, she felt she was pushing the air around her. A strange tabby cat stalked across the drive, head low, something no cat would ever have done if the dear old dog had still been around. Halfway across it paused and, motionless, looked up directly at Sasha with empty yellow eyes. Spooked, she was tempted to turn the light on, though it wasn't yet dark, but that would advertise her presence in the house and if she was to call his bluff her whereabouts had to remain a mystery.

And, she reminded herself, this was just the start of the evening. Once Bruno turned up there was the whole rigmarole of bath, and teeth, and story, and going to bed, before she could even think of flopping down in front of the telly. The Blyths had gone with friends to a show at the Northcott Theatre in Exeter, there was no way they'd be back before eleven. There were sausage rolls and potato salad in the kitchen, she yearned for the moment she could sink her teeth into the flaky pastry, the peppery sausagemeat, the slippery new potatoes in their silky covering of mayonnaise and chives . . . Her mouth watered . . .

How had she let herself be at the mercy of a spoilt seven-year-old boy?

Bugger it, she was going to go to the kitchen, turn on the light, and have some supper.

She went first to the family room and turned on the television. The local news was on, the most boring programme known to man, but better than the endless miners with their placards. She left it chatting away while she put the sausage rolls in a low oven – they were ever so much nicer warm. Then she went back along to the hall and turned the light on there – in for a penny in for a pound. It was definitely becoming dusk outside, and turning on the light made it seem even darker. She went out of the front door and stood on the drive, where the cat had been, looking all around. The metal five-bar gate stood open awaiting the Blyths' return later on, and a woman (it was Wendy Waller) with a spaniel on a lead walked past in the direction of the footpath. She waved cheerily to Sasha.

'Hi!'

'Hello.'

'Lovely evening!' the woman called as she went on her way. 'But they're drawing in, aren't they? We need to get a move on!' This little encounter cheered Sasha up. She was not alone, and the natives were friendly. That posh, energetic woman would definitely have been on her side in the battle of wills with Bruno, just like his sister. For a moment she felt herself at one with the world of beleaguered, right-minded adults.

The front door had a Yale latch and closed with a satisfying clunk behind her. An appetising whiff of sausage roll wafted along the corridor to greet her. Mrs B's note said the potato salad was in the green bowl in the larder. She had not yet turned the light on in the family room, but the telly cast its comforting, flickering glow as she crossed and opened the larder door. There was only one small window high on the far wall, so the narrow room was in semi darkness.

'Hello.'

The disembodied voice came from somewhere below her. Shocked and disorientated Sasha let out a loud shriek.

'It's only me.'

'Who?'

Her hand scrabbled for the light switch. Bruno was sitting cross-legged under the marble shelf at the back. How stupid was she, who else would it have been?

'You gave me the fright of my life!' she scolded. 'What are you doing in here?'

'Getting some cake.'

There was indeed a rather dilapidated Victoria sponge under a plastic cover on the side, but there was no sign of it having been cut, and Bruno wasn't holding any.

'Sorry,' he said, pre-emptively.

'No you're not, you're hiding.'

'Only because I heard you coming.'

'You weren't supposed to be hiding in the house!' said Sasha. She sounded childish, but she couldn't help it. Her heart was still racing with anxiety, and the fact that he'd caused it made her angry, too.

He crawled out. 'Well you were in here and I heard you coming.'

She couldn't be bothered to argue, but snatched the green bowl off the shelf.

'Do you want cake, then? It's bedtime.'

'No not really, I'll go up.'

This docile capitulation was as surprising as the original discovery. He edged past her looking almost crestfallen. Sasha reminded herself that this was a nice little job.

'I'll come up in a bit, alright?'

'OK.'

She watched as he sloped off down the passage. Was she just imagining a forlorn slump to his shoulders? Perhaps, she reflected, she had been too sharp, but he had given her a fright – and meant to as well. Maybe that was only mischief and she shouldn't have overreacted, but he was so – she struggled to find a word – so *tricky*. Even now, as she listened to him scampering upstairs (with a light tread now, she noticed) she suspected the joke was well and truly on her. She'd called his bluff and he'd come right back at her. She cringed when she thought of her shriek; talk about playing into his hands!

In need of the crudest comfort, Sasha turned off the oven and consumed one of the sausage rolls right then and there, opening and shutting her mouth and hopping from foot to foot (it was hot) and shedding greasy flakes of pastry on the floor and down her front in the process. Then she dug into the potato salad with a pudding spoon while the telly burbled on in the background.

Warmed and calmed by the food, she wondered how long to leave him before going up. She'd more or less decided not to get on his case about washing and teeth, and if he was happy looking at a comic, or drawing, she wouldn't press a bedtime story on him either. At least the older sister had understood, so it wasn't just her who found herself on the back foot the whole time.

She sat down in front of the telly for ten minutes to kill time, and then went up. Once again, it was so quiet it was hard to believe there was anyone else in the house. The Blyths' bedroom was to the right of the landing, with a window overlooking the garden and the Fort. To the left was the large spare room with two beds and an old-fashioned wash basin with massive brass taps. Bruno's was the first door along the passage that ran above the kitchen and family room. There were two more along there which were referred to as 'the girls'' rooms, meaning the middle sisters, but they weren't around much as far as Sasha could tell. Sasha had only met the younger one, Honor, and that only once – she was really friendly and nice. In photographs (of which there many around the house, especially in the loos) you could see that the oldest girl – the one who'd rung earlier – was the good-looking one. She was really glamorous in a posh way, with swingy hair and shiny skin – she seemed to have lots of friends and went skiing and sailing. Sasha was glad that the first time she'd spoken to her was on the phone, or she might have been intimidated. Now that she was an ally, she wouldn't be nervous if they met.

Now she turned down the passage, past the family bathroom which was huge, with black and white tiles on the floor, a wicker chair, a giant silver towel rail, and a bookcase of all things with magazines, a basket of stones and shells, and a plant on the top. Bruno's door was open, and she tapped with her knuckle and went in. The curtains were open but the bedside light was on. Bruno was hunched up on his side under the bedclothes.

'Bruno? It's me, I just . . . Are you asleep?'

There was no reply, so she very quietly drew the curtains, and went to turn off the lamp.

'Can I have it on?'

Once again he made her jump, but at least this time he wasn't looking at her.

'Yes. I suppose. For a bit.'

He didn't answer. You never knew where you were with him. Cautiously, trying not to make a sound, she leaned forward so as to peer over at his face. He looked fast asleep. His long dark lashes – God, she'd kill for those lashes – lay softly on his cheek and his hair was like a rumpled fan of black feathers on the pillow. There were a couple of tiny dry leaves caught in his hair. So he *had* been hiding in the garden, to begin with anyway. Sasha felt a beat of something like tenderness for him. He was only seven, a baby.

'Goodnight, Sasha.'

His voice was clear and bright, though the lashes hadn't so much as fluttered.

'Oh – night!'

Sasha hastened back downstairs.

★   ★   ★

Spooked again, she hadn't gone back up to check, or to turn the light off. When the Blyths got back, at twenty past eleven, she told them truthfully that she hadn't heard a sound.

Mr B observed that that made a change. While he found Sasha's money (they had rarely put aside the right amount, and often rounded it up) Mrs B went up to take a peep and came back down shaking her head.

'Tinker . . . He must have turned the light back on, and then gone to sleep.'

'Sorry about that. I didn't hear anything.'

'He'd make sure you didn't! Don't worry, he's fine.'

Sasha pocketed her envelope — she could feel there was some change, so that would be the exact amount this time — and said, 'Thanks for my tea.'

'Tea? — oh, the sausage rolls. Pleasure, were they nice?'

'Delicious.'

In the car on they way back to Salting, Mr B gave her one of his funny sidelong looks.

'Hope he didn't give you any gyp.'

'Not at all.'

He tilted his head in her direction. 'You can speak frankly. I shan't grass you up.'

She had to smile at the way he said certain things in his nice posh voice. 'Well, he was a bit hard to find.'

'Hard to find?'

'We played hide-and-seek.'

'You did? Ye gods — and was that a mistake?'

No matter how friendly Mr B was, Sasha knew better than to diss their beloved Bruno. 'It was fun, but I had to give up.'

'Where on earth had he gone?'

Sasha realized she had no idea where he'd hidden originally — she'd stumbled across him in the larder and nearly shat herself with the shock.

'I don't know. I had to give up, and he came back in.'

'That was decent of him!' Mr B laughed happily. They doted on Bruno. 'I thought you were going to say you'd called the police!'

He had no idea how close that was to the truth. But the remark reminded her of something.

'By the way, I nearly forgot, your daughter called.'

'Which one?'

Her mind went blank. 'Fiona . . .?'

'Felicity.'

'That's it, I left a message by the phone.'

'Did she say what it was about?'

'No – just to call her.'

'Hmm . . .' Mr B slowed for the lights at the top of the high street. 'Sounds ominous.'

Four

It was an eye-opener, thought Robin, to see someone you knew when they didn't know you could see them. So *that* was how she looked to other people, and the world in general. To other men.

Swinging down the colonnade at the side of the square in Meliano, his wife's lissome English limbs and pale blonde beauty left a small but discernible frisson of appreciation in their wake. Her demeanour was composed, even aloof, but Robin recognized the merest hint of self-satisfaction. She knew, alright. His own feelings were mixed – pride, certainly, but also a kind of tender, oh-come-off-it scepticism. To him, who had fallen so hopelessly in love with her, that ice-maiden schtick was only the surface, the start. He intended to spend a lifetime coming to know what lay beneath.

Now she had spotted him as she crossed the square and her lovely, luminous smile lit up her face. Those watching (and there were always people watching) would want to know who it was for. He didn't get up – let them wonder for a bit longer. She had almost reached the table before he rose.

'Hi there!' She leaned across to kiss him. He accepted the kiss and moved to pull a chair out, but a waiter was there before him, flourishing Prosecco over her slender glass in almost the same movement. She acknowledged the waiter with the merest sideways tweak of her head, shedding a shiny leftover sliver of smile in his direction.

'Did you have fun?' Robin asked. 'Buy anything?'

'Not a thing!' She waved airy fingers before folding them round the glass. 'In the end I didn't even have to resist, because I wasn't tempted.'

This might have served as Felicity's motto. Because she was rarely if ever tempted, the potential in her life for indiscretions, faux pas, let alone downright disasters was vanishingly small. Her cast-iron amour propre had served as her shield and protector since childhood, and it was only when confronted with the, as it were, thrown-down gauntlet that was Robin Trevor-Savery that she moved forward to accept the challenge.

Here, she intuited, was a man worthy of her steel. Someone not dancing attendance, or paying court, but entirely at ease with himself and others. Perhaps not quite as devilishly hand-some as was generally thought (and as perhaps he thought himself) but certainly at the top of his game, successful, pros-perous, amusing and single. Oddly, it was this singleness which gave Felicity pause. Why? He was thirty-two years old, eight years older than her, and with no ex or dependents in the background. The sort of man who in the Jane Austen novels that she loved would have been widely spoken of as a catch. The last thing Felicity wanted to be was one more notch on the bedpost of some acknowledged Lothario – lured, laid and left, to general sighing and eyebrow-lifting. If she was, as it were, going in, it must be on equal terms, and with at least an equal chance of success. And although she wouldn't have put it in so many words, that success meant a proposal and a ring. Unreconstructed pre-feminist aims though these were, Felicity took a thoroughly modern and clear-eyed approach to them. Since her teens she had cherished the picture of herself as the radiant mother of a clutch of glorious children. The father of the children had always been a shadowy figure, like the outline in a colouring book, waiting to be filled in. She would know who he was when he came along. The question of romantic love didn't really come into it. There would be a mutual attrac-tion, of course, because he would be attractive, that was a given. But phrases like 'head over heels' and 'soul mate' weren't in her emotional lexicon.

And so it came to pass that she wore Robin's square-cut diamond on her finger for some time before falling in love with him.

They made a golden couple. Locals and tourists alike couldn't help glancing their way. Felicity was an exquisite fawn-like creature of ivory and cream, Robin was six foot three and richly tanned, his sun-bleached hair of that thick, wavy, careless kind which seems to go with a certain sort of patrician Englishman – hair made for fluttering beneath the spinnaker of a yacht, for bouncing from beneath a doffed cap after the hitting of a six, for brushing aside during energetic manoeuvres on the dance floor. Her beauty spoke of a ladylike nature with hidden fires, his of a bold and buccaneering approach to life.

In one way, onlookers intuited correctly – Felicity wanted everything done properly, by the book. This included Robin asking her father's permission.

Robin had laughed at this, though not unkindly. 'Hang on – what if he says no?'

'He won't.'

'But he might. And then where will we be?'

'We don't actually *need* his permission,' Felicity pointed out.

'So why tempt fate?'

Felicity tilted her head, bestowing on Robin her warmest and most melting smile, the smile which had led all sorts of people to imagine they had a special place in her affections. 'He's a sweet old-fashioned thing at heart. He'll be charmed.'

'I'll take your word for it.'

Contrary to what they said to each other, it was Felicity who had more at stake, and who was more concerned about her father's reaction. She was not a rebel, but a driven conformist. It was important to her that all should go swimmingly. Robin found 'Operation Ask Daddy' rather quaint and diverting, but was more than happy to indulge her.

So Felicity had rung her parents to ask if she could bring someone down to meet them. The first time she called they'd been out and she'd spoken to some girl who'd been left in charge of Bruno and was clearly having rings run round her, poor thing.

It was her mother who'd called back the following evening, and she of course had cottoned on immediately.

'*Oh* . . .? Well, yes of course. Someone important?'

'He is to me,' said Felicity winsomely.

'That's wonderful! Darling, I can't wait.'

'I think you're going to like him.'

'I like him already,' declared Marguerite. 'And so will Hugh.'

Felicity took this as it was intended – as a promise that her mother would ensure her father's approval.

They had no need to worry. All their eldest daughter's 'young men' had been eminently parent-friendly, she had never confronted them with tattoos, unintelligible accents, strange hair (on the head or anywhere else), children from previous alliances, substance addiction or even food fads. So they could afford to be sanguine.

As the weekend approached, Robin looked forward to it. He was tickled by what he saw as a sort of delightful and enjoyable game.

'When would be the best moment?' he asked as they sped down the M4 in his racing green Morgan.

Felicity had thought of this. 'Between tea and drinks.'

'We'll be having afternoon tea?'

'Drawing-room tea – or perhaps in the loggia.'

'Loggia!' Robin raised his eyebrows. 'That's posh.'

'It's always been called that – it was when they bought it.'

'Anyway, good. I shall sidle up to your father as the tea tray's being removed—'

'He quite often goes for an early-evening walk.'

'And I can invite myself along.'

'Exactly,' said Felicity, pleased that Robin had cottoned on so quickly. 'Ma will know just what you're up to.'

'And so will he, I imagine.'

'Probably, but he'll play along.'

'Do you think he'll want to know what my prospects are?'

'Of course.'

Robin was marketing manager of a wine company, and there was a half-case of Porterfield's premier cru burgundy wedged behind the passenger seat. All in all he considered his prospects were pretty good.

'They're here!' called Marguerite, having spotted the Morgan through the half-landing window. 'Gorgeous car!'

Hugh came in from the loggia where he'd been reading the Saturday sports section.

'Glad to hear it.'

'You go, I'm just going to whoosh back up for a moment.'

Marguerite applied a critical eye to her reflection in the wardrobe mirror. Verdict: face OK, figure definitely bearing the signs of four pregnancies. But, she told herself, that hardly mattered because the young man would have eyes only for Felicity. She swiped a brush through her hair, felt that looked too flat and fluffed it again with her fingers. Too bad, this was her. She heard voices downstairs, a warm burble of greeting, Hugh's pleasant chatty tones, a bright male laugh – not Hugh's – and Felicity's silvery one. Time to go down.

On the landing she met Bruno, the only one of her other offspring at home.

'Is that them?' he asked, not concealing his avid curiosity.

'Yes.' It occurred to Marguerite that her youngest child was the one person capable of derailing this potentially delicate weekend. 'Bruno—'

'What?'

'Please be nice.'

'I will!' He affected his best look of injured innocence. She knew he was being disingenuous.

'Right you are then.'

She moved to give her son a kiss but he'd flashed past her and down the stairs, and a moment later was accompanying Felicity's young man out to the car.

'What's in the box?'

'Six bottles of wine for your parents. To say thank-you.'

'For what?'

'For having me.'

Bruno paid no attention to this answer. 'Can I take it?'

'I think it's a bit heavy.'

Again Bruno didn't argue but moved seamlessly to the next request. 'Can I get in the car?'

'Sure.' Robin opened the driver's door and Bruno jumped in, turning the wheel and peering over it with narrowed eyes. 'Did it cost a lot?'

'It was pretty expensive, yes. Do you like it?'

Bruno nodded, before adding, 'But it would be better in red.'

'Red's a cliché.'

If Robin had hoped to put this precocious child in his place with a grown-up put-down, he was disappointed, because it was ignored. The others had gone out through the loggia and on to the lawn, so he left the box of wine on the hall chair for presentation later and went back out for the bags.

Bruno was still in the driver's seat. Robin had left his key in the ignition and the boy was twiddling it.

'Don't do that!'

'OK.'

Robin removed the key and put it in his pocket. He took the bags from the boot and slammed it shut, then opened the driver's door pointedly. Bruno got out and watched as he locked the car.

'What about the top?'

'I'm not going to worry about that just now.'

'It might rain. It was on the forecast.'

'I can nip out and do it later.' The child was probably right but he was disinclined to take his advice.

'OK,' said Bruno again, with a suggestion of a shrug, as one might say 'suit yourself'. He sauntered ahead of Robin into the house which for some reason Robin found irritating. In the hall there was no sign of him, and Robin left the bags at the foot of the stairs and went out to join the others in the garden.

'What an absolutely lovely place.'

'We like it,' said Hugh. 'We've been here for, what, over twenty-five years now?'

'With a name like Heart's Ease,' said Robin, 'it could so easily be a disappointment. Like calling a girl Belle.'

'We called ours Felicity.' Marguerite put her arm round her daughter's waist. 'And to date you're happy enough, aren't you, darling?'

'Absolutely.'

Robin detected a bat-squeak of tension and decided to move away from the name thing. 'I'd love a guided tour.'

'Yes, why don't you do that? Hugh will put your bags upstairs—'

'You don't need to do that—'

'Of course, all part of the service.'

'And I'll get some tea. We might even be able to have it out here, or in the loggia anyway.'

'Then thank you.' Robin turned to Felicity. 'Lead on.'

Once they were down the steps at the end of the terrace, he said, 'Tea! Should I pounce after that?'

'You mustn't *pounce* at all. And today's too soon, we've only just got here. Tomorrow will be fine.'

'Received and understood . . . God, this really is delightful . . .'

'It is, isn't it.' She linked her arm through his. 'Actually it's good to see it through someone else's eyes. We're in danger of taking it for granted.'

A little further and she opened the door of the fruit cage. 'Do you like raspberries?'

'Mad for them.'

She picked a handful and held them out. He leaned over and took one with his lips from her cupped hand. 'So sweet . . .'

'Robin—' He had her by the wrist, but she reached to close the door with her free hand. 'Not here!'

He laughed and let go. 'Happy Felicity – I never thought of that before.'

'We all have those names. My sisters are Charity and Honor.'

'And are they charitable and honorable?'

'Jury's out.'

'Ouch!' He tossed the remaining raspberries into his mouth. 'What about your little brother?'

'Bruno, they stopped doing virtues with him. It's not so easy with a boy.'

'He came out to the car with me.'

'I saw. Is it still in one piece?'

'I did forget to take the key out of the ignition, but fortunately I noticed just in time before he set off down the drive.'

'Aah!' Felicity covered her eyes with her fingers. 'The little sod.'

Instinctively Robin agreed with her, but this was a sensitive moment. 'Just doing what small boys do. I believe it's in the job description.'

They were walking along a cinder path with the kitchen garden on their right, and the house to their left. Beyond the kitchen garden between a row of scots pines could be glimpsed the blue of Salting's bay, and the marshmallow colours of the Georgian houses with their sea view.

'Don't you know?' said Felicity. 'You were a boy once.'

'Yes, but I was an angel.'

She cuffed him gently on the arm. 'Well Bruno's the spawn of Satan.'

Robin honked with laughter, relieved to have his feelings so wholeheartedly endorsed. 'That's a bit steep!'

'Most people adore him, so he's monstrously indulged. Thank God I was on my way before he got too bad. No wonder my sister Charity took off at the first possible opportunity.'

'What about your other sister – Honor?'

'She's one of the adorers. And he knows which side his bread's buttered on, he sucks up to her shamelessly.'

They reached the end of the path and stood looking out over the view. Robin lifted a handful of tawny-blonde hair off her neck, and held it to his face, letting it sift through his fingers.

'Sounds as if I had a lucky escape with the car . . .'

'Believe me.'

He kissed the soft, fragrant hollow beneath her ear. 'And shall I meet the saintly Honor?'

'That depends on her old people. They come first at all times.'

It was interesting, thought Robin, as they turned and walked round the back of the house and across the front drive, the subtle differences in Felicity in her home surroundings. Since their divorce he hadn't seen much of his own parents, and then eight years ago his father had died. Till then his mother had been living with her obnoxious second husband in the trackless wastes of Norfolk, but the demise of her first had been a turning point, and she'd gone not long after. The obnoxious one had taken off for Spain, thank God. So this place, Heart's Ease, which was both physically and emotionally home to Felicity, had no equivalent in his life. Seeing her here he sensed (Bruno notwithstanding) its magnetic pull, its role as a touchstone. And he could – almost – understand it. Her parents were certainly charming. Her mother must have been stunning in her day. Even now in what he reckoned must be her late forties, she had a warm, distrait beauty quite different from Felicity's, springing chestnut hair and brown eyes, a figure showing the gentle sag of childbearing, rather sexy in its way . . .

Jesus, there was the boy, staring at him! They were just passing a backyard, with garden sheds and stone steps scuttling down to some sort of cellar, separated from the drive by a tall hedge. Bruno was sitting on the top step, eating a chocolate bar out of a wrapper, but his eyes were fixed on Robin.

'Hi!' said Robin. Bruno raised his free hand.

'What?' asked Felicity.

Robin nodded his head in the boy's direction. 'Your brother.'

'What are you doing there?'

'Nothing.'

'Where did you get that?'

'Honor gave it to me.'

'Why doesn't that surprise me?' murmured Felicity, then sharply, 'Don't just drop the paper!'

Robin glanced Bruno's way once more, to find the boy was still staring.

A pale blue Citroen DCV was parked neatly between the Morgan and the Volvo in the drive. The front door was standing open and Honor appeared, carrying a large round tin.

'Hello, this is so silly, I'm going straight out again. I just came back to collect this . . .!'

Watching the sisters greet each other, Robin observed that whereas Felicity looked nothing like either of her parents, Honor, while no one would have called her a beauty, was the spit of their mother.

Felicity held out an arm to include him. 'This is Robin . . . This is my sister Honor.'

'Hello Honor, super to meet you. I do hope I'll see you again over the weekend?'

Robin shook a warm, slightly calloused hand, noticing as he did so the first genuine blush he'd seen in years.

'She gets time off for good behaviour,' said Felicity.

'I'll be home for lunch tomorrow,' said the still-pink Honor.

'Good. I shan't hold you up in that case. Look forward to it.'

'Don't watch me back out, will you?'

'I wouldn't dream of it.'

He waved, but Felicity was already back in the house so he followed, closing the door behind them.

Five

Marguerite was sitting up in bed in one of her oversized supermarket T-shirts, the one proclaiming *It's nothing a kiss won't cure*. She was holding a novel by the brilliant octogenarian Mary Wesley but not, on this occasion, reading. Hugh, who never wore pyjamas, bounced in beside her, thrusting his arm behind his wife's neck and kissing her warmly.

'Better now?'

'He seems really nice, doesn't he?'

Hugh withdrew his arm and linked it with the other behind his head, adopting a musing expression.

'He does seem so, certainly. Bags of personality. Doing well for himself.'

'Now come on.' Marguerite recognized implied disparagement when she heard it. 'He's absolutely charming.'

'No doubt of it.'

'And that was an incredibly generous present.'

'He's in the wine trade.'

'I hope you're not going to be difficult.' Marguerite fixed her husband with a hard stare. 'Felicity's very keen on him.'

Hugh sighed. 'Believe me, I realize that, or he wouldn't be here. What do you think, do I need to have a word with the bank manager?'

'Well . . . no . . . I mean . . . how do I know? Even if they do want to get married—'

'Ah, finally, the words have been uttered!'

'*Even* if they do, they might want to do it with a handful of friends on a beach in Scotland.'

'Daisy. This is Felicity we're talking about.'

'Alright, yes . . .' Marguerite conceded. 'But anyway listen to us, we're jumping the gun.'

The next day, Sunday, was a model of its kind. At seven thirty a.m. Hugh walked down the lane to church, so as to get it out of the

way, and not to cause embarrassment to their guest who was
probably not a regular churchgoer. By the time he got back at
nine, Bruno had already been picked up for Little League rugby,
and Honor had gone off to minister to the old. When Felicity
and Robin came down for breakfast at nine thirty it was to find
Hugh, suitably shriven and exercised, with bacon and egg already
consumed and tucking into toast and St Martin's chunky. Robin
professed himself amazed and delighted to be offered a cooked
breakfast, Felicity had her usual black coffee and Marguerite, who
had been up since seven, sat down with her muesli to join them.

It was a beautiful early autumn day, and Hugh declared that he
was going to chop wood which was, as he explained, one of the
very few outdoor tasks he did around the place.

'That and feeding the boiler. I'm in charge of fuel.'

Having received assurances from Marguerite that no help
was required towards lunch, Felicity and Robin hopped into the
Morgan and went down to Salting to walk along the beach. Two
miles – first on the prom, and then the unforgiving shingle – was
followed by a comfortable hour and a half in the pub slaking
their virtuous thirst. Halfway through the second pint a young
man came over, a blast from Felicity's past.

'Fliss?'

'Hello stranger!'

'Fliss, this is brilliant – I haven't been in here for ages, and
now I bump into you.'

'Pete, this is Robin.'

'Pete Spurling.' Robin stood and the two of them shook hands
with forceful geniality.

'Down for the weekend?' asked Pete.

'Yes,' said Robin. 'Drove down yesterday.'

Probably only Felicity would have noticed the glint of animus
this information produced, but Robin was not going to be
wrongfooted.

'Why don't you join us?'

'Ah, no, meeting someone, but cheers. Anyway – all well with
you, Fliss?'

'Absolutely. Lovely to see you.'

'Yes, I'd say like old times but hey – nothing's like old times,
is it?'

And with a double-cheek kiss and a raise of the hand, he was off.

Watching him go, Robin asked, 'So the two of you have old times in common, do you?'

She grimaced. 'That's what he'd like you to think.'

'Can't blame him for that.'

Five of them sat down to Marguerite's roast lamb. Bruno had been invited to a friend's following mini rugby. Honor had to be reminded to take her overall off, which provoked more blushing.

'Sorry – I forgot I had it on!'

'I suppose we should count ourselves lucky you're not wearing those wretched rubber gloves,' said Hugh, adding confidingly to Robin, 'she has a box of the blighters on the back seat of her car. That and other unmentionables.'

'Daddy!'

'I tell you what, it's a dreadful warning to us all about the indignities that await us in old age.'

'Hugh, Honor is absolutely right, must we discuss this over Sunday lunch?'

'Oh I don't know,' said Hugh comfortably. 'There's never a wrong time for a clear-eyed look at the future.'

'You work awfully hard, Honor,' said Robin. 'And not many people could do what you do. I'm so impressed.'

'No one quite believes me, but I really love it.'

'Just as well,' said Hugh. 'Someone has to.' His voice softened. 'No, my girl, there's no doubt about it you're the angel of Salting.'

Robin found himself surprisingly pleased that the teasing, however gentle, was over. He understood that the old people were lucky to have Honor – she was a sweetie. Felicity's expression was neutral. She had obviously heard this exchange, or something like it, many times, and was unaffected by it either way. Robin had no siblings, but assumed this was the rivalry one heard about.

'Tell me,' he asked, not entirely without mischief, 'where's Charity? What does she do?'

'Believe me,' said Felicity, 'you don't want to know. She's the brainy one.'

★   ★   ★

By the time they'd finished and cleared, it was after three, and the next couple of hours were given over to the papers. Honor had gone out again and Bruno had returned, and was watching a film in the family room. Later, Hugh told him, there would be Scrabble 'to save them from the God slot' – for a churchgoer he was bracingly dismissive of religious broadcasting.

Robin couldn't remember the last time he'd spent a Sunday with such an unforced traditional rhythm. It was, he realized, delightful, and must surely be the source of Felicity's confidence. His own came from what he'd done, but hers from what she was – a part of this. That and her looks, but beauty was nothing without self-esteem, and she owed that to Heart's Ease.

These reflections had the effect of making him feel more respectful towards the now imminent exchange with Hugh. Up to this point he'd regarded it as a game, now he wasn't quite so sure. He wanted not simply to go through the motions but to get it right. And this was because it wasn't just marriage to Felicity that was at stake, it was the chance of being part of all this – the Blyths and their heart's ease. He had never wanted anything more. The relationship between him and Felicity might be work in progress but this – he had a horrible feeling this was the real thing.

The tea tray, accompanied by Bruno with a plate of biscuits, appeared at four thirty and once he'd downed a mugful and a Penguin, Hugh as predicted got to his feet.

'Right . . . I'm going to take a brisk turn up to the beacon, any takers?'

Felicity and Marguerite were in conversation. This was Robin's cue.

'I'm up for that, mind if I tag along?'

'I'd be delighted.'

Robin looked down at his feet. 'I've only got these or trainers.'

'Those are fine, it's not rough going.'

They went out through the loggia and across the lawn.

'A few weeks,' said Hugh, 'and this won't be possible.' To Robin's sensitized ears this sounded like notice being served – now or never.

'How so?'

'Clocks will change.'

They went out through a small gate between the bushes on the far side, and then forked right to take a path between high tree-lined banks.

'About three-quarters of a mile to the clifftop,' said Hugh. 'That suit you?'

'Perfect. Nice to walk in the country for a change after—'

'Daddy! Wait!' Bruno was pounding up the path behind them. 'Wait for me!'

'Get a move on then.' If Hugh had harboured any idea about Robin's intentions he covered it up well. 'We're going to the beacon, no dawdling and no turning back.'

'I won't – I want to come.'

That was it then, thought Robin. No chance whatever of the gently amusing and courteous man-to-man exchange he'd had in mind. That had been well and truly sabotaged by the little bugger. What were the Blyths doing, he asked himself testily and quite unreasonably, having another child when all the others must have been practically grown up?

Bruno fell in step between them, interruption made flesh.

'Are you here tomorrow?' he asked.

'Some of it,' said Robin. 'We'll be leaving after lunch.'

'Great!'

Robin couldn't tell whether this meant great that they would be there next day, or great that they were going before the day was through. The latter, probably, though he was quite sure any ambivalence was intentional.

'We'll make lunch early,' said Hugh. 'You'll want to be on the road well before two to avoid traffic the other end.'

Bruno moved ahead, weaving around, stopping and starting, it was like walking a particularly insensitive dog. Robin and Hugh fell into conversation about cars, the Morgan especially always proved a fruitful talking point. At one point the path led across a golf course and Bruno had to be prevented from sprinting across in front of a serious-looking four-ball, but one of the men seemed to know Hugh and waved cheerily enough. When they reached the clifftop they paused to admire the view which was spectacular, with the low red cliffs curving away to the west and a wonderfully rough, dramatic headland to the east, between them and the sequestered Salting Bay. Hugh did his best to point out landmarks, describe the role of the beacon and so on, but his commentary was continually broken by the need to contain Bruno, who kept going too close to the edge, windmilling his arms and generally playing the fool. Robin could all-too clearly imagine the casual shove which would end the nuisance once and for all, but Hugh's patience was magisterial – or perhaps he was just used to it.

After ten minutes or so they started for home and this time Bruno hung back, but never far enough behind to open a window of opportunity.

'One of the great mysteries of childhood,' observed Hugh. 'They can be in constant motion when there's no objective, but anything that smacks of organisation and their energy seems to flag.'

'He plays rugby,' pointed out Robin, a diplomatic devil's advocate. 'I didn't play till I was twelve, and it was pretty tough even then.'

'The chap who runs it is practically a saint in my view,' said Hugh. 'I've been to watch and it would drive me to drink in minutes, they all run around in a loose scrum, no one can hang on to the ball or has any idea what to do with it, and they just break off when they feel like it to chat, or fight or whatever . . .' He shook his head. 'Not for me. Girls are easier.'

Once they'd crossed the golf course again and had reached what was effectively the home strait, Bruno suddenly took off, scrambling up the bank and between the trees to run along the rough at the edge of the fairway.

'Mind the golfers, Bruno!' bellowed Hugh to no avail, before adding with a shrug, 'you see?'

Robin wasn't sure what he meant by this, but as far as he himself was concerned this was the moment.

'Ah, Hugh – there's something I'd like to ask you.'

'Really?' Hugh stopped and faced him, smiling. 'Fire away.'

'You've probably realized – I'm sure you have – that I think the world of your daughter.' He almost winced. *Think the world of your daughter?* He'd never used that phrase before nor even consciously thought it. What did he think he was doing, enacting some dimly-remembered scene from a Victorian novel? But Hugh appeared not to notice or, if he did, not to find it odd.

'I'm glad to hear it. She seems pretty keen on you.'

'Yes, it's mutual.'

'Good.' Hugh continued to stand there, smiling in that pleasant, neutral way. 'She's always had more than her fair share of swains and not always treated them as well as she might. You seem to have brought out the best in her.'

'We'd very much like to get married.'

'Would you?' Hugh's smile grew wider and warmer, his eyebrows lifted. He was, Robin considered, a really nice man. 'Would you really?'

'Yes.' There was a form of words for this, that didn't actually involve asking permission, and now, like that earlier phrase it came winging to him out of nowhere. 'Can we count on your blessing?'

'My dear chap, you can.' Hugh's smile practically threatened to split his face. He held out his hand. 'You certainly can.'

'I realize you don't know me.'

'Fliss brought you here, and she's clearly smitten, that's testimony enough. And anyway,' he went on as they began to walk, 'in this day and age, as I understand it, it's a bonus to be asked and not just presented with a fait accompli.'

Robin felt the need to regain some autonomy. 'She was very insistent we do this by the book.'

'And I consider it outstandingly decent of you to go along with her. But then,' said Hugh, clapping him on the shoulder, 'you love each other, so why the devil wouldn't you?'

It was just as they reached the end of the path and were crossing to the gate that Bruno appeared from the other side of the bank, where he must have been walking parallel to them, and shot ahead of them, over the lawn and into the house.

'Mercury,' said Hugh fondly. Robin had been thinking something different.

'What?'

Both Felicity and Marguerite spoke at the same time, and both their voices carried the same note of startled expectation.

'You're getting married!'

'Sssh, Bruno!' Marguerite flapped her hands to quieten him. 'Don't spoil the news.'

'Too late,' said Felicity, walking out. 'He already has.'

★　★　★

Now all of that – the champagne, the fuss and fun, the classic country wedding in June when the rhododendrons of Heart's Ease were at their best – was over, out of the way. The Italian honeymoon was their time to recalibrate. Robin had been captivated by the Blyths, but now that he had signed up he was about to feel the full force of Felicity's project.

Six

1995

Charity had long since decided her family got along very well without her, and vice versa. This decision had been reached entirely without rancour. She loved them or at least she didn't *not* love them, and how were these things proved anyway? She had always considered King Lear a petulant old fusspot with his insistence on proof. Her parents certainly loved her, though she couldn't speak for her siblings. Honor loved everyone, Felicity's attention was focused on Robin and the children, and Bruno had always loved himself most.

Nothing wrong with that – Charity quite approved of amour propre and had always seen to it that her own was in good shape. You couldn't let yourself be governed by other people's reactions and what was going on in their lives. However, she suspected that in Bruno's case being the youngest and the only boy had made him believe the sun shone out of his fundament. The parents and Honor were always swayed by his charm – even when they knew they were wrong they tended to laugh about it – and Felicity, who knew a rival when she saw one, affected indifference.

Charity's position was that she was not prepared to take any shit. Least of all today when she'd been dragooned into collecting Bruno from school after yet another misdemeanour, this time requiring temporary rustication. Before it had been the classic fags-and-booze combo, today it was something far more serious connected with a member of the kitchen staff. Hugh was on a trip to Frankfurt and Marguerite knew that Charity was driving down that day anyway, and asked if she would mind terribly 'scooping him up'.

'I'd be so so grateful, love. I honestly don't think I can face another interview with Mr Macfarlane being ruggedly understanding. I never know what I'm supposed to say, or even to do with my face.'

Alastair Macfarlane – 'Mac' as he was known, though Marguerite couldn't bring herself to do so – was the head of Brushwood, the liberal free-thinking boarding school which Bruno attended most of the time. He was quite famous (in some quarters notorious) in the educational field, for being ahead of his time, devoted to children and fiercely direct with adults especially when it came to protecting their offspring's interests. His tolerance with the young was legendary, but he made it clear with everyone from the start there were some things he just would not put up with. It was one of these – hanky panky with a member of staff – that Bruno was guilty of, the reason why Charity was taking him home in mid-February for a couple of weeks' kicking his heels.

As she drew up in the school's parking area, in the right angle created by the bike shed, the chicken run and the prefab classroom (a 'temporary' addition from three years ago), Charity wondered again why time at home should be considered such a deprivation, especially for a boy of seventeen whose sole preoccupation as far as she could see was to smoke and sniff around the local girls.

She was a little early, so she rolled down the window and lit a cigarette. Her smoke swirled in the cold, dank air.

Bruno was lucky in not having been through an uncomfortable stage. He seemed to move seamlessly from childhood to adolescence without spots or awkwardness, retaining that eerie, unchildlike composure. She could all too clearly imagine the hanky panky of which he stood accused.

'Hey – are you alright?'

The question came from a tall, beautiful girl wearing a Crombie overcoat over frayed pyjama bottoms and DMs, who was standing in the chicken run with a plastic bowl, idly scattering seed.

'Yes, thanks,' replied Charity. 'Just waiting – I'm early.'

The girl continued to scatter while keeping her eyes on Charity. 'Who for?'

'Bruno Blyth.'

'Oh, right . . .' She emptied the rest of the bowl with a sweeping gesture and came out of the run, closing the gate behind her.

'I don't suppose you could spare one of those, could you?'

It took less than a nanosecond for Charity to conclude that this was neither the place nor the moment for prissiness. She held out the packet.

'There you go.'

'Cheers.' The girl took a box of matches from her coat pocket and lit up with exaggerated relish. 'Christ . . . thanks!'

She had a natural, go-hang charisma. Fox-brown hair hanging in long, wavy hanks, pale bony hands with rings on the thumb and forefingers, a mouth with a slightly pouting upper lip. Charity liked her looks.

'You know Bruno, do you?'

The girl nodded on a long exhalation. 'Everyone knows everyone here.' She looked directly at Charity. 'How do you know him then?'

'I'm his sister.'

'Fuck me, really?' She gave her head a little shake. 'You know he's been bad?'

'Yes. That's why I'm here.'

'To see Mac?'

'And take Bruno home for a fortnight.'

'Jammy bastard.'

'Yes.' Charity smiled thinly. 'I did wonder if that was much of a punishment.'

'And all for groping Annelind in the sluice.'

'Sluice?'

'Toilets . . . cloakroom.'

'Annelind?'

'She works in the kitchen. She's nice actually, but let's just say she won't have put up much of a fight.'

This time Charity laughed out loud. 'Sorry, what's your name?'

'Paulina. Hi.'

'Charity.'

They shook hands, a curious note of formality under the

circumstances. Paulina's hand was icy. Charity looked at her watch.
'I suppose I'd better go in and face the music.'

'Ach!' Paulina took a final drag and ground the butt beneath
her boot. 'Mac's a pushover. But he has to draw the line somewhere and shagging the staff is where.'

'Did he actually – shag her?'

'You know Bruno.' Paulina quirked her mouth and flashed Charity
a sidelong look. 'What do you think?'

'OK.' Charity closed the car window and got out. 'Well, nice
to meet you, Paulina.'

'And you. Thanks for the fag.'

As Charity headed for the main building a group of teenagers
who'd been hanging around by the prefab began drifting towards
Paulina, doubtless for the de-brief. One of the boys lifted his chin
in a 'Hi' motion. Charity lifted her chin back, suppressing her
automatic shouldn't-you-be-in-class reflex; that wasn't how this
place worked. Everything was voluntary and self-regulating.

Or, she thought grimly, almost everything.

The door of Macfarlane's room (never referred to as the office)
was standing open, and to her surprise Charity could see Bruno
already there, perched on the edge of an armchair with his hands
hanging between his knees. He looked remarkably relaxed in
an oversize plaid shirt, baggy jeans and Timberlands. She always
forgot how good-looking her brother was, with his thick dark
hair and furry lashes – and as if good looks weren't enough he
was armoured, like Felicity, in the smooth, watertight self-confi-
dence that so often accompanied them.

She couldn't see Macfarlane, but as she tapped on the open door
with her knuckle he appeared from behind it, carrying a book.

'Ah – good morning. Charity, is it?'

'Yes.' She submitted to a brisk, powerful handshake. 'Hello.'

'Take a pew.' He gave the door a push, enough to half-close
but not shut it. 'Won't keep you long.'

The room was not much warmer than the air outside. The
sullen glow of a coal fire was too small and too far away. Charity
sat down in one of the other armchairs. There was a sofa, mostly
covered in books and magazines, and a desk in the far corner
similarly heaped high. Having placed the book on the desk,

Macfarlane lowered his bulk into the free space on the sofa. Bruno twitched a hand.

'Hi Sis.'

'Hello.'

Sis? *Sis?* Where had that come from? The little toe-rag needn't think she was going to enter some sort of conspiracy of cuteness with him. This would be all business if she had anything to do with it, and as brief as possible.

Macfarlane was a big, tall man, probably in his mid-seventies, but his age in no way detracted from the impression he gave of real strength. His shabby tweed jacket was the sort that might have been worn in an early assault on Everest. As well as being physically impressive he had an air that was at once pleasant and wholly authoritative. Even – Charity considered – sexy, a deeply inappropriate reaction in all the circumstances.

'Now then. Charity. I take it you know the score?'

'My mother outlined it, yes.'

'And you drew the short straw.' His gaze rested on her benignly.

'I was due to drive this way anyway . . .'

'. . . and your parents have been before.'

'Our father's away.'

'Of course.' Macfarlane's eyes moved to Bruno. 'Bruno, perhaps you'd like to tell your sister why we're all here. Just so we're all clear.'

Yes, thought Charity. *Let's hear it in your own words, sunshine.*

Without hesitation Bruno said, 'I made a pass at Annelind.' He didn't sound or look in the least discomforted, any more than did the head. 'Worthy of each other's steel' was the phrase that came to mind.

'I see.'

'It was a little more than that,' suggested Macfarlane. 'Remember I've spoken to Annelind and she gave a full account.'

'Sure,' said Bruno. 'It was a successful pass.'

His brazen cheek – the sheer bloody *chutzpah* – took Charity's breath away. Her face was burning and she hoped she didn't look red, but Macfarlane appeared unaffected.

'She said as much.' He turned to Charity, cutting Bruno out of his next remark. 'And you don't need me to list the several ways in which that is completely beyond the pale.'

'No,' muttered Charity. 'Indeed.'

He continued to talk to her. 'As you may know, it's our aim to deal with anything and everything that comes up here, at Brushwood, and in an open and democratic way. But not, I'm afraid, this. We would like Bruno to be off the premises for at least a fortnight, and for his parents – your parents – to impress upon him how wrongly he's behaved and do whatever they think is right. Obviously they can talk to me at any time.'

'I understand.'

'Is there anything you want to ask now?'

Charity had to press her foot to the ground to stop her knee trembling. *Be appropriate.* 'How is Annelind?'

'Alright so far as I know. She's left, of course.'

'May I say something?' Bruno looked from one to the other. 'Certainly.'

'About Annelind. She led me on. She was coming on to me for weeks.'

Charity studied her fingers, spread out on the still-quivering knee. But if Bruno was a cool customer, Macfarlane was cooler.

'She was well aware such a thing should never have happened. What exactly is your point, Bruno?'

'She wanted it alright. It was fifty-fifty.'

A painful pause spread like spilled water, during which Bruno glanced from one to the other of them with an air of aggrieved impatience.

'Here's what I suggest,' said Macfarlane, folding his arms across an impressive chest. 'You go home with your sister, have a talk to your parents and a bloody good think, and come back here in due course if that's what you would like. If, on the other hand, you want to take your A Levels at home, that can be arranged.'

There was another silence. Charity said, 'Bruno . . .?'

'Do I have a choice?'

'Limited,' said Macfarlane, 'as I've just outlined.' He turned to Charity. 'Is there anything else you want to know? It's a great pity your parents couldn't come, I'm afraid you've been put in a rather invidious position.'

'There is one thing.'

She had the attention of both of them.

'How did this come to light? Who told you?'

Macfarlane looked mildly at Bruno. 'Would you like to answer that?' Bruno shrugged. 'Another member of staff overheard Bruno talking about the incident. She told me, and I followed it up with Annelind.' He slapped his knees and stood up. 'No harm done, except to Brushwood's reputation.'

'Thank you,' said Charity.

'Right.' Macfarlane went to the door. 'Bruno, have you got your bag?'

'It's in the Long.'

'Go and fetch it. You can meet your sister outside.'

He watched Bruno go before starting to walk in the direction of the main door. Paulina and the other youngsters Charity had seen outside were still hanging around near the prefab, but paid them no attention.

'Thank you for coming,' said Macfarlane. 'People assume that because Brushwood is a free-thinking school that anything goes, but that's not the case.'

'I completely understand.'

'May I ask what it is that you do?'

'I'm an academic.'

'In what field?'

'My subject's prehistoric icehouses.'

His tone and expression didn't change and she liked him for that. 'Of which I'm almost completely ignorant.'

'You should come to one of my lectures.' She smiled wryly. 'There's always room. But the teaching subsidizes my writing. I'm writing a book for what is an extremely niche market.'

'Excellent.'

'Well' – she stopped by the car as Bruno was advancing with his rucksack – 'this is me.'

Macfarlane held out his hand. 'I hope we meet again in slightly less disobliging circumstances.'

'Yes.'

'And I'll look forward to hearing from your parents.'

Charity had arranged to stay at Heart's Ease for a few days so there was ample opportunity to watch, with a kind of rapt scientific interest, as Bruno finessed his way out of trouble. Of course he had already established that he had made a successful pass, and that Annelind had been not just older, but willing, nay enthusiastic. And Charity recalled Paulina's comment that Annelind 'wouldn't have put up much of a fight'. She rather wished she'd quizzed the girl a bit more while she had the chance, but it hadn't felt like the right moment.

Marguerite put on her seldom-used serious face and established that two weeks at home did not mean a fortnight's holiday. It would fall to Hugh when he got back to have the Big Talk, first with Bruno and then Mac, but he was supremely ill-qualified for the role of heavy father and Charity hadn't the least doubt that whatever the outcome it would go Bruno's way.

'The thing is, Daisy,' said Hugh, 'I can remember all too well what it was like to be that age.' It was the night after the Big Talk and they were in the family room with the television on to cover their voices.

'We all can,' said Marguerite.

'But you were a girl. It's different.'

'How would you know?'

'Because I'm a bloke.' This much was irrefutable. 'There's a period of about two years when it's easier to count what doesn't give you a stiffy than what does.'

'I bet you never molested the staff when you were at school.'

'No, but then I'd never have had the confidence.'

'Hugh!'

'It's true.' He laughed. 'There was an under-matron we all fancied ferociously.'

'Poor woman.'

'She knew, she loved it. Anyway, I'm just saying I feel a bit of a hypocrite playing the heavy arbiter of teenage morals when I know the seventeen-year-old me would have been mad with envy.'

In bed, Marguerite lay awake a long time pondering on this. In the small hours she heard something – the displacement of air to which mothers are attuned – that meant someone was moving about elsewhere in the house.

With no lights on inside, it was possible to see someone sitting in the loggia. Marguerite opened the door.

'Bruno?'

When there was no answer she went over to him. 'Darling?'

'Oh Mum!' To her astonishment he turned and put his arms

round her, burying his face in her dressing gown. When she
clasped his shoulders she could feel them tense, and tremble.

'I'm sorry, I'm so sorry!' He rolled his head from side to side.
Marguerite held him awkwardly for a moment and then reached
for another chair and pulled it over. She sat down, waiting while
he swiped at his eyes and nose with his cuff.

'Bruno, sweetheart . . . Come on, it'll be alright.'

His eyes, still wet with tears, met hers.

'Will it?' he asked. 'Really, you promise?'

Marguerite's heart contracted. He was after all just a boy –
her boy.

'Promise.'

Surprisingly it was Honor – who apart from the parents was
Bruno's biggest fan – who was the most upset. She knocked on
Charity's door when she was getting some reading done and came
straight in, wearing an expression of almost comical shock.

'This is so awful! What can he have been thinking?'

Charity kept a finger in her page. 'I don't suppose he was. Or
not with the bit most of us think with.'

Honor flopped down on the bed. 'I can't believe it.'

'It's not up for debate, Honor.'

'Will they have him back?'

'Yes. In two weeks – provided he sees the error of his ways.'

Irony was wasted on Honor in her current frame of mind. 'Do
you think he does?'

'He'll be fine,' said Charity. 'Take my word for it.'

Hugh took Bruno back to Brushwood just over a week later
where he was given a hero's welcome by his peers and went on
to get irritatingly good grades in his A Levels.

Hugh, Marguerite and Honor were all delighted and gratified
that their boy had put the incident behind him and shone
through in his true colours. Charity and Felicity, if they'd
discussed it at all, would have found that they were of one mind.
Bruno had as usual got off lightly.

However, Charity found that she would be driving south
again in early July and would be able to collect her brother from
Brushwood at the end of his school career.

Seven

'It's just till he finds somewhere,' said Marguerite. The fingers of her free hand — the one not holding the phone — were firmly crossed. 'Hugh and I'd be so much happier if we knew he was with you and Robin.'

'He'll have to behave himself,' warned Felicity. 'Our nanny's only twenty-two.'

Marguerite laughed gaily. 'Oh for heaven's sake! All that's long past.'

'Dream on, Ma. What will he be like with the whole of London to choose from?'

'He's young, he deserves some fun.'

Even to Marguerite herself this sounded pretty lame, and her daughter's incredulous tone left her in no doubt.

'Deserves? Ma, please.'

'Darling . . .' Marguerite kneaded her brow. 'I'd deem it a favour, I really would. You can set house rules.'

'Oh I shall, believe me.'

Marguerite closed her eyes on a silent prayer. 'Do I hear a yes?'

'I'll need to talk to Robin.'

'But basically you'd be happy with it?'

'I wouldn't go that far. But I would like to help you out.'

'Thank you!'

'Don't thank me just yet. Let's see what Robin says.'

'You worry too much,' said Hugh. They had walked along the prom, and were now sitting on the shingle at the end of the spur of beach that overlooked the river estuary and the rocks on the other side.

'I worry,' said Marguerite. 'I don't know about too much. You don't worry at all.'

'I try not to. It's the most useless and pointless of all emotions,' said Hugh gently, covering his wife's hand. 'Someone has to stay away from it.'

'You don't think Robin will veto the idea, do you?'

Hugh chuckled. 'I'd be amazed. Depends on how Felicity presents the case.'

'Well quite . . .'

'But he's the second most uxorious husband I know.' Hugh gave her hand a little shake. 'And he's devoted to you as well. I think we can rely on him to do the right thing.'

Robin, walking back to the office from an exceptionally convivial client lunch at the Bonne Femme, was suffering a slight attack of cold feet. Two weeks from today, instead of returning in the evening to the peaceful delights of his well-run home and family, he would have only uncertainty to look forward to, in the form of his wife's teenage brother, with whom even 'a short while' might prove too long.

He realized he'd been press-ganged, however elegantly. Felicity, when she'd raised the topic, had clearly already made her mind up that it was something they should do. The fact that she didn't relish the prospect any more than him just made it harder to refuse – if she could do it, so could he. They had the space, and the resources, why shouldn't his brother-on-law (a sensible grown-up title which somehow didn't suit Bruno) stay for a couple of weeks while he found his feet in London? It would have been churlish to object. This was a favour to the wider family – to Marguerite in particular – and should be performed with a good grace.

Still, it was a bit of a bugger.

'Lucky you,' said Honor, stirring bèchamel for a lasagne. 'Their house is to die for.'

Bruno was leaning up against the worktop, watching. 'So everyone keeps telling me.'

'The only trouble is you won't want to go anywhere else afterwards.'

'You might want to turn that off, it's started to boil.'

Honor switched off the gas. 'Where are you going to look, anyway?'

'Don't know yet.' He pulled a shrug face. 'Ma favours West Hampstead because she used to live there.'

'Gosh, you'll never afford Hampstead!'

'*West* Hampstead – it's not smart, she says.'

'Oh, fine. Anyway,' added Honor comfortably, 'I expect the TSs will be able to help with that.'

'If he thinks I'm going to trudge round with a copy of the *Advertiser* looking at god-forsaken bedsits with him, he can think again,' said Felicity.

'I'm sure that won't happen,' said Robin. 'We can point him in the right direction, but it'll be character-forming for the lad to conduct his own researches.'

In this interim period – what he thought of as the calm before the storm – Robin had quite frequently found himself in the role of devil's advocate. Perhaps Felicity had secretly hoped he would object to Bruno's coming, so she'd be let off the hook, because now that it was arranged she was making heavy weather of it.

It was a matter of common consensus among their wide circle of friends and acquaintances that the Trevor-Saverys, Fliss and Rob as they were generally known, had an enviable lifestyle. In fact they were one of the few couples of whom it might be said that they *had* a 'lifestyle'. Meaning that they – especially Felicity – had formulated a plan, and worked on it. Lucky for them that Robin was now CEO of Porterfield's so executing the plan had been well within their means.

Their house in Hampstead, in one of the more recherche zones overlooking the bathing pools, stood out from its neighbours in just the right way. A 1930s mansion, cool, pale and shiny, it sat there like a spaceship, all gleaming glass and elegant curves, unashamedly different. Inside, clever Felicity had created exactly the right mix of chic minimalism and habitability. With three children under ten this was a hard act to pull off, but she'd achieved it triumphantly. Mind you, they had the space, so the children's bedrooms were in a kind of annex, and they also had a full-time nanny which helped. People agreed that they were marvellous parents and had the balance just right. Felicity had given up paid work (there was no financial imperative) till Noah, Rollo and Cecilia – nine, six and three respectively – were all in school, but she was no idle luncher. She was on the fundraising committees of two charities, a volunteer at the local hospice, and heavily involved in an important initiative (spearheaded by a famous Hollywood actress) to do with the provision of sanitary products for girls in the Third World. All this kept her busy. Plus the house was absolutely amazing, the scene of sparkling dinner parties (the TSs still gave those) as well as convivial kitchen suppers and Christmas parties where the whole place was transformed into a silvery winter wonderland. And the children of course were *lovely*.

In short, they were a fortunate couple who spread delight rather than envy. Carpers were in a minority.

The night before Bruno was due to arrive Felicity lay awake fretting. Part of the trouble was that she hadn't seen him for ages and wasn't sure what to expect. After getting three respectable A Levels (God knows how, Felicity had no time for that weird school) he'd taken off on a gap jolly with a friend – six weeks in Australia and around the dodgier youth meccas of the Pacific Rim. Whether this had broadened his mind wasn't clear, but she'd heard no reports of disasters. She'd invited the parents up to Hampstead for the weekend, but they'd declined in order to keep the home fires burning for Charity and Honor. They had been up earlier in the summer and been a great success, you could take them anywhere.

Now the TSs were back from three blissful weeks in Maine, and awaited the arrival of Bruno, an unknown quantity.

'Mum! Mummee . . .'

'Who's that?'

'I'm wet!'

Cissy came paddling across the bedroom, trailing dampness. Robin rolled on to his back.

'Anything I can do?'

They both knew the question was rhetorical and in a moment he rolled away again.

Felicity accompanied Cissy back to her room and embarked on the process of changing first her nightclothes, then her sheets, then sitting next to her during a potty session in case there was more to come out. Given the hour and her mother's undivided attention, Cissy became chatty.

'Can we read *Tiger*?'

'Not now, it's sleeping time.'

'*Tiger for Tea*!'

'Not now. It's night-time. Have you done anything?'

'Ate *all* the food in the cupboard, drank *all* the water in the tap, ate *all*—'

'No tiger now, Cissy. Come on.'

'No, no, wee's coming!'

Felicity sat with her arms round her knees. Her feet were cold. She was overcome by a familiar weary boredom. She could admit it to herself – much of the activity associated with small children *was* boring. Daily, hourly, she thanked her lucky stars that she was able to employ a nanny. She simply didn't know how other women did it, the long hours of time-filling, the sheer plod of childcare. At least with Noah there had been the excitement of the first grandchild, and a boy (over nine pounds, she still winced to think of it, thank God for epidurals) – all the flowers and champagne and general sense of celebration. She had a nursery nurse to tide her over the first month and after that she had stopped trying to breastfeed, she couldn't believe the ceaseless struggle was good for either of them. Rollo had been much smaller, so his arrival had been easier, and he wasn't so hungry either, but two – dear God! Nothing had prepared her for the ceaselessness of it. Marguerite had come up, but that was before they were in this house and the spacious Edwardian semi down the hill had felt crowded. Their first nanny had arrived when Marguerite left, and though she hadn't survived the move they hadn't been without one since.

'Effant book. Effants!'

'No, no elephants now.'

Felicity lifted her daughter off the potty – it was still empty – and hoisted up her trainer pants and pyjama bottoms.

'Into bed.'

'Can I come in your bed?'

'No, you're going to sleep in your lovely bed.'

'My big girl's bed.'

'That's right.' Felicity pulled back the duvet and hoisted Cissy in. 'There. Do you want Sheepie?'

'No, not Sheepie!' Cecilia's tone implied that this was the most ridiculous, villainous suggestion in the world. 'Not Sheepie!'

'Who would you like?'

'I want to come in your bed.'

'But you're going to go in your lovely Big Girl's bed which is much better.'

After a not brilliant night with Cissy occupying the centre of the bed, Robin left early the next morning, the rucksack containing his clean shirt on his back. He collected his road bike from the garage and was through the gate and just about to mount when the nanny, returning from her night off, slowed down to turn into the drive in her red Japanese runaround, a necessary perk of the job. He paused and raised a hand in greeting.

'Morning Ellie!'

She sent him a little wave, opening and closing her hand like a bird's beak. A very confident young woman, and why wouldn't she be? The nanny business, he had come to realize, was a seller's market, and though Eleanor was undoubtedly indispensable and a treasure, she knew her own worth and had negotiated a very comfortable package chez TS.

Robin didn't grudge it her. Now he took a couple of scooting steps and swung his leg over the saddle. The Tempo Ultegra had set him back north of five k but it was worth every penny, not for the exercise alone but the psychological benefits.

He needed to be calm. Tonight Bruno would be here.

Noah and Rollo were at that age when small boys seemed to ricochet from place to place like released balloons, creating small explosions of mess wherever they touched, and making a lot of unnecessary noise. Felicity fondly believed that Rollo was actually a quieter child, but this theory remained untested because Noah was rambunctious and where his older brother led, Rollo followed. This morning Cissy was cranky after her disturbed night, so Felicity was particularly grateful for her nanny's cheerful Kiwi competence. Ellie had an enviable ability to distract the boys – this time with some mad song about thunder down under, which if it wasn't lavatory humour sounded enough like it to enchant them – so that they followed willingly, and while she was doing that she somehow got Cissy into her shoes and sweatshirt. This morning the boys were strapped into the back of Ellie's car to be taken to St Cuthbert's C of E Primary up near the Vale of Health, and Cissy into her seat in her mother's Audi. Her playgroup was a quarter of a mile further away, en route to the hospice where Felicity was due to provide comfort to the residents both in the day room and on the ward. Cecilia would be dropped off by Felicity, and then picked up by Ellie at midday. On this occasion the boys had a lift home with another mother after football on the heath, but Ellie would give all three children their supper, and make sure the chicken casserole was defrosted and in the oven for later. Officially her day ended after the children's bedtime, but she was agreeably flexible.

'He's catching the train that gets into Paddington around four,' Marguerite had told Fliss. 'So allowing for some faffing around he should be with you between five and six.'

Felicity had not offered to meet him, and was glad her mother hadn't asked. They needed to start as they meant to go on. Bruno had been halfway round the world, the journey from Paddington to Parliament Hill should cause him no problems. There was one thing though.

'Is he solvent at the moment?'

'He should be. He swears he is – he's been working down at the beach cafe since he got back. And Hugh's slipped him a few bob for extras. So don't stand for any sponging.'

'Don't worry, we won't.'

'It's very, very good of you,' Marguerite had said again with feeling.

'Remind me again when he starts college?'

'Two weeks – beginning of October. He'll be off your hands by then.'

Bruno was due to start one of those mixed degrees that were so popular – Felicity couldn't remember exactly but it was something like Sanskrit, Philosophy and Design – at what would once have been a poly, now the University of North London.

The campus was in Cricklewood, so even when he was in his own place that was three years within easy reach. During that time they would be the first resort in a crisis. All the more reason not to featherbed him when he was here.

St Teresa's Hospice was a model of its kind. Felicity felt better the moment she crossed the threshold. Modern, comfortable, tastefully decorated, peaceful but not hushed, everywhere an air of gentle wellbeing. She could never have done what her sister Honor did – all the mopping and wiping and spooning and sponging – she knew her limitations, and that was beyond her. She wasn't even much good when one of the children was sick, the sound, sight and smell of vomit made her retch, and she was more relieved than she dared admit that the end of nappies was in sight. She could never have coped with the less obliging psychological aspects of terminal illness, or even old age. These days she was painfully alert to any signs of forgetfulness in her parents. Children were mentally and physically demanding, but at least one had the reassurance of knowing that they were probably likely to grow up and grow out of whatever it was, whereas with the older generation it was only likely to get worse.

The receptionist (another volunteer) greeted Felicity with a warm smile – she was a popular member of the team.

'Morning Felicity!'

'Hello Jean, lovely day.'

'It's always the same isn't it, the moment the kids go back to school . . .?'

'Absolutely.'

Felicity passed through reception, down the bright corridor with its tasteful framed landscape photographs and into the kitchen. The timetable on the wall showed that sharing ward duties with her this morning would be Angela, a recent graduate from the induction course whom she hadn't met before. Felicity was glad she was there first, to establish a microscopic degree of precedence over the newbie. All the volunteers had to take the twelve-week course, but there was no substitute for real hands-on experience.

She set out rose-patterned cups and saucers (everything was attractive and good quality at the hospice) trays with pretty cloths, and plates of biscuits. She filled a jug with elderflower cordial, and surrounded it with glasses. The next task was to visit the ward and take the patients' orders, something which could take a little while because you didn't want to rush – conversation was just as important as refreshment.

She was just about to set off, armed with notebook and pen, when a woman entered from the corridor carrying a long-spouted plastic watering can.

'By a process of elimination, Felicity, I presume?'

'Yes.'

'Angela Hall, good to meet you. Not sure of the form so thought I'd just find something to do' – she brandished the can – 'and get stuck in.'

'Well done – hello Angela.' Felicity concealed her small discombobulation beneath the prescribed beaming niceness. 'I was just off to take hot drink orders, why not come along?'

'Good idea. Unless there's anything' – Angela cast about – 'but it looks as if you've done it all.'

This went some way to soothing Felicity. Angela was a neat, homely, well turned-out woman in her sixties, with bobbed grey hair. Everything about her proclaimed lack of vanity, as well as order, dependability and good sense. So probably not a rival but a good henchwoman.

On the other hand there was no denying that on the ward she was a natural – chatty, thoughtful, considerate and (most importantly, they'd had this drummed into them) a good listener. Felicity was conscious of raising her own game slightly to, well, not compete exactly, but to show she was an old hand.

Felicity tried not to have favourites among the patients. Apart from anything else you never knew how long they would be there for and it was unwise to become too attached. But she was especially fond of one chap, a retired sales director, who had been in a few times over the past few months for respite care. David Thorpe's aggressive cancer had done nothing to dim his love of the ladies, and they had established a mildly flirtatious relationship. This morning Angela reached him first and Felicity glimpsed their handshake, her attentive enquiries . . . But Angela's good manners couldn't be faulted. As Felicity approached she stood back, and David said, 'Ah, here she is, the angel of the urn.'

Felicity raised her eyebrows at Angela to show it was a joke. 'You know perfectly well there is no urn.'

'Bet there's one out in the galley.'

'Anyway, what's it to be this morning?'

'I'll have my usual skinny macchiato with almond milk and a cinnamon stick.'

Felicity spoke as she wrote. 'One flat white.'

'She's a hard woman,' said David to Angela.

'I'm learning that.'

Back in the kitchen, as they prepared the orders, Angela said, 'It's impressive how stoical people are. I'm not sure I'd be so philosophical.'

'This place does all it can to help the patients to be comfortable and calm.'

Angela smiled indulgently. 'That Mr Thorpe is fond of you.'

'I don't know about that. It's just his manner.'

'Does he have family?'

Felicity tried to decide whether this was a loaded question and decided on balance that it wasn't.

'He's divorced with two grown-up children. They come quite often, they're nice.'

They began loading the trays on to a trolley – itself a thing of beauty, made of sparkling brass and glass, with a lace cloth.

'What about you, do you have any children?'

'Three under ten,' Felicity said modestly. 'The youngest only just turned three.'

'My goodness, such a busy time . . . I remember it well – or at least, I say that, but actually it's a blur!'

They headed back to the ward, with Angela bustling ahead. Felicity, with food for thought, followed after with the trolley.

Eight

Bruno and Sean sat in a Victorian pub that nestled in the lee of the Royal Free Hospital. Bruno's giant rucksack lay propped against his chair. On the table were two pints of Bullshot ale, and a packet of smoky bacon crisps. Bruno had been told not to turn up at the TS's house before five, and it was two-thirty so there was time to kill. The original timing had been predicated on his getting the train from Exeter to Paddington, but he had decided to save the fare and hitched a ride – well, two to be precise – which had set him down near Hendon at about one.

Since the two of them had returned from South-East Asia Sean had taken up residence in London – Kilburn – and extended an invitation to Bruno (not mentioned to the family) to shack up there on the sofa indefinitely. There might even be a permanent billet if Sean's current flatmate moved out which was always likely, they were a floating population. But Bruno was attracted by the idea of a couple of weeks with his sister and brother-in-law first. Fliss was a bit up herself but Robin was OK. And even though they had three kids they were loaded, so he expected the conditions to be quite luxurious.

They had already scoped out the house from beyond the iron gate, and Sean had expressed admiration.

'Fucking hell, it's a palace!'

Bruno, not letting on that he hadn't been before, played it cool.

'Her husband's really rich.'

'You're not kidding . . .' breathed Sean. 'I mean, fucking hell.' He peered at the metal console on the gatepost. 'They're not taking any risks either.'

Bruno affected nonchalance. 'Let's find a beer.'

Sean described himself as being 'in the music business' but they both knew that a) his work life was fluid and b) he was a not-even-glorified gofer to a couple of hard-living A and R men who treated him like shit. But it would do for the moment, and the A and R men had cash to spray around so the job, though low status, was surprisingly well paid.

He didn't think much of Bruno's college plans.

'That'll bore the scuds off you, man. What are you doing that for?'

'It'll pass the time,' said Bruno loftily.

'I'd have thought you'd have had enough of being a student.'

'I'd had enough of school, being a student's different.'

'If you say so.'

'If something comes up I can always drop out.'

Sean shook his head. 'I couldn't do it, I fucking tell you.'

'All that cheap booze and women?' Bruno never said 'girls' – he had his reputation to think of. Sean gave him a sardonic look.

'That what they told you?'

Nobody had told Bruno anything, but he was perfectly happy with the current plan. He had no burning ambition to do anything in particular, and the prospect of two or three years in London subsidized by his parents and the government, was quite appealing. Academically he'd always been able to cream the competition without much effort, and he was pretty confident he could do so now with English, Media and Religious Studies. Sean thought this last was particularly hilarious.

'You're having a laugh!'

'Doesn't mean I'm religious.'

'No, but – come on, dude!'

Teasing of this kind was water off a duck's back to Bruno. 'And you know what, I might be a vicar, they're always looking for those, it's like the army.'

The thought of this was so excruciatingly funny they'd both cracked up.

They stayed in the pub till quarter to five, consuming another pint each and in Sean's case a chilli sandwich, the house speciality.

'You not eating?' he asked round a large dark red mouthful.

'Don't need to,' Bruno reminded him. 'I'm having my dinner at the big house.'

Much later they left the pub and went their separate ways. It was a fair walk to the TS's, and Bruno had already done it once that day, so he spent some of the train fare money on a taxi up the hill, and pressed the button by the gate. A young woman – not his sister – answered.

'Hello, yes?'

'It's Bruno.'

'Oh hi there. Push and enter.'

The gate swung open slowly, and closed just as majestically, and soundlessly, behind him. He crossed a wide sweep which seemed to be made of white bricks in a herringbone pattern and as he did so the front door opened. At least something opened, less a door than a vast sheet of cloudy glass that slid back to reveal a tall red-haired young woman, presumably the one who'd answered the intercom, with a seriously cute small girl beside her, dressed in dungarees and blue desert boots. This he assumed was his niece Cissy, whom he hadn't seen for over a year.

'Welcome Bruno. I'm Ellie. I'm the nanny.'

'Nice to meet you.' They exchanged a handshake. Bruno grinned. He was preternaturally gifted at sniffing out an ally.

As the plate glass slid shut behind him, the little girl said, 'Is your name Bruno?'

'That's right.'

'My bear's called Bruno.'

Bruno had little experience of small children but sensed Ellie's eyes on him. 'I'm in good company then, aren't I? I know your name, you're Cissy.'

'Cecilia called Cissy,' she said, no doubt parroting what she'd heard others say about her.

Ellie said, 'I'll show you your room. Felicity should be back any minute.'

'I want to come.' Cissy was already heading for the stairs at the far end of the hall. The staircase was wide and shallow, made of blond wood, curving in an elegant sweep past a window that stretched from floor to ceiling. 'I know where it is.'

'You probably know anyway, don't you,' said Ellie. 'You'll have been here before.'

'No.' Bruno felt a squeak embarrassed to admit it. 'I remember their old house. This is a bit different.'

'Not everyone's cup of tea,' said Ellie, crossing the enormous white-carpeted landing. 'But I really like it.' She wore loose fatigue-style trousers with many pockets, a black T-shirt and Birkenstocks, an ensemble that seemed to declare unequivocally that though an employee she was in no way subservient.

Beyond the landing was another short flight of steps of normal size. Below this was a second landing with four doors. Ellie pushed open one, then another. 'Family bathroom, that'll be you, separate loo' – she waved a hand at the other doors – 'airing cupboard, sewing room, don't suppose you'll be needing those.'

They went up another couple of steps beyond which was a

short corridor with broad, low windows on either side which made it feel like a bridge. From here Bruno could see a big garden, laid mainly to grass, with a central round patio, roofed but open-sided like a bandstand. A large structure covered by a waterproof cover, a barbecue probably, stood next to the patio on which was an assortment of black rattan furniture.

'This is your room! This is your bed!' announced Cissy.

They were now in a whole separate part of the house, with what appeared to be several bedrooms. Opposite was an open door, with beyond it a double bed with grey-and-white striped linen, on to which Cissy was attempting to climb.

'Down off there, young lady,' Ellie shooed, 'you've got your boots on.'

'Can I take them off?'

'Sure, but you still can't jump around on the bed.'

'I don't mind,' said Bruno. Cissy began yanking at the velcro on her boots and he went in and set down his rucksack. The room was less palely glamorous than what he'd seen of the rest of the house, but it was still chic in its way, with pale grey linen curtains that puddled on the floor, a rough-woven cream rug, and a bedside lamp like a sinuous chrome snake. There was just one picture, a huge rectangle of variegated blue swirls.

'Cupboards, drawers, wash basin . . .' Ellie tapped and tweaked various doors, all with concealed handles. 'Bathroom you know about.' She stood with hands raised. 'All OK?'

'More than.'

'I'll leave you to dump your stuff, come down when you're ready. Cissy' – she held out her hand – 'you come with me.'

'I want to stay and help Bruno.'

'He doesn't need help.'

'It's fine, I'll come down now,' said Bruno. Ellie cocked an eyebrow and he added, diplomatically, mostly to Cissy, 'I might not find you otherwise.'

So it was that when Felicity got home with the boys fifteen minutes later she heard voices from the kitchen and found the three of them sitting round the island. Bruno slipped off his stool.

'Hi Fliss.' They exchanged a cautious, skimming kiss.

'Welcome, when did you arrive?'

'Not long ago.'

'All well, Ellie?'

'Fine. Cissy's got a new friend.'

Thundering footsteps heralded Noah and Rollo. Bruno had to suppress a slight sense of shock as his sister affected the introductions. These vivid, restless, unpredictable small people were the first boys in the family since his own arrival. Did he have anything in common with them? Had he ever been like this, so crackling with energy, so confident, so . . . entitled? Noah was slim and fair like his mother, with a cool regard. Rollo had a mop of brown hair and was brown-eyed too, a sweet-looking boy. From old photographs Bruno knew that Rollo looked a little as he had at that age.

'How long are you going to be here for?' asked Noah, opening the fridge, which Ellie immediately closed again. 'Oh come on! Are you staying here?'

'Just for a while.'

'Are you next to me?' This was Rollo.

'Umm . . .' Bruno didn't understand the question but Felicity answered for him.

'He is, yes, but no pestering.'

'I wasn't going to pester.'

Noah looked at his mother. 'When's supper?'

'When Daddy comes back. We'll have it early this evening, all together.'

Ellie said, 'I've put it in a low oven, and the veggies are ready on the top.'

'Thanks, Ellie.' Felicity looked at her watch (Tag Heuer Bruno noticed). 'You can drop out now if you like.'

Bruno heard the reluctance in her voice, and saw her face brighten as Ellie said, 'Tell you what, Cissy, if you're going to have grown-up dinner why don't you and I go and get you bathed now, and you can have it in your PJs?'

'Ellie, you're a star,' said Felicity. 'It can be bedtime straight after.'

'Will you be having supper?' asked Cissy.

'I hope so,' said Bruno. She looked at her mother.

'Of course he will,' said Felicity. 'He's staying here.' Ellie and Cissy left and she added, 'Boys, why don't you show Bruno around?'

'Want to see the garden?' enquired Noah, as if this were the least-worst option.

'Lead on.'

Robin, still in his return-commute kit of suit trousers and sweat-shirt, took a beer from the metallic Smeg fridge, snapped off the top with the opener beneath the rim of the island, and stood next to his wife, both of them looking out into the garden.

'I know what you're thinking,' said Felicity, 'but it won't last.'

Bruno, Noah and Rollo were kicking a ball around. Or at least Noah and Rollo were kicking the ball and Bruno was somewhat unsuccessfully keeping goal.

'You think he's just ingratiating himself with us.'

'Or with them, anyway.'

'He's letting them win' – Robin took a swig – 'which is a step in the right direction.'

'What do you mean "letting"? He's never been any good at sports. Not that kind. He skis well, swims . . . Show-offy things.'

Robin stroked her hair. 'Let's take what we can get.'

Marguerite put the phone down with a sigh which Hugh, attuned to both moods and sighs, recognized as one of cautious relief (he was alive to the nuances).

'Well?'

'All is calm, all is bright.' She held up crossed fingers. 'At the moment.'

'No reason why that should change,' said Hugh. 'And it's not for very long. I mean, he could find somewhere tomorrow, that's what the college noticeboard is for.'

There hung between them a moment of silence while they both tried to imagine Bruno sensibly studying the noticeboard, notebook and pencil in hand.

'Hm,' said Marguerite. 'Times have changed. Anyway, Felicity says they're going to give him a day or so's grace and then send him out to get on with it.'

'Did you speak to our hero in person?'

She shook her head. 'He'd gone out for a walk with Robin.'

'Really? How far *is* the nearest pub?' Marguerite ignored this, and he went on, 'I still think it's a pity he didn't get into hall,' said Hugh.

'We both know he didn't not get in as you put it, he didn't want to and didn't try.'

'Still much the simplest option and less bother all round. Charity liked being in hall as I recollect.'

'Yes, she did.' Marguerite gave another sigh, this time containing a distinct tremor of anxiety. 'But that was Charity.'

Bruno reckoned he would stay ten days with the TSs. To stay for the full fortnight might be pushing his luck, and 'finding' somewhere on the very last day might give rise to suspicion. Also, he wasn't going to wait to be chivvied. On the morning after his arrival he got up at a time he barely recognized and presented himself in the spaceship-like kitchen for breakfast. It appeared that Robin had already left. The household was in transit. Ellie was at the sink. Felicity, immaculate in faded jeans, cream shirt and a camel-coloured blazer was clearly about to set off somewhere. The boys were wolfing down Nutella toast, Cissy was sitting next to them drawing with a felt-tip pen.

'Bruno, look at my picture of you!'

He glanced obediently at the giant-headed stick man with its explosion of corkscrew curls and mad grin.

'That's very good.'

Felicity said, 'Morning. On a weekday it's a case of help yourself, cereal or toast, yoghurt and whatnot in the fridge.'

'Thanks.'

'Plans for the day?'

'Thought I'd go down to college, see what goes on. Start looking.'

'Right.' He thought he detected a note of surprise. 'Super. OK, Ellie, I'll be off.' Felicity kissed the children. 'Have a good day and I'll see you later.'

When she'd gone, Ellie said, 'You can cook eggs or whatnot if you want to.'

'Toast is fine. Where do they keep the coffee?'

'Instant or real thing?'

'Don't mind.'

She popped open one of the invisible cupboards. 'In here.'

'Where's your mum off to?' Bruno asked the children.

Rollo shrugged. Noah said, with the air of one who'd learnt his lines, 'She does loads of charity work.'

'No, really,' added Ellie as if he might not believe it. 'Hospice, NSPCC, clean water . . . what else?'

'Loads,' repeated Noah.

Once Ellie had left with the children for their various destinations Bruno made two slices of French toast and ate them in his fingers, wandering about the ground floor of the house. There was something pleasantly transgressive in knowing that if he dropped even a morsel of the delicious, greasy slabs they would leave a mark and show exactly where he'd been. Everything was spotless. At least there was a playroom, and it was pretty normal, untidy with toys and gadgets, but with a sofa and a telly of a size you wouldn't normally find in a kid's room. The drawing room was on the first floor, with a sliding glass door on to a big rounded terrace – on top of the extended kitchen, he worked out. From here there was an incredible view of London, from this distance a city of dreams. He felt suspended between worlds. Free as air, ready for anything, alive with possibilities. His mother had rung last night, but he was quite glad he hadn't spoken to her. He had fled Heart's Ease and its comfortable expectations. All of this seemed as strange as any of those sticky, lurid places he'd visited on his travels – stranger in some ways, because his family actually lived here.

He heard a soft hum, and turned to see someone in the drawing room. A cleaning lady, stocky, dark, not so much as sparing him a glance as she hoovered. The two of them were socially invisible to one another. As Bruno came back in she glanced up briefly and he raised a hand and mouthed, 'Sorry', but she didn't acknowledge him, continuing to hoover as he walked discreetly round the edge of the room.

Felicity had provided him with a key, and instructions about the security gate. As he closed it behind him and set off down the hill towards the bus stop, he felt almost lightheaded with freedom. London lay quite literally at his feet.

On the bus as it thrummed its way into the centre of town, another thought floated into his head and hovered there, not troubling him exactly, but giving him pause. That big, shiny house was currently empty except for the saturnine cleaning lady. Robin was adding to his millions, Ellie had taken the kids to their respective destinations. His sister was out Doing Good. There was a kind of contradiction in there. Felicity was obviously some kind of Lady Bountiful, but her kids were left largely in the care of someone else.

Was doing good, Bruno wondered uncritically, the same as being good?

Nine

Honor considered it a privilege to look after the old. She was aware that twentieth-century Britain was not a culture where old people were automatically accorded respect and care, rather the reverse, and she liked nothing more than in some small way to redress the balance. The respect bit came naturally, and she didn't find the personal care onerous or distasteful as many did. Even people in the business, so to speak. She had from time to time worked shifts at Lilac Tree House and it had been an eye-opener what some of the staff got away with. There was quite a lot of casual, impatient roughness, and often a neglect born of hastiness – food removed uneaten, water not topped up, beds imperfectly made and so on. She had also noticed a loud, bracing, impersonal way of talking that had nothing to do with conversation and was in fact a sort of verbal bullying. She wasn't by nature a whistle-blower, but she had tried to make good as she went along, and when each locum period came to an end she returned to her private work with a sense of relief. She could never beat the system, but she could provide a much nicer alternative.

She had learned that biological age was relative. Some of her lovely people (she hated the term 'clients') were barely there at seventy, others had full command of their faculties, and their memory – if not always of their waterworks – at a hundred. Life was a lottery, and some people drew a fortunate gene pool. What life wasn't was a competition. Honor hated the judgemental school of thought which decreed that people who'd smoked, or drunk, or eaten too much along the way were responsible for their decline. Many of those people in her experience were generous souls who'd led full lives and had good stories to tell. And if people were picky and stroppy, well, if you were in constant pain or discomfort, or chronically lonely, you had some excuse.

She tried not to have favourites, but she always looked forward to seeing Mrs Butterworth, who could remember the German airship raids of 1915 as well as the Dunkirk evacuation and the Battle of Britain. She had lost her childhood sweetheart at Ypres, but had been married three times since: first to his older brother who had died in 1921 from TB contracted in the trenches, then to a dance band musician who had proved to be a 'wrong 'un' and from whom she'd been divorced in short order, and most recently (forty years ago) to 'a lovely gentleman', Arthur Butterworth, editor of the local paper, to whom she'd remained happily married until his death in 1971. None of these unions had produced children, but this was not a cause of regret for Mrs Butterworth. Avis, as Honor had been invited to call her was warm, worldly, and in spite of terrible legs, failing eyesight and the aforementioned unreliable bladder, unfailingly good company. Honor recognized a woman even now at ease with herself, without rancour, guilt or jealousy, satisfied with a rich past but still interested in the here and now.

As far as Honor could see, women tended to become either fat or thin in old age. In Avis's case it was the latter. There was almost nothing of her, but with her bright eyes, dyed red hair and animated expression she was like a flickering flame, burning low these days but still vital, and giving off light and warmth.

This morning, Honor arrived at Avis's terraced bungalow at seven thirty to help her get up, wash, and move to her daytime position on the sofa. Until recently she'd sat on the end of the sofa with her feet up on a padded stool, but these days she lay full length with a light fleece over her legs, a pile of cushions behind her, and a table with her 'necessaries', as she called them, drawn up alongside.

The 'necessaries' included a machine for listening to audio books, plus a wireless kept tuned to Radio Two (both with extra-large On/Off buttons), a water beaker with a lid and a spout, a box of tissues, a dish of mints and (most importantly) a lipstick – Tropic Rose – and a gold powder compact with a mother of pearl lid.

Medication and pills, of which there were many, were not considered necessaries. The miniature plastic chest of drawers containing them stood on the sideboard between the Christmas cactus and the photo of Arthur in his prime. The pills were the one thing that made Avis grumble, but even the grumbling was a sort of joke. They got most of the early morning ones out of the way as soon as possible, a few had to wait till Avis was eating her porridge.

'Any more of these and I'll rattle like a maraca,' she commented, swilling down the handful Honor passed her. 'I look like a flipping maraca, don't I?'

'I'm not sure I know what one looks like,' said Honor. 'Do you?'

'Skinny with a bump on the top,' explained Avis. 'My father didn't care for skinny women, just as well when you looked at my mother, but if he saw one he used to say "There goes another one, death's head on a mop-stick"!'

Honor loved Avis's fruity humour. Her father featured a lot in their conversations, and Honor had long since decided that she liked him. A picture of Avis's parents stood near the one of Arthur. Her father was small and dapper, beaming bright in a suit and a billycock, his wife high and wide on his proudly held arm, and looking even bigger in her puffy sleeves and voluminous skirt and hat like a galleon.

As they went about the lengthy business of porridge, tea, bathroom and dressing, they chatted comfortably. Not all of Honor's people could do this, because while the personal care was going on they were too worried, or wobbly, or just plain embarrassed, which Honor perfectly understood – she was sure she'd have been the same herself. But Avis just carried on as if nothing was happening, and she took a lively interest in Honor.

'Now tell me, sweetheart,' she asked, as Honor dropped her kaftan over her head and felt for her twig-like arms in the capacious sleeves. 'How's your young man?'

This wasn't forgetfulness, but a joke between them. Of course Honor realized she wouldn't know when it *did* become forgetfulness, but it amused them both to have the conversation about Honor's imaginary boyfriend.

'He's waiting for me.'

'That's nice. A girl should keep a man waiting. What line is he in?'

Honor understood this, too. 'He's in the clothing line.'

They started at a snail's pace for the sofa. 'Maybe he can get you something nice.'

'What sort of thing?'

'Oh . . .' Avis's breathing was becoming heavy now, they were nearly there. Honor steadied her as she sank down, her eyes closing for a moment.

'I'd like some nice fluffy bedsocks.'

Avis wagged a crooked finger, the nail an immaculate carmine. 'Undies . . . Pretty undies.'

They both laughed, but Honor could feel the old lady's piercing bright eyes on her. She busied herself arranging the cushions, and the fleece, pulling the table with the necessaries to within easy reach.

'Would you like a drink, Avis?'

'No thank you, I've had my tea. Any more liquid and you'll never get away.'

'Do you want the radio on?'

'Not for now thank you, dear. Sit down, sit down.'

'I'll make my cuppa and be straight back.'

A minute later Honor sat on the Parker Knoll with its pink tapestry upholstery and wooden arms. She enjoyed these moments, when the tasks were done and there was time to chat. Her old people might live circumscribed lives but so, for her own reasons, did she. She was glad to have a routine, and to know her work was essential – that it made a difference. When her father teased her about what a 'tie' it all was, she tried to tell him that she was happy to be tied. She didn't want to rush around, or go abroad, or be out every evening. She had created a life that suited her. Indeed it was one of Hugh's maxims that people 'wrote their own script' as he put it – but he still wasn't able to see that that's what she was doing.

Just as Avis couldn't quite believe she didn't hanker after a 'young man'.

Now Avis asked, 'But you're alright, are you?' as if something had passed between them which implied Honor wasn't.

'I'm very well thanks. Let me see . . . The house is quieter because my younger brother has moved up to London—'

'London? London! What will he be doing up there? I lived for a while in Maida Vale, it was full of streetwalkers in those days, but they were quite nice girls in the main. Sociable – well they would be, wouldn't they?' She sank into a husky chuckle from which she took a moment to emerge. 'They never caused me any trouble, and it kept the rents down. That was after Ronnie ran off, and I hadn't got two pence to rub together, I was living on a greasy rag . . . Who did you say was going?'

'My brother, Bruno. He starts college up there soon. Not in Maida Vale though – that's posh now, I believe. Million-pound houses.'

'A million? Cripes, I don't know . . . A million . . .!'

'A tart would have to be doing pretty well to live there now.'

'You're right!' This provoked another chuckle which turned into a cough. Honor passed her the beaker and helped steady it while she drank. Once that was over, with the usual satisfied exhalation, Avis wagged the finger again.

'I may have been broke, but I never did that. I could have done, I thought about it, but no' – she shook her head emphatically – 'never that.'

'I'm glad to hear it,' said Honor. It amused both of them that she should sound slightly prim, when in reality she was not easily shocked.

'Then with Arthur we were in Dollis Hill,' went on Avis, rehearsing a chain of memories that was as familiar as a well-walked path. 'That was nice. Wonder what that's like these days . . . Then when he got the Salting Packet we came here. A bit different for us two Londoners . . .' She considered this for a moment, before sloughing off what Honor thought of as her 'mind's eye' look and focusing once more on the here and now, particularly Honor herself.

'That's a lovely place, up there where you and your family live.'

Honor agreed that it was. 'We're very lucky.'

'It's got that name, that pretty name . . .'

'Heart's Ease.'

'Heart's Ease. Lovely garden, lots of those great big bushes with the big flowers.'

'Rhododendrons, all round the lawn.'

'I've been there. Years ago they used to have the church fête up there. They had a fortune teller inside one of those bushes, like her tent.'

'Yes, I've been told that.'

There followed a pause, not an uncomfortable one, during which Avis's eyes remained on Honor speculatively. Then she seemed to reach a decision and looked away, playing with the edge of the fleece.

'You know there were goings-on – before that, long ago.'

'No.'

'Oh, big scandal.' Avis shook her head. 'She ran off with the gardener.'

'No – who?'

'Like that book, the dirty book . . . well I took a look and it wasn't all that . . .'

'*Lady Chatterley*?'

'That's the one.' Avis darted an affirmative finger. 'The lady who lived in your house ran off with him. Never seen again.'

Honor was fascinated. 'I haven't heard any of this.'

'Oh yes. Set Salting tongues wagging, believe you me.'

'I can imagine,' agreed Honor. 'Was this lady married?'

'Now you're asking . . .' Avis rolled her eyes. 'Widowed, I think. That's what I heard.'

'I suppose that's not so bad. She didn't run out on her husband.'

'He was a wrong'un. Like Ronnie.'

'Who, the husband?'

'No, no, no the gardener chappie. That's what I heard.' Avis blew out her lips. 'That's sex for you. When it's all sex. Nice, but no good.'

Even from her inexperienced standpoint Honor felt compelled to demur. 'Not always, surely. Not always no good.'

'It depends. These two were stark raving mad for it, and off she went.'

'What, and she never came back to the house?'

'Didn't want to. Imagine. That lovely house – where you

live,' Avis reminded her as if she needed reminding. 'Never seen again.'

'So she sold it.'

'Had to.' Avis rubbed her thumb and forefinger together. 'He was a bad lot.'

Honor found herself reflecting on this a good deal during the day. When in her early-evening break at home, she asked her mother about it she was surprised to learn that she knew nothing of the story.

'Heavens above, it all sounds terribly – I don't know – sort of glamorous? Outre, at the time.'

'Avis says tongues wagged.'

'I bet they did. I mean, the fifties weren't exactly noted for wild goings on. If it had been the sixties, another matter.'

'She was a widow.'

'And a merry one by the sound of it.'

'I don't know.' Honor considered this. 'I'll have to see if I can find out more.'

'Yes, do!' Marguerite, in possession of a gin and tonic, was enthralled. 'You move in the right circles.'

Funnily enough it was Hugh who recalled something, when Marguerite was passing on the story over supper.

'Honor was very intrigued with the whole thing,' she said, to indicate that it wasn't just her.

'There's a grave in the churchyard of a chap who lived here. I noticed because it mentioned the house. Maybe he was the wronged husband.'

'He wasn't wronged, she was his widow.'

'If she was a free agent, I don't see what all the fuss was about.'

Marguerite pulled an exasperated face. 'She ran off with the *gardener*, darling, and was never seen again! You must admit it was quite fruity, especially then.'

'There are gardeners all over the television.' Hugh was enjoying himself. 'And they're absolute models of respectability.'

'Well, this one definitely wasn't. Avis said.'

'Who's Avis when she's at home?'

'She's the very old lady Honor looks after down in the sheltered housing.'

'I guess she'd know. I'll look at that grave again on Sunday.'

'You must tell Honor.'

'I will,' said Hugh. 'If you think she'd be interested.'

Armed with the information, Honor made a point next day of making a detour via the church between shifts. A gentle drizzle was falling and she dragged on the pac-a-mac that she kept in her tote. Following the spell of fine weather the mac was dry and crackly with disuse, and stuck out where it had been folded. She thought she must look like a particularly angular ghost drifting between the gravestones. The spots of rain tapped in an uneven rhythm on her shoulders.

Her father had said the grave was up in the far corner but it was some time since he'd spotted it and he could be no more precise than that. She drifted along the uneven row, peering from time to time. The drizzle became proper rain and she put her hood up. Old, no longer fashionable names, spoke quietly from the mottled stone. *Horace . . . Ethel . . . Wilfred . . . Lily . . . Gilbert . . . Stanley . . .* She peered more closely.

Stanley Govan. There followed dates, and the name of his regiment.

> *Formerly of Heart's Ease*
> *Soldier, and dear husband of Barbara*

Odd how that 'formerly' made it sound as though his heart, at the time of his death, had no longer been at ease. And yet Barbara – she had a name now – hadn't bolted until afterwards. 'Dear husband of Barbara', was that rather lukewarm? Or was it just that these days everyone was conditioned to more extravagant expressions of grief?

Honor stood looking at the grave, the rain and her hood providing a sense of privacy. She did her sums. Stanley had died in his seventies, a relatively young man by today's standards. But then if he had been a soldier he would have been through both world wars, either one of which experiences would knock the stuffing out of anyone. So Barbara surely must have been much younger than him if she had been of an age and mind to run off with someone after his death. And she would have been quite entitled to find love again, so the mysterious gardener must indeed have been a 'bad lot' as Avis put it, for her to *need* to run off, and for the whole thing to be such a scandal—

'Good morning.'

The voice made Honor jump.

'Sorry . . .!' The man of about fifty, whom she half-recognized, laughed pleasantly. 'Didn't mean to make you jump.'

'That's alright. I was just, you know, looking around.'

He was wearing a waxed jacket and wellies. No hat, but he had hair like a dog's coat, wiry and curly, that was not flattened by the rain. 'Interesting, isn't it, grave-browsing?'

'Yes it is.'

'I'm Ed Jones, by the way, I'm the vicar here as of a few weeks ago – I think we may have met?'

'Honor Blyth. Yes, we have – I come sometimes with my father.'

'Ah, right. From Heart's Ease?' He nodded at the grave. 'This chap lived there.'

'I just found that out.'

'I believe, though don't quote me on this, that it was his parents' before him.'

'Oh, really?' Honor was ambushed by a sharp sadness. So their house had been the dream house of that Victorian couple, Stanley's parents, passed on to him with love and in the expectation of happy continuity. But the woman, Barbara, had thought nothing of that when she ran away, heedless of her dead husband's legacy. Honor thought she had just been plain selfish.

She was mortified on behalf of Stanley, the soldier, formerly of Heart's Ease. She almost hoped there was no afterlife, it was too horrible to think of him looking down on what had happened after his death, seeing his widow betray him and his lovely house sold to strangers just for the money . . . Except, she reminded herself, *they* lived there now. Her family, the fortunate, faithful, affectionate Blyths, who valued the idea of home and knew how lucky they were to live where they did. So perhaps their presence had restored Heart's Ease to its rightful character. She hoped so.

Ed Jones was speaking. '. . . raining just a bit. We're doing coffee in the church this morning, would you like to join us?'

'I'd love to but I'm working . . .' She pulled back the cuff of
her mac to look at her watch. 'I'd better get on to my next shift.'

He accompanied her back towards the church. Now she could
see the inner door ajar, and the lights on, a baby buggy and a
couple of umbrellas in the porch. At the junction of the paths
he said, 'Right, well, nice to see you outside of official duties as
you might say. I must go and join the ladies. See you again soon
I've no doubt.'

'Yes. Bye.'

He was very nice, she thought, the new vicar. Manly but kind,
a good combination.

Of course, one of the reasons Avis was so well informed about
the Heart's Ease scandal was that Arthur had been editor of the
Packet, and so a kind of living archive. Anything of any interest
that had happened in Salting for the past century was stashed
away in the cuttings library, now on microfiche. The *Packet*,
though not exactly going strong – it was mainly an advertising
vehicle these days – was still delivered free to convenient
households in the town, and Honor promised herself a bit of
sleuthing. She decided not to revisit the subject with Avis just
yet, because Avis tended to take over rather and it was, after all,
the Blyths' house that was the cause of interest.

That evening Bruno rang. Or at least Robin rang initially, and
Honor answered. She had once overheard her father say to her
mother, 'Honor has a bit of a crush on Robin', which she had
immediately and for the first time recognized as true. Up till
then she had just known that she liked her brother-in-law very
much, as everyone did, because he was so charming and friendly
and apparently interested in them all. She'd never told her
father that she'd heard his remark, but it had made subsequent
interactions with Robin a lot trickier what with her heart pattering
and the wretched blushing – at least on the phone he couldn't
see that!

'Felicity's out at her book club, so as Bruno and I are fending
for ourselves with the aid of a few beers and a curry, we thought
we should ring and see how you all were.'

'Thank you,' said Honor. 'We're all fine.'

'How's work going?'

'Very busy, but I like that.'

'I suppose it's a growth market, what with the demographic mushroom.'

Honor knew this was a sort of joke, and if anyone else had made it she would have thought the less of them for it, but Robin she was prepared to forgive. 'Sort of. How is Bruno, anyway?'

'I'll put him on in a minute. You know, Honor, if you ever want a few days in London, to do whatever you want to do, you have only to say – we'd love to have you.'

She wondered if this open invitation had been generated by her sister, or whether he'd only just thought of it.

'Thanks, that's really kind.'

'I mean it. You could be a free agent.'

'Thanks.' She couldn't picture herself as a free agent, least of all in London where she was sure she'd be a fish out of water. What exactly would she be free to do, that she wanted to do, and couldn't do here?

'Don't forget.'

'I won't.'

'Good. Now here's your little brother . . .' There was a brief silence, then Bruno's voice.

'Hi.'

'How are you?' She was smiling, it was good to hear his voice.

'Very cushy.'

'Is Robin still there?'

'No, he's gone to get the film started. The rug rats are in bed.'

'Have you found somewhere to live?'

'Actually I may have done.' Honor thought she detected something slyly suggestive in his tone, but just then Marguerite appeared, so rather than follow this up, she signed off and passed over the receiver.

Hugh was in the drawing room, reading the current scurrilous political memoir. As Honor came back in, he closed the book and looked up.

'I'm glad he finally saw fit to get in touch, your mother's been fretting.'

'I spoke to Robin first – I think he applied some pressure.'

'Good man.' There was a glass of whisky on the table next to Hugh, and he took a sip. 'Where was our Fliss?'

'At her book club. The kids were in bed.'

'It's high time we saw that lot,' mused Hugh. 'They change so rapidly at that age, particularly the little girls. Remember? Cecilia will be ruling the world in no time.'

Honor wondered if he'd thought that about her. She could easily see how it might have been true of Felicity and Charity.

'Not you so much, my girl,' he went on, reading her thoughts. 'You looked after the rest of us from the moment you could walk.'

She tried to work out if this was a good thing and decided that on balance it was. She would definitely rather look after people than rule them.

Marguerite came back into the room with a brisk step and a cheerful expression.

'Gosh, that's a relief. Why do I worry?'

'No idea,' said Hugh comfortably. 'Why do you?'

'He thinks he may have found somewhere, but he won't be able to move in for a week or so.'

'Any details?'

'No, you know Bruno. "Just a place in North London with a couple of other guys" – one he used to be at school with apparently.'

'Dear God.'

'No, come on, that's a good thing. Much better than strangers.'

'Better for who?'

'Stop it, Daddy,' said Honor. 'You're stirring.'

Ten

Mac didn't often get into London these days. The school was over sixty miles from the city, and the local village station not particularly easy to get to. Nor (infuriating this) was there anyone in the ticket office except at 'peak times', i.e. between seven and eight thirty in the morning. Driving in was out of the question

– he was fond of his car, a classic Mercedes, and was old enough to remember when he'd have liked nothing better than a spin into town with the prospect of enjoyable hours ahead – but now the traffic and the hassle and expense of parking rendered the whole thing a trial.

However, this fine September Saturday he was 'bunking off', leaving Mrs Lewis the deputy head at the helm, and catching the ten o'clock to town. This was almost unprecedented. Mac was a dedicated man, and Brushwood was his calling – his raison d'etre. He had no wish to escape the school, it was his home and where he most wanted to be. He knew the school's regime was described disparagingly in some quarters as 'laissez-faire', but those who used it were ignorant of his ethos. The children (they were all children to him) must be listened to, and they must also learn self-reliance. That could only be learnt in the context of reasonable freedom – that is, as much as was consistent with their safety and wellbeing, which he also took seriously. But presiding over such a delicate balance, whilst providing an education, and assuming all the responsibility that even his pupils' parents had a right to expect, was tiring, and he was no longer young.

So this day out was a treat, and he was quite heady with pleasure and excitement as he stood on the platform and saw the yellow light of the London train appear in the middle distance, closing fast, full of promise.

He had worked out a schedule for this outing. The main focus of the day was lunch, but it would have been a pity not to make the most of the trip to town. He was going to spend a couple of hours in the V & A and then, depending on how things went and if there was time before the rush hour, perhaps the British Museum in the afternoon. These side attractions had the added benefit of making the lunch less freighted with importance.

Being free and at leisure in the city was so exhilarating that when he emerged from the tube at South Kensington he didn't go into the V & A right away but walked up Exhibition Road to the park. The Albert Memorial glittered magnificently in the sun, the trees of the park many textures of greenish-bronze, like verdigris. At the sand track he had to wait for a couple of riders to pass, smart girls who tipped their caps as they went by. He liked that – these little niceties, neither expected nor encouraged at Brushwood, were a sort of guilty pleasure. Basic politeness based on consideration for others was of course essential, but the school's no-frills, self-determining ethos meant Mac would rather the children's energies went into areas other than social window-dressing. He touched his own finger to his forehead as the girls trotted past.

He had dressed rather formally for his day out, in the lighter of the two massive suits he had had tailored for himself in the distant past. He was proud that both suits still fitted – Brushwood democracy demanded that everyone, pupils and staff, do their bit in maintaining the kitchen garden, the livestock and the games field, so he was fit. Outside the classroom he often wore a boiler-suit, but the world was a smart-casual place these days, and he owned little that would have come under that heading. He hoped that formality was an error on the right side.

He had almost forgotten the particular pleasures of a London park. When he'd been here as a young man at the LSE, parks had not featured in the student repertoire, but they had been a big part of that brief period when he'd been an impecunious young married teacher. Adele had missed her native Lyons, but she had enjoyed the green spaces and they'd spent hours strolling, picnicking, feeding ducks, listening to the band concerts, people watching . . . In fact this was the part of his fleeting marriage that he chose to remember because even though they both (he suspected) knew they had made a dreadful mistake, they had been happy walking arm in arm under the trees. It was back in the tiny second-floor flat in Paddington that the tension had pressed in on them, forcing them to confront their differences. And then, when Adele had lost the baby – a stillbirth for which she had to endure a terrible dry labour, and both of them a pathetic funeral – that had been the turning point. No more strolling side by side, pretending. Now they looked straight into one another's wide and terrified eyes and saw the truth staring back. Adele had returned to Lyons, and after due and distant process the marriage was over.

Mac sat down on a seat overlooking the Italian garden. Perhaps that was when the seeds of his philosophy had been sown. You had to know your*self*, your own mind, for self-determination to happen. And that was far from easy. Self-awareness had to be learned. Many people – probably the majority – if they knew anything about Brushwood, thought the regime slack, lacking in rigour, that the children just 'did as they liked', but such was not the case. If a pupil made a wrong decision, then he or she had to live with the consequences, at least for a while. The school council, composed mainly of peers, with one or two members of staff, assessed situations as they came up, and its judgements were surprisingly sound. This system had the added advantage that those under scrutiny were far more likely to accept the outcome.

There were some instances, naturally, when Mac had the power of veto, or when he simply had to make a ruling.

On the very instant that he thought of Bruno Blyth, he saw him. And since there was little doubt Bruno had seen him too, there was no option but to keep going. Not that Mac had any qualms about encountering past pupils, even troublesome ones, but it was a question of context, and today's was delicate. The freedom he'd accorded himself felt compromised by this chance meeting. Still, since the encounter was now inevitable it must be taken by the scruff.

'Good grief, is that Bruno?'

'Hi there.'

Mac held out his hand and after a split second Bruno took it and they exchanged a brief, manly tug.

'How's everything going? I hear you got in.'

'Yes, term starts next week.'

'Those were good A Levels.'

'Thanks. They were alright.'

'Bragging rights for Brushwood, anyway.' Mac made a split-second decision. 'Are you hurrying off somewhere, or can I buy you a coffee? There's a hotel opposite the gates.'

'Sorry, thanks, but got to go.'

Mac was relieved. 'Good to bump into you, Bruno.'

'Sure. Bye.'

'All the best.'

Mac walked the next couple of hundred yards at speed, before sitting down on a bench. Bruno Blyth would have been most surprised to know how discombobulated he felt, and the reason.

He set off again, turning east towards the Round Pond and the bandstand, from where he could cut through to Kensington High Street and walk along to the restaurant. He had abandoned all ideas of going to the V & A. A girl in bright pink Lycra zoomed past on a skateboard, swerving and swooping like an exotic swallow. A jogging couple overtook him, one on each side and very close, making him flinch. A football bounded across the path ahead, chased by a youth with dreadlocks, holding up a hand with a 'Sorry mate!' Mac felt his age. Relative fitness notwithstanding his reactions were not the same, and nothing to be done.

Was he, he wondered, about to make a massive fool of himself?

Bruno had been a bit startled too. What the f . . .? That was parks for you, serve him right for taking a short cut, but he had a hangover which had made him nearly heave on the bus, and he certainly couldn't face the Tube. He wasn't at all sure now why he'd agreed to meet this girl, Camilla, Priscilla, whatever, in Kensington, at an hour on a Saturday he barely recognized. He'd fancied her ferociously last night and she was the kind of posh confident girl who was going to make you work for it, so coffee in Ken Market it was. Coffee! He grimaced. Even the head's offer had brought the taste of it into his mouth. He reminded himself that in a few days' time he would have moved in with Sean and this particular state of mind and body – dehydrated, queasy, disaffected – would become the norm.

Mac walked briskly along the broad walk, then round the pond with Kensington Palace to his right, and south towards the high street. The prospect of Bertorelli's restored his confidence and energy. Generous platefuls of aromatic pasta, blizzards of parmesan and black pepper, seeping chunks of garlic bread, all served in the surroundings he remembered and was fond of, with murals of the Italian lakes, pepper grinders like small cabers, and rough, quaffing red by the litre . . . He could almost taste it already. The Brushwood menu, while wholesome and largely organic, was not exciting. Perhaps they should do something about that . . .

He had been walking fast, and was perspiring under his suit jacket by the time he arrived, half an hour early. He should have checked his watch sooner, then he could have wasted some time in the park. There was a coffee shop, one of the new chains that had sprung up everywhere in recent years, and he crossed the road and went in. It was surprisingly busy, with people having what he supposed was lunch – wraps, sandwiches, cakes and salads in tubs. Queueing, he confronted the bewildering array of options. What in God's name was a caramel frappuccino? It was trumpeted as New! so perhaps he could be forgiven. He found a space by the window. The tall stool didn't look inviting, but there wasn't room to stand, so he hauled himself up and perched, his boots resting awkwardly on the bar which didn't seem to be at the right height for anyone of a normal build. His 'medium white Americano' would have done three reasonable people, and the handful of tiny packets of sugar weren't nearly enough, so he could scarcely taste it.

However, the massive coffee did mean he could legitimately stay in place for the required amount of time. He'd been there about twenty-five minutes when he saw her arrive at the restaurant, and go in. Damn, he'd particularly wanted to be waiting for her. But less than a minute later she came out again and walked briskly the few metres to a nearby bookshop.

He abandoned the last third of tepid khaki liquid, hurried out and just caught the green crossing light.

Charity had finished a paperback on the train and had dropped it off in the first charity shop she passed. Since it now appeared that she had arrived first and there was a bookshop more or less next door she took the opportunity to pop in and look for something else. The latest Black Swan paperbacks were prominently displayed near the entrance, and she took only a second to choose. She was rigorously selective with academic and work-related books, but when it came to fiction she was easy to please – she knew what she liked and needed to look no further. The particular author she was into at present specialized in writing about relationships, families in particular, and apart from the intricacies of the plots she enjoyed the author's insights. It was reassuring to know that, in this writer's view anyway, her own family's idiosyncrasies were nothing out of the ordinary.

Happy that she had the return journey's reading taken care of she popped the novel in her bag. In the restaurant, she saw that he'd arrived and was sitting at a table next to the wall, his head framed by a technicolour Mount Vesuvius. He was looking at the menu but not with great concentration because the moment she entered he looked up and rose to his feet.

'Hello there! Excellent. Where would you like to be, on the chair or facing the action?'

Charity opted for the banquette and they changed places. She submitted to napkin flourishing and menu provision.

'I hope you haven't been waiting long?'

'Three minutes at most. May I suggest we choose, and then we're free to talk.'

'Absolutely.'

'Carafe of cheerful red do you?'

'Perfect.'

They made their selection – mixed antipasti for two, then liver and onions for her, lasagne and deep-fried polenta chips for him – and the carafe arrived and was plonked down on the table for them to do as they wanted. Mac poured two generous glassfuls.

'Good health!'

They clinked. Mac's spirits were lifting by the second. In fact he couldn't believe his luck. This smart, good-looking, inde- pendent young woman was sitting across the table from him, talking animatedly and with every sign of enjoyment. She was telling him how fortuitous it was that there was a bookshop next door . . . that she was a fast reader, used to, as she put it, 'hoovering up facts', though what she had bought . . . she showed him . . . was the purest entertainment . . . He listened, enjoying her dry, slightly ironic way of talking and her thin, mobile face as she did so. It struck him that Charity Blyth was the sort of woman he hoped his female pupils turned out to be: self- confident, unfussy, plainly turned out though in his view far from plain, with clear and clearly-stated views. And (a surprise this) who chose *fegato alla veneziana* with fried potatoes. With a bit of luck they could pool the spuds and the polenta.

She had asked him something – the faint wake of her question still showed on her face. He'd been caught out in daydreaming.

'I'm sorry, I'm a bit' – he tapped his left ear – 'and it's a convivial atmosphere in here.'

'I said I don't suppose you get much time off during term time?'

'Well, I'm sure I could have more but l certainly don't take it. The school's not large and I feel, rightly or wrongly, that I should be there, taking care of things.'

'Of course.'

'But all work and no play . . . I owe myself an occasional treat, and this is definitely one.'

'Just this?' She gestured with her glass. 'Or do you have any other plans for the day?'

Mac made a series of lightning decisions. But he had never been a player of tactical social games, and wasn't about to start now.

'This is why I'm in London,' he said simply. 'But I've made the most of it. I was going to look round the V & A, but it was such a glorious morning I walked round the park instead. If I have the time I might well do something else this afternoon.'

'I know what you mean. Even if you live in the country a London park has a special charm. And just the' – she waved the glass again – 'the sense of everything being there if you want it. I love my work, but where I am is a cultural desert. And that's not to imply I'd spend every spare moment in galleries and museums even if I could. But it's nice to have the option.'

They talked a little about her work, and moved on to films – Mac seldom went to the cinema these days, so it was interesting to hear both her recommendations and her scathing critiques. They had a surprising amount in common.

Prior to Charity's coming to collect the malefactor, Mac had only met the parents, who were charming. He'd liked them for selecting Brushwood for their youngest because it would be right for him as an individual, not because of some fixed ideology or determined objection to all other forms of education. He was glad of anyone who shared his views, but the Blyths were not his usual clientele. They had asked searching questions in a polite way, and made it clear that once committed they would

be fully behind the enterprise even if (in Mr Blyth's case especially
he suspected) it was all somewhat alien.

Charity had to remind herself that she was lunching with a man
almost old enough to be her grandfather, let alone her father. And
yet surprisingly, this was not an issue. It was a long time since she
had sat opposite anyone, male or female, with such presence. There
was a certainty in his manner and an impressive solidity to his
frame. And she still found him alarmingly sexy.

After Bruno's rustication she had seen him only once more,
when she'd been to collect her brother at the end of term. He
had spotted her, sought her out in the melee of parents and leave-
taking, as she'd hoped he would. There had been an exchange
which had been on the face of it formal, wishing Bruno well and
so on, but she had known. She had felt his interest, echoing hers.

His invitation hadn't beat about the bush. Not an email, or
even a call, but a handwritten postcard:

> I wondered if you were going to be in London in the
> foreseeable future. I greatly enjoyed meeting you again and
> would like to renew the acquaintance under more propitious
> circumstances.
> Alastair Macfarlane.

He had added his phone number. The card was a photograph
of Brushwood, looking attractively sylvan in the days before it
had been a school – the address was printed along the top. For
some reason she had chosen to do things his way and reply in
kind, on one of her business postcards.

> Good idea, I'd like that. I'll be in town doing a couple of
> days' research first week in September. My time will be my
> own, so can be flexible re time and place.

At this point he'd rung, but missed her and left a message with
time and venue, short and to the point. *No need to ring if this all
suits you.*
And here they were.

★   ★   ★

When they came out of the restaurant Mac wanted to be sure they could separate. He didn't want to be going the same way as her, to have to walk side by side on the crowded pavement, cross roads, make all those small on-the-hoof decisions that had to be made by a pedestrian in London.

'Which way are you going?' he asked.

She pointed over her shoulder, in the direction of the West End and Marble Arch.

'Right,' he said, 'so I'll say au revoir.'

They shook hands. 'I've enjoyed this a lot,' said Charity. 'Thank you.'

'My absolute pleasure.'

'Perhaps I could return the favour some time?'

'Indeed. At any rate, let's stay in touch.'

They set off in their respective directions — Mac's entirely notional, he simply wanted time to think — and each resisted the urge to glance back at the other. Fortunately the bookshop presented a perfect escape route and he marched in. Neither staff nor customers could have guessed, from this elderly gentleman's craggy, frowning exterior, the fizzing emotional tumult within.

Bruno returned to Hampstead out of sorts. The meeting with Camilla had not been a success, her desirability of the previous night's party faded in the light of day and her toffish self-possession stopped him from gaining any purchase socially, let alone physically. Jesus H, she actually wanted to shop! He'd felt like some old married fart out of a TV sitcom following her around that shitty market. He'd known at once that it was so not going to happen.

And tomorrow, Sunday, was the day set down for his removal to Sean's place in Kilburn, an event about which he had mixed feelings, followed as it was by the start of term. He had settled in surprisingly well at Fliss's. The living conditions were let's face it pretty luxurious, and as long as he kept his head down no one was on his case. He'd come to acknowledge what he'd always suspected, that his eldest sister didn't care about anyone much except herself. Robin was a top bloke, and the kids were actually OK, but she just wanted to swan around being thought wonderful by everyone in all those charities she spent her time on. He could imagine the dreaded Camilla turning out like that, she was the same type.

He thought wistfully of Annelind, the rustle of her overall over yielding curves, the soft dark down on her upper lip, her heavy-lidded eyes, the mint on her breath . . . He had been overwhelmed by lust, and she'd have swallowed him up if he had lasted that long. The encounter had been brief, messy and inconclusive. There'd been no thought involved on his part. And when he was able to reflect, he never for a second imagined the whole thing would blow up in his face. But he'd been an idiot to mention the incident, that sort of thing went round like wildfire at school, and when questioned Annelind had spun it her way. And of course he just had to act cocky, calling it 'a successful pass' as if he'd had any say in the matter.

What a dickhead! At least only his mother had seen him cry.

The whole experience had left him with a determination never again to be out of control. Getting carried away was a mug's game.

Mac bought the latest, much-lauded translation of *Beowulf*. He didn't go anywhere else, but returned to the station and sat happily on the train, the book open in his hand, not reading but dreaming.

Charity settled down at her usual table in the reading room of the British Library, a place she found always particularly conducive to work, but not today. After a fruitless hour she packed up her things again and left for the UC hall where she was staying. She considered ringing Fliss, to see if she was at home for a visit, but decided against it. Today must stay a secret for now.

Eleven

Bruno didn't invite his brother-in-law in. Robin thought he understood why. The disconnect between worlds was notoriously tricky and this, by the look of it, was a veritable chasm. He watched with some trepidation as Bruno hauled his massive rucksack from the back seat of the Audi TT (at one point Robin had to stifle a yelp of sympathy for the leather upholstery) and leaned in briefly.

'Cheers mate, thanks for everything.'

'Pleasure. You know where we are. Don't be a stranger.'

'I won't.'

The door swung shut with a mighty clunk and Robin started the engine at once. But as soon as he'd crept forward on to the vacant double yellow just ahead (thereby giving the impression of departure) he paused and looked back in time to see the front door close behind Bruno.

This was a god-awful street. His own student days in Leeds had been relatively privileged, his father having invested in a small house where three of them lived pretty comfortably. These were down-at-heel houses in a rundown neighbourhood, dirty and unloved. The terrace visibly sagged in some places as if the subsiding houses were only being held up by their neighbours. Bins overflowed, walls crumbled, guttering dangled, outside paint-work was leprous and flaking, roofs were gappy with missing tiles. The pavement was littered with fast-food containers, cans and plastic bottles and bags. One of the lampposts had a kink where some careless or drunken driver had ricocheted off it. The street was stranded – at one end was a small and rather dismal industrial estate, at the other a stretch of urban freeway. Nearly all the houses were multiple occupancy, Robin could see the bell console by each door and the drift of sodden junk mail on the step that no one could be bothered to discard.

He felt genuinely sorry to be leaving Bruno here. Was he really this desperate? Speaking for himself he'd quite liked having the lad around. Fliss seemed to regard him with suspicion, but Robin had seen no evidence to support this view. Bruno had been an easy guest, played with the kids, got on with Ellie and not been unduly messy. If it had been left up to Robin he might even have suggested a more long-term arrangement, but he knew better than to mention this to Fliss.

As he pulled away, Robin was aware of the familiar black-bat thoughts closing in and flitting around. A casual observer would never have suspected him of such thoughts. He kept up appearances. It would anyway have been at best disloyal, at worst wicked to confess to anyone that he found it hard to understand his wife.

He wanted to, and there had certainly been a time when he had – or at least been so romantically, blindly in love that it hadn't mattered. But over the ten years of their marriage, nothing had changed. His love for her was still there, but it was under strain. Small, marginal reservations had turned into solid doubts. For one thing, he was far from sure whether she loved him. He knew he'd been the chosen one, the man who had come up to scratch. To begin with he'd found that amusing. And he had fallen for her family, especially her parents who had welcomed him so warmly and of whom he was immensely fond. The whole set up down at Heart's Ease (the name, for goodness sake!) was beguiling, and he had bought into it. He didn't think of himself as naive, but in this instance he had been. He had been reckless in not stopping to consider what was actually between him and Fliss. A one-sided partnership was no partnership.

He filtered on to the dual carriageway and cruised in the slow lane. The advantage of a car like the TT was that one had nothing to prove.

The truth was that Fliss's energies, both physical and emotional, were directed elsewhere. She ran a tight ship, the fact was often commented upon, but her husband and family came second. With all her altruism and good works – she was undoubtedly (and probably consciously) sailing towards an OBE in ten years' time – the rest of them were sidelined. Not neglected in any physical sense, but when he saw how some other families were he had to acknowledge something was missing. They were managed, administered, their every need attended to except a certain base level of availability and attention. Fortunately the children didn't seem to notice this. They took for granted that they would be ferried about by Ellie on weekdays and there was nothing unusual in that, most of their peers had nannies or mother's helps. Most mothers worked now, it was the nature of Fliss's preoccupation which made it peculiarly ironic. She didn't need or want paid employment, but she sought, indefatigably, the validation of her good causes. He used to be proud of her, now he was beginning to think the set-up rather strange. And this feeling extended to their sex life. She rarely said no, and she was always . . . co-operative, he'd put it no higher than that. Sometimes he felt that their moments together were just another of her boxes to be ticked.

He turned off at the slip road and stopped as the light before the roundabout turned red. Next to him was a Volvo with a young woman at the wheel, and a baby and a toddler in the back. The woman was undoing a wrapped biscuit with one hand and her teeth, against the clock. As the light went amber she passed the biscuit over her shoulder to the toddler with seconds to spare, catching Robin's eye as she did so. Slightly embarrassed she pulled a comical smile as if asking, What can you do? He smiled back. There was something engaging in her harrassed, hard-pressed competence.

'So how was he?' asked Fliss, stirring at the stove. Cissy sat at the island with play dough. Ellie was in the utility room, loading washing. 'Did it look alright?'

'Honestly? It looked horrible. Not that I went inside.'

'Horrible enough to warn the parents?'

'Good lord no, he's young, he'll be alright.'

That was it, there would be no further interrogation. Robin wasn't sure if he was glad or disappointed. He would have liked to express some anxiety without it being pounced on or dismissed. Considering this was Felicity's young brother they were talking about, she was oddly uncurious. The sound of a computer game buzzed and blipped from the other room.

He took a beer from the fridge and sat down by Cissy, commandeering a lump of dough and rolling it into a snake.

He said, 'I imagine Hugh and Marguerite will want to come up and see him some time anyway. Then they can see for themselves.'

'They might.' Felicity took off her apron. 'Or they might just think that squalor goes with the territory.'

Cissy rolled and rolled a ball of dough. 'Where's Bruno?'

'He's gone to live somewhere else,' said Robin.

'Will he come back?'

'No,' said Felicity firmly. 'He's got his own place now.'

'I want to see him.'

'He'll come and visit us, don't you worry,' said Robin.

'Why don't you go and tell the boys that lunch is ready?'

Ellie breezed through. 'I'll tell them – I'm off now if that's
OK.'

'Thanks Ellie.' Robin smiled at her departing backview.
Something went missing when Ellie wasn't around.

The family sat round the kitchen table for Felicity's Greek lamb
stew. It contained olives which Cissy and Rollo laboriously
removed. The plan for that Sunday afternoon was their default
one for the rare occasions when nothing was planned. Robin
would take the children for a long walk over the heath while
Felicity did 'admin'. This was not, as it might have been with
a different sort of parent, code for putting her feet up with a
book, or the television. She would be at her desk, laptop open,
sending emails about fundraising events, organising agendas
and actions, researching venues and contacting potential helpers.
When it came to her charity work her energy and eye for detail
(not to mention her barefaced cheek, Robin considered) knew
no bounds. She didn't mind being thought cheeky, in fact
she took pride in it, and in the fact she had enough charm and
clout to be effective.

Robin put Cissy in the pushchair – she was old enough to
walk a reasonable distance, but if the boys were to be kept amused
for two or three hours, the buggy was a necessity – and set off
down the hill towards the bathing ponds and the path through
to the heath. On the path that skirted Parliament Hill he spotted
friends, the Lachelles, also taking a constitutional mob-handed.
They were going in the same direction but currently paused by
a bench as Lilian struggled with the toddler's welly. Their eight-
year-old daughter Sasha clambered on to a nearby bench and
jumped off. Anton, in a cap, scarf and norfolk jacket only a
Parisian could get away with, stood in attendance with his usual
dégagé air. The family's springer spaniel orbited round the group,
tail waving joyously, and it was the dog the boys spotted first.

'There's Hector! Hector, hey Hector . . .!' And they were off.

'I want to go!' Cissy strained at her straps. Pleased to see the
Lachelles Robin released her and followed his children.

Anton relinquished cool for a broad smile.

'Rob, my dear old fellow, how nice!'

They exchanged a handshake and a shoulder-clasp. Lilian touched her cheek to both of his. 'Hi darling. Exercising the troops?'

'Absolutely. Would you by any chance be going our way?'

'Well, we were somewhat unadventurously heading for the swings and slides.'

'Suits me.'

Normally Noah would have balked at the playground – too many little kids – but now they were hooked up with the Lachelles it was different. He'd be able to pull rank – swing higher, spin faster, show off on the zip wire – so everyone was happy. The baby Joel, welly replaced, had dropped off in his buggy.

'What have you done with Felicity?' asked Lilian. 'Time off for good behaviour?'

They knew, and he knew they knew, that 'time off' didn't compute where Fliss was concerned, but they were dear souls who were fond of them both, and playing along.

'She's taking the opportunity to catch up on a few things.'

Lilian peered round at her husband. 'Hear that my little cabbage?'

'You can catch up on as many things as you wish,' said Anton. 'Be my guest. Why not start with that pesky curtain rail?'

'See what I have to put up with?' said Lilian comfortably. She tucked her arm through Robin's. Her physique was the opposite of Felicity's. He adored his wife's figure – tall, slender and long-limbed was his preferred shape in a woman – but right now there was something comforting in the feel of Lilian's solid, sweater-clad curves against him, warmly companionable and easy.

They proceeded slowly at the pace of the two smallest children who were diverted and delayed by everything from the first conkers to stray sweet papers. Sasha and Rollo jogged ahead and had to be reminded not to go too far. Noah looked after Hector, throwing his ball and making him sit, stay and come. Robin knew he would have loved a dog, but it was hard to imagine one in their house. Marguerite and Hugh still had a dog at Heart's Ease, a whiskery rescue mutt who took liberties and got away with it. Fliss took a dim view.

'They went ages without one, I can't think what possessed them to get one at this stage.'

Robin had shrugged. 'They're just used to having a dog.'

'What's wrong with a cat? Much cleaner, they can be more easily left, and they don't need walking. In fact a cat isn't needy at all.'

Just as well, thought Robin, that he and the children had learned to be cats.

Cissy had to go back in her buggy for the last quarter of a mile, or they'd never have reached the playground. When they got there Lilian sat on the bench with Hector on his lead while Robin and Anton supervised the little ones and the other three charged about with Noah telling them what to do and how to do it. There were plenty of people there on a Sunday afternoon, but the atmosphere was restful. This was a nice part of town. Robin felt soothed. Everything was alright, and would be. He was a fortunate man, they were a fortunate family. At this distance he thought fondly of Fliss sitting at her laptop, her hair in its casual Sunday topknot, doing her good works. Good God, what did he have to complain about, he was married to the most beautiful woman anyone knew, and who was actually making a difference.

After an hour or so, Lilian asked whether he and the children would like to come back for tea.

'I want to show off – believe it or not I actually have a homemade cake in the tin.'

Anton confirmed that this was so. 'And I've tried it.'

The Lachelles' house was only a few hundred yards from the TS's, but this being London and a different postcode the area was pleasantly bourgeois rather than smart. Here there was no landscaping, no security gates, and no view to speak of. The house was one of those once-Pooterish Victorian semis which had come up in the world, no longer pretentious but welcoming and comfortable. Lilian worked as a producer for a London radio station specialising in local news and indy music, Anton ran the food and wine department of a high-end supermarket – that was how he'd met Robin. They weren't rich, but hard-working and reasonably prosperous. The front garden had been converted to parking, the back was a long narrow space with tussocky grass, a couple of apple trees at the end, a slightly skew-whiff Wendy house (homemade by Anton) and a scattering of children's toys.

Near the house was a patio, with a wooden table and chairs and groups of tubs and amphora still overflowing with plants.

The adults and toddlers gathered in the kitchen while tea and cake were produced, the older children larked about in the large living room which ran from the front of the house to the back.

Robin had few worries about his children – they were a happy bunch and remarkably self-sufficient. But sitting at Lilian's kitchen table he felt relaxed and carefree knowing everyone was happily occupied, and that it wasn't his responsibility. They came in to collect cake and squash, and Lilian issued no injunctions about taking them into the living room. 'Let's face it, we could do with the peace and quiet.' The two little ones sat at the table for a few minutes and then scrambled down and went to join the others. Outside at the end of September the sun was low and the garden had that poignant, overripe look which marked the change from summer to autumn. Fallen leaves lay thick on the grass and the patio and the tomato plants against the south-facing wall, still with a few tomatoes, were beginning to straggle and droop.

Anton was talking about the residents' association.

'. . . The woman from two houses along is keen for me to be on the committee, but I absolutely do not want to be. The last thing I want to do when I come home is go to some wretched meeting.'

'I think she fancies you,' said Lilian. 'Don't you reckon, Rob?'

'How should I know, I've never met the woman.'

'Thank you,' said Anton.

'No,' said Lilian, 'but you get the idea. Over-excited retiree, elegant Frenchman—'

'Married Frenchman.'

'—she'd love to be the one to snare him, if only to ensure a quorum.'

'Describe this public-spirited temptress,' said Robin, 'so I can picture you fending her off on the doorstep.'

'She's not bad,' said Lilian, 'for her age, which must be over sixty. You know, she dresses well, got that tufty blonde hair, little boots—'

'Sheep dressed as lamb,' put in Anton.

'Mutton,' corrected Lilian. 'Though actually that wouldn't be fair, she's not.'

'Whose side are you on?' asked Robin. He enjoyed the Lachelles' amiable wrangling. They teased each other a lot, could even get quite heated over small things, but you sensed they did so because they could, because their relationship was sound. He and Fliss rarely if ever argued. Not that he wanted to argue, but – well, it would have been nice to have had the confidence to do so. He sometimes feared that if they did argue over some trivial thing it would quickly turn huge, personal and damaging. He was shocked to realize that he was afraid of what he might say. It was all too big, too fundamental . . . Who knows what might come out of his mouth if things got heated?

An hour went by and Lilian suggested a glass of wine. Anton didn't associate himself with the suggestion, he still affected to disapprove of the casual, unthinking imbibing of the Brits. Though tempted, Robin declined.

'We must head home.'

'Why not give Fliss a ring,' said Lilian. 'She could come over for a cheeky one and run you all home. It'd be nice to see her.'

'Thanks, but no – she's busy. I'll start rounding them up.'

He and Anton spent the obligatory ten minutes calling, threatening and cajoling, and then Lilian came with them as far as the pavement. Cissy was in the buggy, the boys balanced on the low wall.

'So glad we bumped into you, Rob. You and Fliss must come to supper soon.'

'We'd like that.'

She folded her arms, cocked her head. 'You OK?'

'Yes, why?'

'You're strangely subdued.'

'No, nothing. Got the work-tomorrow blues.'

'Ah! Tell me about it!' She held his arms and kissed him on each cheek, firm and friendly. 'Au revoir. Don't be a stranger. Bye kids!'

By the time she heard her family return, Felicity had long since finished what she had to do. In the children's rooms all their stuff was laid out ready for the next day. She had brushed out her hair and done her nails, but she went back to her desk and waited for a moment before answering Robin's call.

'We're back!'

There followed the thumping and pattering of the boys' feet, followed by the clunk of the fridge door, the rattle of plates.

'Mummee!'

She met Cissy at the top of the stairs and picked her up. As she carried her back down she inhaled the sweet beauty of her daughter – the sweetness and beauty of the young. A parent wasn't supposed to have favourites, but having a daughter held a special importance for Felicity. Cissy would grow into an enchanting teenage girl, a lovely young woman, with all the associated pleasure and pride. She often thought about what it would be like to get older, to lose one's looks, but with a beautiful daughter one's legacy could continue . . .

Robin's breath was caught by the sight of his wife and daughter in the doorway. His earlier thoughts shamed him. He adored Fliss, and Cissy was so like her.

'Hello my dutiful darling.' He went over to kiss her. 'Did you get everything done?'

'Nearly,' she said. 'It's ongoing.'

Twelve

These days, Marguerite pictured Christmas like a huge lighted ship – an ocean liner or giant cruise vessel – bearing down on her, full of promise, but also slightly threatening. Before the ship hove alongside there were so many decisions to be made! Many of them by oneself, some by other people in order that one's plans could be put in place, logistics organized and provisions and presents bought before the stampede. When Hugh accused her affectionately of thinking about the festive season far too early, she heard the voice of someone who didn't have to think about it at all, because all the prompting, shepherding, enquiring and suggesting was done by her.

Also, and she found this to be true of many, that the Good Ship Christmas didn't have quite the magic as when the children were young. Grown-up life was complicated and emotions not straightforward. There were tides, there were shifts, there were sea changes of which one might be unaware . . . She never wanted to place a burden of expectation on her offspring, but neither did she want them to feel that Heart's Ease was anything but home, where they were welcome at any time and at however short notice, with no questions asked. She had heard people speak resentfully of having to put in an appearance with two sets of parents in forty-eight hours, a species of social tyranny which was so pointless and soul-destroying as to have nothing to do with the spirit of Christmas. The family must come of their own free will, but then if they *didn't* want to come . . . It didn't bear thinking about.

Hugh was altogether more down to earth. Fifty per cent of 'the squad' as he called them were now 'self-starting' and had their own establishments. Even Honor would move out eventually, and who knew what Bruno would get up to now that he had a pad in London? Hugh could easily imagine the two of them spending Christmas on their own or even going abroad! But Marguerite knew that though she'd put a brave face on it she'd be secretly devastated and probably mope.

Still, she did like to *know*. This year in particular seemed uncertain. So when Fliss rang, she was caught off balance.

'. . . We wondered if you'd like to come here?' said Fliss almost casually. 'There's plenty of room, and the children would love it.'

'Oh, darling, well, what a lovely thought . . .' Marguerite was flustered.

'Take your time. Discuss it with Dad.'

Marguerite thought she detected the merest glint of impatience. Any invitation from her eldest daughter needed to be welcomed at once and with open arms.

'Alright, yes, that sounds wonderful though, I'm sure . . .'

'You don't sound all that keen.'

'I suppose I was just thinking of the others, you know, we've always been here to welcome all comers.'

'All the more reason for the two of you to have a break.'

Marguerite gave a brittle laugh. 'I suppose! But just the same I'd better check—'

'Bruno can come here too.'

'Oh really?' This came as a surprise. 'Has he said so?'

'We haven't asked him yet, but he's hardly likely to turn it down. And if he does, you can bet he'll have good reasons.'

This brisk dismissal of the Bruno problem made Marguerite self-conscious about mentioning the others. She'd have to do some detective work before giving Fliss her final answer. They were adults after all. Or adults when they chose to be, children when they didn't, but that was how it worked. It seemed to her that she'd been a pretty good mother of babies and small children, but that the role had become more challenging as they got older, requiring a set of skills that she didn't possess, or which didn't come naturally to her. Not much more than a decade ago, Heart's Ease had seemed perfectly named, a kind of domestic Camelot where family life was bathed in a rosy glow. She felt it herself, and saw it reflected in other people's faces. These days her heart was rarely easy.

An unforeseen difficulty presented itself when she mentioned Felicity's invitation to Honor.

'Oh wow, that's so nice. Did you say yes? I'd love to go there with the children and everything.'

Agonising though it was, Marguerite knew that to leave the situation unclarified for even a single second would be to make things worse.

'I think she meant just us – me and Dad.'

'Oh, really? Oh right, sure, of course, I wasn't thinking.' Honor, caught out in her false assumption, was equally flustered. 'Yes, my God, they don't want everyone descending on them!'

'I think Bruno may go, he doesn't live very far away.'

'Yes, yes, sounds sensible.'

Marguerite wanted to put her arms round her daughter, but stopped herself – that might be making too much of it.

'What – I mean, if we do decide to go—'

'Oh but you must!'

'If we do, what do you think your plans would be?'

'It depends, I might very well work, make sure some of my old people are having a nice time. I actually like doing shifts on Christmas Day.'

'You're so good.' Marguerite allowed herself a smile. 'Like *Little Women*.'

'Who?'

'You remember, the March girls?' Honor's earnestly enquiring expression remained blank. 'Never mind. As long as you wouldn't mind.'

'Of course I wouldn't, it's a great idea. You must go.' Honor added, as though it were an afterthought, 'What about Charity, any idea what she's up to?'

There had to come a time, thought Charity, when one didn't necessarily spend Christmas with one's family. She'd always been happy to do so, but these things shouldn't be cast in stone. Not that the parents had ever applied pressure, quite the opposite – their line was that they would be laying on the festivities at Heart's Ease for any of the family who wanted to join them. But it was easier to say no if, like Felicity, one had a family and household of one's own. Once Rollo and then Cissy had come along they'd stayed in London, and arrangements had been made to get together with the parents at New Year. Charity's pleasantly monastic small flat wasn't suited to seasonal celebration, and she'd have been perfectly content to let the day pass her by, but she knew that it made her mother happy to have her offspring around her.

Looking at Mac's postcard, she reflected that this might be the moment to break with tradition. The card was another featuring Brushwood in the old days – he must have had a stash of them – and she realized that as before he'd committed the invitation to writing so as to give her time to think.

> I shall be rattling around here over Christmas, and I wondered if you'd like to come over for any part of the holiday to share the contents of my bachelor larder and my Scrabble board. I'd be delighted to see you.

She was amused by his faux self-deprecation. One of the things that drew her to him was his solid, old-school confidence. Besides, it was clear he saw nothing odd in their friendship, and was right in assuming that she didn't either.

They'd met three more times since that first lunch in London – an RSC production in Stratford, and dinner in a pub not far from the school, one evening when she'd been driving back from a meeting and realized she was going to be close by. At half-term he'd suggested (without irony) 'a hike' and they'd met halfway and done fully ten miles, which had felt like more due to the gradient. Charity had been ashamed of her lack of fitness, and commented on it.

'Your work keeps you pinned to your seat,' said Mac. 'Whereas mine requires a surprising amount of hard labour.'

So far there had been nothing of a romantic nature between them. Or at least no physical manifestations. But Charity could feel the thrilling hum of a kiss coming down the line. She couldn't remember when she had last enjoyed a man's company so much, in fact she surprised herself. Her reaction to people and situations was always measured. Some found her almost too cool, she knew that. She found incontinent emotion suspect both in herself and others and did all she could to keep it in check. But now, with Mac, she found that it was not possible to calibrate her feelings, and that to be just a little out of control could be pleasant, exhilarating even.

So the news that the parents had been asked to spend Christmas in London was all it took for her to accept.

> Thank you for your kind invitation, and the answer is Yes.
> Shall I show up p.m. on Christmas Eve? And what shall
> I bring?

As before, once she'd accepted, he rang.

'I generally make a turkey stew and buy a supermarket pud, but a bottle of something warming is always welcome. May I ask if you're a whisky drinker?'

'Given the season I am. It's on the list.'

'Some cheese, perhaps?'

'Stilton and proper cracked and gum-fizzing cheddar?'

'Gum-fizzing! Exactly. Yes. No more than that please, I shall enjoy prowling the aisles. And in case you're worried I allow myself to be extravagant with the fuel at the solstice so even the spare room will be decently warm.'

'I'll leave my hottie at home then.'

'I wouldn't go that far. The boiler's not much younger than me, it might prove a useful precaution.'

She considered he'd managed the passing of the bedroom

information quite gracefully, in a way that was both gentlemanly and practical.

When her mother had asked what she would be doing, and whether she'd be alright, she was able to allay her fears without being specific.

'Of course! I'm going to spend a couple of days quietly with a friend.'

'Are you sure? Because you know we always love having you all.'

'But it's good to have a change, Ma. I mean good for you two to have a change. Go to London. Have fun. I certainly shall.'

Marguerite mentioned that Honor would be at home on her own.

'Lucky her,' replied Charity bracingly, 'in sole charge of the drinks cupboard and the remote.'

Marguerite made a murmuring sound, somewhere between a demur and a laugh. They both knew that putting pressure, however gentle, on Charity to keep her sister company was futile, but it had been worth a try.

'Go,' Charity repeated. 'Enjoy yourselves, let Fliss and Rob wait on you.'

Marguerite put down the phone and looked at the dog, who was sitting nearby, watching her fixedly to shame her into a walk. He wiggled his whiskery stump of a tail and shifted from foot to foot.

'And then there's you, Archie,' she said. 'What shall we do with you?'

As a child Bruno's parents had always bought an advent calendar (not one containing chocolate, which Hugh considered unchristian) and now he almost wished he had one so he could count the days until he could legitimately flee to Fliss and Rob's. He reflected that it had probably been a mistake to go there in the first place, because it had spoilt him. Freedom, he was discovering, was not all it was cracked up to be. And anyway, he'd been pretty free at the TS's, they weren't fussed what he did, with whom, where or when so long as it didn't interfere with them, and the result was he'd hung out at the house quite a lot, enjoying the comfort, as well as the contents of the bottomless fridge-freezer. The kids were cool, the nanny was a pretty good sort, and he hadn't minded being pressed into babysitting once or twice.

At Sean's place it was different. Grotty didn't begin to cover it. Rank. Minging. No one could call him fussy, but this was gross. The flat itself wasn't too bad, in the sense that it didn't actually have damp or dry rot and the plumbing by and large worked so long as it wasn't overtaxed (which happened fairly often). The landlord was a smooth Sri Lankan who asked no questions so long as the rent was on time, and who had Dyno-Rod and a fleet of other useful businesses on speed dial. No, the trouble was that Sean simply didn't care. Worse, he seemed to think that it was rock and roll to let everything reach the status of a health hazard and beyond. Clothes, dishes, surfaces, floors and furniture seemed melded together in a homogenous mass, covered in grease, grit, dust and hair. You could feel the gunk of ages under your feet if you went barefoot to the loo in the night. Every handle and light switch was haloed with grime, the windows were streaky inside and out, and the cords which adjusted the blinds, themselves fluffy with accumulated dust and dead insects, were black with use.

To make matters worse, Bruno hadn't the tiniest space to call his own, in which to have his own albeit modest level of order. The other sub-letter, Phil from Swansea, had the second bedroom, and worked nights at a furniture warehouse, so his living conditions were a mystery. But Bruno was on the sofa, the sofa was in the living room, and no concessions were made. Thank goodness for his headphones, with which to zone out unwanted music, telly, and conversation, but there was nothing he could do about Sean's beer-fuelled, single-sex social life. It was weird how one's capacity for enjoyment was in direct ratio to the availability of an escape route. Once you were trapped, Bruno found, you were sunk. Hell was indeed other people.

He'd checked out the noticeboard for other places, but they were either too expensive or too far away which would incur greater travel cost. There might be more, he was assured, after Christmas when a number of people dropped out of their courses. Also, he had shamefully to confess to himself that he wanted to stay within hailing distance of the TS's. At least here he knew that Paradise was within easy reach, if not exactly on offer. Fliss had invited him over to Sunday lunch on one occasion but he'd turned it down, making up an excuse, because he knew he couldn't face leaving there in the early evening and coming back to this shithole.

It wasn't all terrible. Sean was an old friend, and a funny guy who'd always been able to make Bruno laugh. They still from time to time got pissed together and shared a few laughs. Bruno had to remind himself that it was pretty decent of Sean to put up with him in the living room. Sean was as tolerant with a spare body on the sofa as he was with the general grime and chaos. Once when Bruno had dropped off at two in the morning in spite of everything, he'd woken up to find the remains of a Big Mac resting on his belly where it had been absentmindedly left, as if he were a spare surface.

College was OK, the course wasn't demanding and he'd made a few friends among his fellow students – he'd never had trouble with that. But he had to find somewhere else to live in the new year. The squalor made him homesick.

At the end of the month he spotted a familiar sparkle in the window of the local newsagent's. Minutes later he emerged with a plastic carrier containing a naff Santa advent calendar. WTF.

Thirteen

Honor tried to like all her clients, because they were mostly in a bad way, or needed her, and getting to like them was part of the job. She'd found that understanding had to come first. Even the more challenging, impatient and rude ones had their reasons. Sometimes their behaviour was quite simply a symptom of Alzheimer's, sometimes it had its roots in pain, or loneliness, or a long-felt sense of grievance. Just occasionally they were 'miserable gits' (a phrase she'd heard used at Lilac Tree House though she'd not have used it herself), but that was life, and everyone was different.

No, the problem as often as not was the relatives, if they were around. As often as not they weren't, and were more than happy to let her take care of things. She didn't work through an agency, and her rates were as modest as she could manage, but by definition those who employed her were reasonably well off, and throwing money at the problem. Very occasionally she was employed directly by the client (Avis was one such) and these people tended to be likeable, perhaps because they were realistic about their problems, and had taken charge of their own lives.

Mr Dawson – Honor always stuck to surnames unless invited to do otherwise – had a son, Graham, whom she didn't care for. He lived on the new Park Grange development on the inland edge of town, with his wife Sandra. They didn't have children because Sandra had never wanted any. It was unclear from Graham's tone whether he shared his wife's view or resented it. He was certainly not a man you would ever think of as having a secret sadness, being brisk, facetious and always a squeak louder than the situation called for. He was Mr Dawson's only child.

Mr Dawson himself, a widower for twenty years, was a perfect gentleman, one of Honor's 'sweeties'. He had the kind of good manners that were based on thoughtfulness and not just show, which made everything so much easier. Not that it mattered, intimate personal care was an important part of the job and Honor was happy to do it, but when the person concerned was accepting and appreciative the tasks could invariably be managed more simply. He wasn't as chatty as Avis, he had a natural reserve which Honor respected, but he did sometimes talk about his wife. This was a safe subject, which made him happy, and Honor would often prompt him with a gentle question when they were having a cuppa together. She knew for instance that Mrs Dawson – Pamela – had been a wonderful cook.

'Did you used to do much entertaining?'

'We used to have a little dinner party about once a month, for close friends. There were two couples we used to play bridge with. And then there was some business entertaining that went with my job.' (Mr Dawson had been a bank manager.) 'She was such an asset to me, in every way.'

Charity would have jumped on this as old-school sexism, but Honor completely understood. The Dawsons had been a team, with a happy and stable marriage based on mutual respect as well as true love. You could hear it in the old man's voice, and see it in his eyes when he looked at his wife's picture.

'She was very elegant, wasn't she?'

'Yes, yes, she was . . . She wasn't in the least extravagant, but she knew what suited her. I took it for granted till we went out somewhere, and then I used to feel very proud. Extremely proud.'

There were no confidences, Mr Dawson was essentially private. He did occasionally mention Graham, saying that he was lucky to have such a kind son and daughter-in-law who lived not far away, and who were so good to him. Honor was glad to hear him say this, but reserved judgement on Graham, whom she encountered about once a fortnight. The moment he arrived, the front door banging behind him, a shout of 'Hello, hello, hello, what's going on then?' all peace was destroyed and for the next half an hour or so the atmosphere in the room jangled with an artificial bonhomie. Under the hollow 'banter' (a word Graham was fond of) there lurked an undercurrent of something unpleasant that she couldn't quite put her finger on. Discontent? Resentment? It reminded her of the blank-faced grins of circus clowns she had seen as a child. They weren't truly funny and were full of a boisterous violence that scared her.

She had never met Sandra, but on those rare occasions when they took Mr Dawson out for the day she found herself worrying about him. She was sure they 'showed him a good time' (another of Graham's expressions), but were they attuned to the old man's needs? Did they listen? Did they rush him, just a little? He was such a gent, and so appreciative, it was hard to imagine him speaking up for himself. She was always glad when she went in the next day and found him alright, if a little tired.

This was one of those days. Graham and Sandra had taken him shoe-shopping in Exeter, with a 'slap-up lunch' in a hotel in the Cathedral close. Mr Dawson looked worn out, but that she told herself was only natural. She waited till the morning's rituals were out of the way before broaching the subject.

'So how was your day out? Did you have a lovely time?'

'Yes, thank you. They're so good to me.' He pointed at his feet in maroon leather slippers. 'Did you notice?'

'I did.' She had provided an arm to lean on as he stepped into them. 'Those are very smart.'

'They're less trouble than my funny old lace-ups,' he said. Honor could hear Graham, or possibly Sandra, saying this. She knew Mr Dawson had been proud of his conker-coloured brogues, and liked to keep them polished. She occasionally gave him a hand with that, and he was fussy about how it was done. The slippers were nice, and certainly expensive, but she couldn't help thinking that 'less trouble' was code for 'old person'.

She held the sugar as he helped himself – 'I should stop, but at least I'm down to one lump' – and sat down in her usual chair with her mug of instant.

'How was lunch? I hear The Mitre's wonderful.'

'Very swish. I was persuaded to go for something different, and it was surprisingly delicious.'

Honor wondered what the different thing was that Graham had insisted his father try, but decided not to ask. Talk of lunch reminded her of something.

'Are you going to them as usual on Christmas Day?'

'No, not this year.' He raised a finger as if this was his idea. 'I shall be doing for myself, with the assistance of the van ladies. I've booked already.'

Honor experienced one of her little heart-squeezes of sadness. Silly, but she couldn't help herself. Avis, for instance, was often alone on Christmas Day, but Avis was different somehow – she deflected worry with her gossipy independent cast of mind. Mr Dawson, in spite of the proximity of Graham and Sandra, seemed far more vulnerable.

'And,' he added, 'I shall be able to watch the Queen.'

Honor sensed this was not the moment to express unhappiness. Positive reinforcement was the thing.

'Excellent,' she said. 'And their food is great, I bet they do a super Christmas dinner.'

But in the car on the way to her next stop she couldn't shake the image of Mr Dawson sitting in his neat living room on Christmas morning, wearing his polished brogues in honor of the occasion, undoing his present from Graham – and a less lavish one from her – and waiting for the ladies in the van.

Shortly after that, an idea began to take shape in her head. Once there, it grew and settled, so that by the time she was home that night it was a fully-formed plan.

'Of course not!' said Marguerite, bright with relief. 'Invite whoever you like!'

'It won't be a wild party,' Honor assured her.

'Go wild if you want to,' said Marguerite. 'Just let us know of any breakages.'

'Of *course*—' began Honor, before realising she was being teased. 'But there won't be.'

Hugh was a man of uncertain faith, but regular habits. He was of the opinion that unless one was a thorough-going atheist one might as well put in the hours, enjoy the peace, and quiet, and who knows? A chap might derive benefits in the form of unconditional approval and a place in the sunny uplands of the afterlife. Marguerite, who was far more emotionally attached to the Almighty, and especially to the New Testament, was at best a sporadic church-goer. Neither of them had passed on the habit to their offspring, but Honor quite often accompanied her father down the lane because she liked this short walk together.

This was stir-up Sunday – the first in Advent – and the service was well attended by current standards. About thirty people were there to see the first of the candles lit on the advent wreath. It was also one of those grey, raw days when it seemed colder inside the church than out. The ancient iron pipes that ran underneath the pews were hot enough to melt plastic (as more than one owner of an inexpensive handbag had discovered) but did little to improve the overall temperature, so Hugh was not inclined to hang about. The call of a pint of Devenish at his own fireside propelled him down to the lychgate before he realized his daughter wasn't with him. When he spotted her in the clump by the porch, she waved with a 'Go on!' motion. He waved back and set off – knowing Honor as he did, she'd probably got stuck in conversation with some aged person whom she was too polite to leave, or the vicar, for whom she had a Thing.

Honor hovered until the last of the congregation had gone.

Quite a few of them had chatted to her, but she'd been waiting to talk to the vicar, who came over at once.

'I'm glad I caught you,' he said, as if he hadn't noticed she'd been waiting. 'I wondered whether you'd found out any more about our friend the brigadier.'

She was so pleased he remembered the conversation. 'A little, yes. Rather sad, actually – years after he died his widow took off with someone else, literally ran away, and then sold the house and was never seen again.'

'I suppose,' reflected the vicar, 'that she was entitled to find happiness. But to disappear like that suggests something strange and dramatic, doesn't it. And of course' – he smiled quizzically at her – 'it's your house we're talking about.'

'Yes.'

'If we were on television,' he said, 'my next question would be "How do you feel about that?" . . .'

'It's not at all a sad house, if that's what you mean. Quite the opposite actually.'

'Just as well, with a name like that.'

'I know!'

They laughed. There seemed nothing else to say. Honor wondered why she had hung around like this to say, well, not very much.

'Were you going to walk?' he asked. 'Because I could give you a lift.'

'Oh no, no thank you, I'm fine thanks!' And why was she so gushingly emphatic? 'I'm with my father, we like the walk.'

She moved off so fast that she was out of breath by the time she'd turned into the lane, and had to rein in her hectic pace.

Oh dear, she thought, *how tragic am I? I've got a crush on the vicar.*

She knew her parents worried about her – not much, but in a mild way. They wished she had what they probably described as 'a social life'. This didn't have to include a man, but she was sure that was what they hoped. No one could believe that her work *was* her life, both social and otherwise. But that didn't stop her recognising this heady sense of excitement.

She'd experienced it at least once before, most notably when she was only fifteen, with a charming friend of her father's. Of all the Blyth siblings she was the most teasable – Felicity seemed to have been born with the ability to flirt, Charity was protected by her cleverness, and Bruno, well – normal rules did not apply.

She had been infatuated with that friend of Hugh's, and the whole family had known it, so the teasing, however affectionate, was relentless. There was *no way* she would let this latest crush be known. It occurred to her that they probably hoped her Christmas guest was someone quite different, evidence of the elusive social life. She wasn't going to disabuse them.

Marguerite looked up from an article about yet another rising star from the seemingly inexhaustible supply of 'un-actressy' young actresses in the colour supplement. 'What have you done with Honor?'

'She was chatting, so I carried on.' Hugh went to hang up his coat and scarf.

'Many people?'

'Not bad. But freezing.' Coming back in, he picked up her hand, kissed it and laid it against his cheek. 'Feel that.'

'Ouch!' She snatched it away. 'Chatting to the rev?'

'I couldn't see, but I wouldn't be surprised. Can I get you anything?'

'The Worra-Worra's in the fridge,' said Marguerite, their word for the Australian sauvignon that was their current favourite. While Hugh went to the kitchen, Marguerite lowered the magazine and gazed thoughtfully into space. She did wish Honor had a bit more life. Her youngest daughter was in danger of turning into a Barbara Pym character, and she deserved so much more than that.

All Marguerite wanted was for her children to be completely happy, so she could stop worrying and do the same.

'I can come and collect you,' said Honor, 'and bring you home afterwards, whenever it suits you. You don't have to hang about.'

Mr Dawson's cheeks showed faint pink patches, and his eyes were moist, but his voice was steady and urbane as ever.

'That really is extraordinarily kind of you. Are you absolutely sure?'
'Absolutely.'
'I can't help feeling that you must have better things to do on Christmas Day.'
'Not at all. I have visits to make early morning and evening, but that's all.'
'I'm afraid I can't be of much help. All that was Pamela's department.'
'Don't worry,' said Honor, 'I shall keep everything easy.'
'In that case,' said Mr Dawson, 'I shall let Graham and Sandra know I'm invited out. It will set their minds at rest.'
Honor was sure they'd be delighted. As, to be fair, she was.

Fourteen

The hospice's carol service was always early in the season, because it was also a fundraiser, and they wanted to steal a march on all the others that were happening at this time of year. This year the calendar dictated that it fell on the first Friday in December, which was a bit too soon really. On the other hand, said the volunteers, the supermarkets had been a-jingle with seasonal goods for at least a fortnight, so why hold back?

Felicity was going to do a reading, and on this occasion sing, too, in the small choral group. Carols notwithstanding the service had a humanist flavour, so her reading was Betjeman's 'Advent', and the choral pieces included 'Winter Wonderland'. Robin, whose last church attendance had been their wedding, nonetheless revealed a conservative streak in this regard.

'I detect mission-creep. It's either a carol service or it isn't.'
'Let's call it a Christmas concert.'
'I'll bring the children along this time'
'Oh no,' she said. 'They'll be bored to death. And remember it's out of doors, so it's quite cold too.'
'Let's see,' said Robin.

Working for her charities at this time of year was rather like being a vicar – it was a busy period. There was always a big push to get donations while people were susceptible, softened up by Christmas music, sugary TV advertisements and the sly nudge of seasonal guilt. As soon as she received notification of the children's Christmas events she realized that it was going to be tricky getting to the boys' concert because it clashed with the big mainline stations' collection day for Clean Water, to which she'd been committed for ages. They were that bit older, and wouldn't mind she told herself – she would ask Robin if he could make it – and it did look as though she might be able to make Cissy's nursery nativity.

She had done the right thing asking the parents this year – children and grandparents should see each other at Christmas. She experienced a warm, self-righteous glow as she ordered the organic bronze turkey, made a cake and pudding, and started her 'Christmas cupboard' with presents. So much of Christmas was about re-creating the past, making these preparations she felt like a good and dutiful child, looking forward to her parents' happiness and approval. At Heart's Ease arrangements had been very simple, but she remembered everything as wonderful – the excitement of the rustling, bumpy largesse of Hugh's old rugby sock stuffed with small things, the cold walk to church, the enormous and delicious lunch which they wolfed down on a tide of excitement about the presents to come, with Hugh saying things like 'This is a religious festival, not a bunfight' to general jeers. After lunch there was the Queen to be sat through before Hugh, still wearing his paper cracker hat, distributed the presents from under the tree. Even then they had to wait till everyone had their pile before diving in. Marguerite, armed with a pencil and pad, would flit madly from child to child keeping track of who had what from whom so that that agonising thank-you letters could be written. Felicity could never understand how her mother, and her father (a fresh glass of port in his hand) could bear to wait so long to open their own presents.

After the frenzy of unwrapping came the pleasant wind-down of the day, with Hugh collecting up the discarded paper, 'Like a looter on a battlefield' he always said, which they never got. And then some undemanding games which Charity didn't join in, but nobody minded. After Bruno's arrival the balance was disturbed because they had to rewind arrangements to take account of a little child's different schedule and requirements. Honor had loved the rewind and revelled in it, and Charity took it in her stride but Felicity, at the top end as it were, had been put out. It was as though her feet had been caught in cement.

Still, the memory of childhood Christmases was what drove her. In her house everything was always perfect – shiny, delicious, fragrant and tasteful, 'just like Harrods' as Charity had once put it – the box trees sprinkled with white lights, the greenery both real and artificial swagged and trailing in abundance, clusters of church candles everywhere . . . But she could never recapture the special atmosphere of the past, that intangible something which had nothing to do with money or effort, which in fact involved a good deal less of both than she expended.

The hospice in December was always lovely. Felicity helped with the decorations, for which she had a special flair, and prepared exquisitely wrapped fairings for the residents – tiny soaps and wrapped chocolates. There was a small tree in the hall, and larger ones in the ward and the day-care centre. Outside, the unremarkable single-storey building was strung with fairy lights just below roof level, which transformed it into something like a fairytale cottage. In the garden at the back the biggest tree, a Norwegian spruce planted in the middle of the lawn, was also picked out in lights – the centrepiece for the carol concert. All the visitors would stand around the tree and the principals – the patrons, padre, mayor, readers and singers – would be on the terrace just outside the building, so that the residents could see and hear them. It gave Felicity goosebumps to think of it.

Today she was on the tea round with Angela, now a full member of the team. They moved down the eight-bedded ward, one on each side, putting the nicely laid trays on bedside cabinets or tray-tables as was appropriate, helping people get comfortable and where necessary helping them to drink their tea.

David Thorpe's deterioration had been abrupt and dismaying over the past couple of weeks. He wasn't in good shape. Family members were coming in every day. The exuberant manner and careful self-presentation were gone, he looked an old man. His skin, now waxy and translucent, stretched and hung at his jowls, and on the underside of his arms. His eyes were small and dull above speckled pouches. His lips were dry, and he'd developed the habit – all too familiar to the volunteers – of keeping it slightly open as if to enable what little breath there was. And then there were his hands . . . Felicity could hardly bear to look at them, the backs sunken between the fragile bones, the veins like blue worms beneath the surface, the nails mauve.

His deterioration repelled and frightened her, so that she hung back. She usually managed well with patients in extremis – that was after all what the hospice was about – but David's descent from handsome flirtatiousness to skeletal near-death was simply too shocking. He seemed scarcely to see her, or if he did he showed no recognition. She was not exactly happy for Angela to take over, but recognized it as best for all concerned. Resignedly, she watched as Angela saw him right, lifted him correctly, poured tea into a sippy cup and helped him drink it, all of it quiet and practical and without resorting to cheery chat.

What, she wondered as she washed up afterwards, was the matter with her? If ever there was a moment to simply be friendly (she hated the word 'caring'), to touch and minister and nurture (another tricky word) their fragile friendship, this had been it. For Angela there had been apparently no challenge, or if there was she didn't let it show. She was the same with everyone, calm and pleasant.

Felicity was overcome by something new to her – self-doubt. And with it a nagging anxiety. It was as though some emotional muscle that had till now been strong and taken for granted had suddenly begun to hurt. Tears crept down her cheeks and she swiped at them with the cuff of her marigold, making her face damper. Angela came in with water flasks that needed filling.

'Felicity . . .? Are you OK?'

'Yes!'

Angela set the flasks down beside the second sink and began to fill them from the jug of filtered water. Without looking at Felicity, she said, 'It is very sad to see Mr Thorpe in such a bad way.'

Felicity nodded.

Angela ran the cold tap slowly to refill the filter jug. 'He's so fond of you.'

'Oh, I don't think . . . You know what's he's like . . .'

'You and he really spark off one another.'

'I suppose.'

'Definitely. I bet he'd like a bit of that more than ever just now.'

Felicity had been moving the brush round and round inside one cup for the past minute. Now she simply stopped, with both gloved hands plunged into the suds. She could feel something perilously like an enormous sob rising up through her chest, disturbing the muscles of her face, causing her shoulders to tense. She couldn't speak, and she wouldn't look round.

Angela put the flasks back on the tray.

She said, 'I suppose this is why we have supervision. Awful to say, but I thought it sounded like unnecessary mollycoddling when they told us about it, but actually it's sensible. My reactions haven't been tested yet, heaven knows what they'll be. Anyway . . . I'll be back in a tick and help with that drying-up.'

The moment she'd gone Felicity let the sob spill out of her. She ripped off the rubber gloves, tore off a couple of squares of kitchen towel and effected repairs. By the time Angela reappeared she had put a good face back on, and the subject was not re-opened.

That evening once the children were in bed she said to Robin, 'I've had a bit of a rethink.'

'What about?'

Supper was a pre-cooked tagine, and they were having a G and T each in the drawing room.

'The hospice concert.'

'You're backing out!' It pleased him gently to mock her ceaseless activity.

'No,' she said. 'I think after all that it would be nice if you brought the children.'

'Umm . . . OK.'

'What does that mean?'

'It means that after our last conversation I've agreed to a work thing that afternoon. The Germans are in town.' He must have noticed her disappointment, because he added, 'Maybe Ellie could be persuaded.'

'No, it's alright.'

'Are you sure?'

'It's my fault for changing my mind late in the day.'

'Aah, sweetheart . . .' Robin leaned towards her, and moved her hair from her cheek. 'That's a lady's prerogative.' She flashed a brief, colourless smile. 'Anyway, they don't know about it so they won't feel hard done by, and as you said—'

'I know what I said.'

'*OK*.' He adopted a different, more practical tone. 'But don't worry, is all I'm saying.'

But for some reason Felicity did worry. A couple of days later she asked Ellie.

'I'd have loved to do that, I really would, but as soon as Robin gets back I'm meeting my cousin who's over, so the times won't fit. I suppose I might be able to reschedule—'

'No! No, Ellie, don't think of it.'

'If you're sure. Time is a bit tight.'

'Of course, of course.' Felicity was cross with herself now for asking. 'It's not important.'

An unprecedented sense of inadequacy was starting to spread in Felicity, like ink through a blotter.

It may have been this which prompted her to ring Honor, who could always be relied upon to calm one's nerves because her own life was, let's face it, so dull. And she was curious, in an idle sort of way.

'Fliss? Is that you?'

'There's no need to sound so surprised.'

Honor regrouped. 'Super to hear from you. How are you?'

'Fine – busy, as always.'

'I can imagine! And everyone – Robin, the kids?'

'All well. Look, Honor—'

There was a pause which Honor jumped to fill. 'The parents are so looking forward to coming to you.'

'Actually—'

'It'll do them so much good to be away, not doing everything here as usual. A lot for you though, how are—'

'I wondered,' said Felicity firmly, 'what you'll be doing.'

'Me?'

Felicity waited. Her sister, the saint. A person could be too self-effacing, she thought.

'I'm going to have a friend round.'

'A friend?' Felicity was sceptical. 'Or one of your oldies?'

Another pause. Honor knew her sister couldn't be fooled. 'An old gentleman. But he is a friend.'

'So you'll be working even on Christmas Day.' Felicity could hear how sharp she sounded, it was so easy to push Honor just because you could, because she would never rise to the bait.

'It's not work, he's good company. Please don't tell the parents.'

'Why? They won't mind.'

'No, but they probably think . . . Gosh, I don't know – something different, and I've decided to let them.'

'If you say so, it's none of my business. What about Charity?'

'She told Ma she had plans. I don't know what they are.'

'Right.' The call wasn't having the soothing effect she'd hoped for. 'I just wanted to check no one was going to be lonely.' This wasn't strictly true, but Honor could be relied upon to think the best of her.

'How sweet of you,' she said. 'We shan't be.'

'Bye then. Speak soon.'

'Of course, loads of love to everyone.'

As Felicity put the phone down, out of sorts, Noah came into the room, carrying a cardboard folder. She sensed a school project, her least favourite thing.

'Mum, we're doing something about this village in Africa . . .'

It was on the tip of her tongue to say Robin would be home soon, and he was so much better at this sort of thing – which was true. But something stopped her.

'Let's have a look.' She patted the sofa next to her. 'I'll help if I can.'

'You can,' said her son, opening the folder. 'You do that clean water thing.'

Her heart sank at the well-worked pages covered in childish maps, annotations and drawings.

'Mum?' Noah looked commandingly from the pages to his mother's face. 'What else do you think I can put?'

Concentrate she thought. 'Let's see.'

Fifteen

No one who knew – or thought they knew – Hugh and Marguerite Blyth, would have suspected that they were a couple who hadn't planned a big family, or indeed any family at all. That for a long while they had been a couple complete unto themselves.

Hugh had first seen Marguerite in a pub on Dartmoor in 1958. He'd been with a group of friends applying hairs of the dog to the hangover acquired at the previous night's twenty-first celebrations. She'd come in with another girl, a friend of one of the friends, and a dog called Butch. He knew the dog's name because it was large and boisterous and needed frequent admonishment, so the name was uttered often and shrilly by the other girl who appeared to be the owner. In spite of his fizz headache and sandpapered eyes Hugh noticed that the second girl – the one not shouting at the dog – was very tall and exceptionally pretty, like a Thomas Hardy heroine with her mop of wavy hair, brown eyes and pink complexion. And in her walking boots and parka she didn't look like a girl to be daunted by scaling tors in driving rain.

But noticing her was only a momentary thing, because he was with the others, and she was talking to someone else and he was never going to see her again. She was just a girl in a pub.

Only she wasn't 'just' anything. There had been a moment when she'd taken charge of the obstreperous Butch, pulling him against her leg (a fine strong leg) and rubbing the side of his head gently but firmly until he quietened down and rested his chin resignedly on her knee. Hugh admired her way with the dog, and envied the animal that calming, authoritative touch. With typical directness he went over as she and her friend were about to leave, petted the straining, bounding Butch and commented on her dog-managing abilities.

She'd laughed self-deprecatingly. 'It's like when you get off the stiff lid of the jar, someone else has already done the groundwork.'

That was when he realized he'd fallen in love.

'Makes you sick, doesn't it?' put in the friend cheerfully. 'Unfortunately I'm the one who has to live with him. We're off, you'll be glad to hear.'

She towed the dog outside. It was now or never.

'Do you live near here?'

She shook her head. 'Just spending the weekend.'

'I wonder if I could have your phone number.'

He was blurting and he knew it, but she expressed no surprise.

'Sure, have you got something to write with?'

He took a biro from his breast pocket and held it over the back of his free hand. 'Fire away . . .' It was a London number. 'Thanks.'

'OK. Nice to meet you – I don't know your name.'

'Hugh Blyth.'

'Marguerite Dancy.'

'Cheers.'

Six months later they were married, in the somewhat chaotic and makeshift manner of the time. They weren't as impecunious as some – back then Hugh, until recently a successful club rugby player, had a job with the training development programme of the RFU, and Marguerite, not long graduated, was secretary to the managing director of a well-known outdoor-clothing brand, popular with the county set. As a sideline, she did occasional modelling for their catalogue, standing on windswept hillsides and tussocky river banks and leaning on stiles and five-bar gates in a fetching assortment of tweeds and corduroys. Hugh found these images almost unbearably sexy, and would occasionally amuse himself by leafing through the latest Huntsmoor catalogue admiring his wife.

He was not the only one, apparently. At an early stage in their marriage Marguerite went on a photoshoot in the grounds of a stately home in Yorkshire. In another part of the grounds a film crew was working on a historical romance with two instantly recognisable stars. During one of the many inevitable longueurs the male star, Frank Doran, had wandered off and watched some of the shoot. What started as only idle curiosity soon became more focused interest.

'He did what?' asked Hugh.

'Chatted me up.'

'Really?'

'There's no need to sound so thunderstruck.'

'I can imagine why anyone would – I just think it's a bit of a cheek, you a respectable married woman and all.'

'He didn't know that.'

'You told him, I hope.'

'I gave him the brush-off,' said Marguerite matter of factly. 'I didn't think I owed him an explanation.'

'I'm delighted to hear it.'

That encounter remained a joke between them. Any man with a pleasantly flirtatious manner (and there were plenty where Daisy was concerned) was referred to as 'doing a Doran'. And since Doran's career went from strength to strength there was also a good deal of byplay along the lines of 'I should have said yes' or 'bet you're regretting turning that one down'.

Years later, when Marguerite was in hospital having just had Charity, Hugh was rifling through her top drawer looking for contact lens lotion and turned up an old envelope, so dusty and dog-eared he at first thought it was just part of the lining paper. There was a postcard in it which he took out, without much interest initially, only to find he was staring at a publicity photo of Frank Doran – white open-necked shirt, slightly tousled hair, that famous grin bracketed by crescent-shaped dimples. To remove all doubt, there was Doran's signature racing across the bottom, with 'To the lovely Marguerite', and a couple of kisses.

On the other side were a couple of lines in the same dashing hand.

> Sorry I couldn't persuade you – but you can't blame me for
> trying.
> Stay fabulous, F.

At once Hugh returned the card to the envelope and slid it back beneath the earring box. His fault for looking, those that pried got what they deserved. Driving back to the hospital he told himself that he was never, ever, going to mention the bloody thing; that anyway Marguerite had turned Doran down (more than once apparently) so what the hell; but that she had kept the picture all this time – why, if not to keep some sort of remembered flame alive?

Much later again – they were at Heart's Ease, and Honor was little – they'd been to the cinema and he came in from driving the babysitter home to find Marguerite sitting on her side of the bed with her back to him, her head bowed. For a moment he thought she was crying.

'Darling? You OK?'

'Yes.' She turned, envelope in one hand waggling aloft the postcard in the other. 'But look what I found!'

He knew it simply wasn't possible that she'd only just found it, or not remembered where it was. So it must have been on her mind all this time, in however small a way, and this was her chance to come clean.

'Let's see.' There were two ways to go, and Hugh chose safety. 'Good grief, it's that chancer. Your famous admirer.'

'Yes, but read what he says.'

Hugh dutifully turned the card over and re-read the message before handing it back. 'He's right, I can't blame him for trying.'

'He was quite persistent.' Marguerite held the card in two hands, looking down at the picture. She glanced up. 'I don't think I mentioned that.'

'Handsome bastard.' Hugh heeled off his shoes and began unbuttoning his shirt. 'Not used to being given the bum's rush.'

'No!' Marguerite gave a short, bright laugh and put the card back in the envelope. 'Oh well . . .'

'Don't throw it away,' said Hugh, when it became clear she wasn't going to. 'It's a useful reminder of what a glamorous wife I have.'

She dropped the envelope on the floor and lay on her side on the bed, watching him.

'Come over here and say that again.'

Later that night, Marguerite woke up in the small hours. She wasn't sure why – perhaps Honor had made some sound that had disturbed her subconscious and sent one of those reflexive maternal messages to her brain. Swinging her legs out of bed, her feet landed on the envelope still lying on the carpet where she'd dropped it. She picked it up and without allowing herself a second thought, tore it in two and dropped it in the waste-paper basket.

Honor was asleep, and so were the others. She came back to bed and hitched over so her length was measured against Hugh's, her long thighs resting on the back of his, her face pressed into his shoulder. Still spark out, he gave a little grunt of contentment.

Heart's Ease was at peace.

Though a large family hadn't been part of the Blyths' plan they discovered with a kind of baffled pleasure that parenthood suited them. They were naturally liberal parents with a loose, non-prescriptive approach – the term 'parenting', as if bringing up children were a job, was not yet in the lexicon, and definitely not what they did. It was a question of expectation – they had none, beyond the certainty that they would love their offspring. They accepted that with this would come inevitably a degree of make-do and muddle-through, a good deal of mess and untidiness, much of it emotional, and a sprinkling of non-fatal fallings-out. They never anticipated plain sailing, and that was just as well.

Just as well, too, that the house had been named Heart's Ease before they took it over. Everyone agreed that to call a house that would be to tempt fate. On the other hand they weren't going to change the name – Marguerite was sentimental and a touch superstitious, and Hugh reckoned it would cause confusion with the mail. So they left it as it was, in the hope that the name would prove to be not a designation but an incentive.

And so it had proved, by and large. The only aspect of family life which came as a surprise to Marguerite was how different all her children were. Not only were they unlike either parent, they were so unlike each other! If there was a common thread, some evidence of shared DNA, she was blowed if she could see it. Fliss so astonishingly lovely, and so driven, where did that come from? . . . Charity so cool and clever . . . Honor, who always put others before herself . . . And then Bruno, who'd burst untimely into the world and kept them guessing ever since. It was all too easy to see him, as the baby and the only boy, as exceptional. Without making excuses for some of the worst of his excesses – the incident at Brushwood being an egregious example – she felt him to be troubled. But to mention this, especially in front of his two older sisters, was to be found guilty of special pleading. What, they might well ask, did Bruno have to be troubled about?

She was very glad that they would be seeing him at Christmas, for his own sake and because his presence would provide a necessary texture, a flavour of imperfect home, to the extreme glossiness of the TS seasonal celebrations. Also, she wanted to see where he lived now, a topic on which he'd been dismissive to the point of secrecy.

'I don't think we should insist on seeing it,' said Hugh.

'I shan't insist, but I shall show reasonable maternal interest.'

'That might be interpreted as insistence.'

'I'm not that delicate a flower!' Marguerite shook her head at him. 'I know what these places are like.'

Hugh made no comment.

She thought of that night, the night of Bruno's birth. She remembered the birth of all her children very distinctly, the particularity of each labour, the individuality of each baby – but Bruno was the only one to have been born at home.

She easily re-lived the walk back to Heart's Ease, stumbling along at Hugh's side, her legs cold and damp, the sense of the baby hanging perilously low, no longer suspended in its protective sack of fluid, the head engaged and beginning to grind down. Every so often Hugh would put out his hand to steady her, but he didn't overdo it, he knew her too well for that. In labour, Marguerite became ferociously independent, it was her and Mother Nature locked in this painful but productive struggle and they needed to be left well alone to get on with it.

At home she had been hit by the first contraction halfway up the stairs, so she had to clutch the banister, breathing heavily, till the moment passed. Down in the hall Hugh called the hospital but by the time he'd got through to the ward she was having another, and being an experienced hand he'd told them it wouldn't be long and put the phone down. Mavis had been wildly excited, running up and down with her tail going round and round like a propellor, desperate to be part of the action.

Once Marguerite reached the bedroom she did allow Hugh to help her get her skirt and tights off, because bending down at this stage was almost impossible. The curtains weren't drawn and they could see and hear the sprays and arcs of distant fireworks at the beacon and over the bay. Neither of them made the obvious joke, they were all business.

'I'm assured someone will be here soon,' said Hugh, pulling back the duvet, 'though something tells me they'll miss the main event.'

'Something's bloody right!'

He turned off the overhead light and switched on the lamp on the dressing table.

'Would you like some water?'

'Don't care . . .'

He left the room as another contraction hit, the fourth in, what, a couple of minutes. She heard him in the bathroom, running the tap till it was cold, filling a glass, coming back over the landing—

'Fuck a duck!' Marguerite never swore except when she was in labour, and there was always something comical about it, as if a generally hidden Mrs Hyde were bursting forth.

Hugh waited, before proffering the glass. 'Here, have a gulp.'

She grabbed it and chugged down half the water. She was still sitting on the edge of the bed but she'd reached the stage where her whole body seemed to have gone into one continuous spasm. Grimacing and cussing she'd lurched and hauled herself up and on to the mattress. Hugh propped all four pillows behind her and spread out the towel he'd brought from the bathroom.

'Aaaah! Hell's bells! Fuck, fuck!'

'You're doing well. I can see something.'

'Bully for you!'

'Never thought I'd actually have to do this.' His voice was pleasantly conversational as he peered, but he was more nervous than he showed and Marguerite knew it.

'You're not doing it now! It's me that's got to fucking do it!'

And then something happened. Or at least, didn't happen. Because everything stopped.

The baby's dark, greasy head was already crowning, Marguerite's body was stretched and expanded to its maximum, like a pulled-back catapult. But for a full minute the pain ebbed . . . the fireworks ceased . . . even the dog downstairs had gone quiet. There was a stillness in the room that was almost palpable, cushioning all three of them in an extended moment of stasis.

Marguerite was vaguely aware that she should have been afraid, should have been asking, frantically, *What's going on? Is everything alright? Is the baby OK?* But none of those questions occurred to her, because somehow she knew it was the baby who was casting this spell. The healthy, conscious baby – who had rushed, exploded its watery sack, beaten on the door, demanded to start life NOW – had suddenly paused, unsure of what lay ahead, taking a deep, thoughtful breath before making its final entrance. And she had no choice but to allow it that breathing space. It was almost as if the baby, not enamoured by what it saw, might sink back and withdraw completely. She'd read of animals who reabsorbed their young in times of stress, could that be about to happen now . . .? But she was not stressed. After the powerfully surging pain of the last twenty minutes she was still, and quiet.

Hugh looked up to his wife's face, then back to that sliver of dark head that he fancied he could almost see breathing.

Now Marguerite said, 'What's going on?' but in a very different voice, soft and curious.

'He's thinking about it,' replied Hugh. He'd said 'he' and they both knew that's who it was.

They heard the girls' voices out on the church path, the click of the garden gate. And then the baby made his entrance on a crescendo of effortful pain and glorious relief. Seconds later he was wrapped in his shawl and in his mother's arms. No beady sagacious stare such as she remembered from her newborn daughters, his eyes were closed and his head slightly averted.

Hugh kissed his son's brow briefly, and the top of his wife's head, lingeringly.

'The troops are back. I'll go and deliver the glad tidings.'

She gazed down. The room was very quiet. 'No crying he made' went the carol, but that referred to someone who was goodness made flesh. In her son's case his silence could have meant . . . well, anything.

Because of the general assumption that Bruno was indulged, Marguerite when she looked back feared she had been guilty of

benign neglect. Their whole largely successful approach to child
rearing had been characterized by a certain laissez-faire – all would
be well if the basics were in place – but maybe Bruno had needed
closer attention. Either she or Hugh really should have gone to
the school that time . . . There had been reasons, and Charity
had managed perfectly well (in fact had been well suited to the
task) but it was their place to go. It was pretty bad, what Bruno
had done, they should have been a great deal more focused, more
on the case.

She was winding herself up, as she always did at this time of
year. She loved Christmas and New Year but they were a barometer of change, this one especially. And always, relentlessly, it was
getting later, and harder, to put things right.

She had a bit of a weep and immediately chastised herself for
being a silly, sentimental cow. No point in wringing her hands,
the children were adults now and she and Hugh must put their
best foot forward and not turn into neurotic old fusspots.

Sixteen

The TS's party was important to Felicity, and not just because
she loved the house to be beautiful and filled with beautiful
people. She was a gifted hostess, entertaining was her stage – the
milieu in which she was most comfortable and could shine
effortlessly.

The party was also important because it marked the seasonal
shift from social and work preoccupations to family. It took the
form of an extended 'drinks' from six to nine so the children
were allowed to stay up – Ellie would be there to keep an eye
and would scoop up Cissy halfway through and take her to bed.
Noah and Rollo helped with coats and passing round (a trio of
fourteen-year-old St Paul's girls, the daughters of friends, were
front of house and the boys were surprisingly amenable to their
instructions).

After the party, there was the endless list with all the bread-
and-butter tasks of the season. But that was a while yet. First

was the hospice carol concert. The choral group were going to sing their seasonal medley, finishing with 'Jesus Christ the Apple Tree'. She hadn't known the piece before, but she had fallen in love with both the beautiful Elizabeth Poston melody and the much older words, possibly American. There were lines that touched some chord in her so deeply she could barely sing them:

> For happiness I long have sought
> And pleasure dearly I have bought

She didn't know why they got to her so much. After all, she had always been happy, hadn't she? And could scarcely have been said to have paid dearly for her pleasures – Robin might have done, but he could well afford it, and dear man that he was he always said that it was *his* pleasure to provide hers.

But there was something about the simplicity of those lines that created a wincing pain in her heart. The pleasure referred to was worldly, unworthy, and the happiness elusive. It was a chimera, if you went after it you were going to be disappointed. Felicity *wasn't* disappointed, not that she knew of. She knew how fortunate she was. But increasingly she recognized that something wasn't quite right.

There was a last rehearsal scheduled for the afternoon. The six of them met in the Gerald Hayworth Suite, named after the hospice's founder. The suite was used for training workshops and the like so the acoustic wasn't brilliant, but it was quiet and well away from the wards. As Felicity came through the reception area she saw someone she recognized. David Thorpe's son, a shy, studious-looking man of about her age with none of his father's chutzpah.

'Chris? It is Chris, isn't it, Chris Thorpe? Hello.'

His stare was distant, baffled. 'I'm sorry, I can't . . .?'

'No reason why you should. Felicity.'

'Ah.'

'Just leaving?' She hadn't been to the ward today and they were trained not to ask relatives how a patient was.

'Yes. Not good news, I'm afraid. Dad died this morning.'

She rode out the inner bump of shock that always, still, accompanied news of a death. 'I'm so very sorry to hear that,

Chris.' She didn't reach out – that wasn't her style or, she sensed, his. 'He was such a lovely man.'

'I suppose so . . .'

His brow was furrowed with the effort of trying to see his father as others saw him.

Trying to help, she added, 'He really was someone who put on a brave face – until very recently he could make us helpers laugh, even when he was so ill. A real charmer.'

Chris, hands in pockets, looked down at his shoes, then up, looking very directly at Felicity as though a decision had been made.

'Plenty of people thought so, certainly.'

'I'm sure.'

'Many women.'

She didn't reply – what could she have said? She had been passed something – if not the black spot then at least some unwelcome information. She'd never believed you couldn't speak ill of the dead – death didn't confer sainthood – but they were in a hospice after all. For all she knew, Dave's body was still lying tranquilly in the departure room, awaiting removal to the funeral director.

'Anyway, there's a lot to do,' said Thorpe, moving away. 'I'm going to see my mother, who will be extremely upset.'

'Of course,' murmured Felicity. He strode away, pushing the glass door open with his shoulder. So there was ill-feeling. David Thorpe's offspring may have loved their father, but they hadn't forgiven him.

Dorothy on reception, who had been very busy till that moment, glanced up.

'Oh dear. Sounds as if there's a lot still unresolved there.'

'Yes.'

'Families are so complicated, aren't they?'

Felicity considered this as she headed towards the Hayworth Suite.

Yes, they were.

Honor hadn't planned to invite anyone else on Christmas Day. It was just going to be her and Mr Dawson, cosy and relaxed. But something about the rhythm of the conversation, the scarlet grin of the electric fire and the winking coloured lights on the all-in-one tree, meant that the question just slipped out naturally.

'Avis, would you like to come for Christmas lunch?'

'Is that an invitation?'

'Yes it is.'

'I don't get so many of those as I used to. Lovely! Rather! I can wear my leopard tippet!'

No beating about the bush. Deal! Done and dusted in three seconds. Honor was a touch taken aback. Was this an awful mistake? Would poor Mr Dawson think she was trying to set him up with animal-print Avis? What if they hated each other on sight, which was not beyond the realms of possibility? They were chalk and cheese, Avis with her brassy bonhomie and Mr Dawson with his gentlemanly reticence. She owed it to him to tell him someone else would be coming, but that it was important not to make the festive occasion sound like nothing more than an extension of her job. Next day she broached the subject, choosing her words carefully.

'We've known each other for quite a while, she's great fun.'

'I shall look forward to meeting her.' Honor detected a hint of apprehension. Perhaps 'fun' had been the wrong word.

'And she's such an easy person. It will all be very relaxed.'

She hoped it would be. She had never 'done' Christmas before and just hoped she'd be able to manage the lifts, the mise en scene, the cooking, not to mention the general required jollity which her parents had always generated with such apparent ease.

From the moment she'd been invited, Avis had never failed to mention the occasion with lively enthusiasm. Mr Dawson on the other hand went quiet on the subject. Honor could have kicked herself. Avis, astute as ever, cocked her head, fixed Honor with her sagacious birdlike eye and said, 'Don't worry, pet, I'll be good as gold. I promise not to frighten the horses.' She'd never heard the expression, but she got the gist.

Not wanting her guests to feel obligated, she'd suggested that the three of them not bother with presents.

'Too late, I'm afraid,' said Mr Dawson. 'I already have a little something for my hostess, and shall bring it along on the day.'

Avis's objection was predictably more extravagant.

'No presents? You're joking! If you're going to give us a lovely Christmas dinner the least I can do is show a little appreciation!'

Traditionally, Honor and Hugh went carol singing in aid of the church. Most of the twenty-odd singers were not choir but members of the congregation – 'poor bloody infantry' as Hugh put it. They performed a two-hour, early-evening circuit of the village, the younger members of the group collecting door to door with a watchful adult, winding up at the vicarage for mulled wine and mince pies.

This year the night of the carol singing was particularly beautiful, the moon a silver paring and the stars shone out brilliantly, so that the words of the hymn felt particularly relevant: 'When like stars his children crowned; All in white shall wait around.' Honor found herself looking up and thinking, *There they are!*

They sang their hearts out and were all quite hoarse by the time they reached the vicarage. The vicar himself had been going round with them, carrying a battery-powered lantern and organising the carol choices. The vicarage was a four-square Georgian villa with twin chimneys, windows set symmetrically on either side of and above the door. All the curtains were drawn back and the lights on in honor of the occasion. As the vicar led the way across the drive the door opened and Mrs Jones – Catherine – came out on to the step with their two small children huddled in dressing gowns and slipper-socks.

'Here we are!' called the vicar. 'And we must sing number twenty-one.'

That was 'It came upon the midnight clear' with its message of the ancient splendours of peace. Catherine and the children applauded warmly at the end, the youngest child ran to her father, and they all trooped in, following Catherine into the big, shabby drawing room where the tree stood – still with some cardboard boxes, leads and bags stuffed hastily behind it.

'We just finished that about ten minutes before you got here!' announced Catherine, she was one of those women who seem born to laugh. Coats were loosened, hats and scarves removed, and the vicar circulated with the mulled wine in an assortment of china mugs while Catherine took the mince pies out of the oven. Hugh was in boisterous conversation with another bloke, so Honor took her mug over to the window, to admire the tree and survey the scene. Behind her, the nighttime front garden with its mature trees screening the drive from the road, was inky black. Next to her the tree fizzed with a cheerful jumble of colour and light, little crackers, and at the top a trio of angels made (some time ago by the look of it) out of clothes pegs. The room hummed with the heartfelt sound of seasonal wellbeing and a job well done.

'Thank you for coming along, Honor.' Ed Jones was standing next to her. 'It's appreciated. Something tells me the time is fast approaching when we'll struggle to get enough people together for this.'

'I bet you will,' she said. 'People don't have to be religious to enjoy singing carols.'

He laughed. 'Ain't that the truth? Four weeks from now it'll be a case of if I ever have to summon all ye faithful again it will be too soon. Which is a pity in a way.'

The smallest child – a boy of about two – came over and clasped his father's leg. The vicar put down his mug on the windowsill and lifted his son. The toddler's hand was a soft, importunate starfish against his father's cheek. Honor experienced a pang of hopeless, unidentified longing, tinged with nostalgia. There was a relaxed completeness here which had been present in her own childhood home but which, with time and growing up, had become diffuse and scattered.

The vicar was asking what she'd be doing on the day.

'I'll be at home,' she said, 'as usual.' And then adding in case she'd sounded plaintive, 'Which is what I like.'

'Up at Heart's Ease?'

'Yes.' She felt his eyes on her – interested, curious, in a good way. She hoped she wasn't blushing.

'Did you find out any more about the brigadier and his flighty lady?'

She shook her head. 'Only what I could find in the local paper.'

'Poor things – can you imagine.'

'But he'd been dead for a long time, so he didn't know.'

Jones raised his eyebrows humorously. 'Ah, but who can say?'

Hugh joined them. 'Well, I've swigged and scarfed and it's probably time we were going. What do you think, my girl?'

'Right.' She swallowed the last spicy mouthful and put her glass down next to the vicar's. 'Ready.'

The vicar accompanied them into the hall, still carrying his son who had gone floppy with tiredness.

'So I shall see you on the big day if not before.'

'Not on the actual day, no,' Hugh wound his scarf. 'We're going up to London to stay with our eldest daughter.'

'Ah, OK, but you . . .' He addressed Honor. 'You're not going?'

'No.'

'No need to worry about her,' explained Hugh, 'she's entertaining friends. A rough bunch I have no doubt.'

They both laughed, kindly. Honor and Hugh said thanks and farewells and set off up the lane. They walked in silence, the beam of Hugh's torch bobbing in front of them. At about the halfway point Hugh put his arm around her shoulders and gave them a squeeze.

'My girl. Thanks for coming. I enjoyed that.'

Honor, inexplicably a little tearful, didn't reply.

Seventeen

'I realize it's a longshot,' Robin had said on the phone, 'and I'm sure there a thousand things you'd rather be doing, but I'd deem it an enormous favour.'

'Sure, no, don't see why not,' Bruno heard himself say, well aware that it was a lie, and there was no end to the reasons why not. 'I mean, if you can't find anyone more . . . if you think I'm the man for the job.'

'Great!' Robin's relief positively crackled over the line. 'Absolutely, you're a star – taxi both ways on me.'

So here Bruno was, about to take his nephews and niece to some sort of carol do at the hospice. What, he wondered, had happened to him? Not that he had any objection to helping out, God knows he owed Fliss and Rob, but both the event and his role in it were well outside his area of expertise.

The taxi was a good idea, he wouldn't have wanted to be

marshalling the kids on public transport. Noah went on the jump seat and he sat between Rollo and Cissy. They were rather sweetly delighted with the experience, you'd never have known they were children to whom travelling around London by car was as natural as breathing. Something about the interior of the cab, the larger floor space, the way they sat facing each other, the driver in his own little world and they in theirs – they were enchanted. Cissy sat slightly pressed up against Bruno, but gazing out of the window. Rollo sat on his hands, kicking his heels back against the seat, humming with pleasure. Noah made conversation.

'We've never been here before.'

'The hospice? No?'

Bruno was glad to hear it. A building full of the dying didn't strike him as the ideal place for a family day out. He'd been glad when Robin mentioned the concert would be outside. And this was one of those dank, dingy days when at least it wouldn't be too cold and the early dark would be scarcely noticeable.

Noah said, 'I'm going to be rather embarrassed to hear Mum sing.'

Bruno thought he might be too, but didn't say so. 'Did you ever hear her sing before?'

'Once,' said Noah. 'She's in this choir?'

'I haven't heard her since I was a kid. We used to sing in the car.'

'Really?' Bruno fancied he could see the thought dawning in his nephew's head. 'Like we are now?'

'Well no, not in a taxi with . . . you know . . .' Bruno nodded at the driver.

Rollo, his interest piqued, turned to look at him. 'What did you sing?'

'All kinds of old cr— All kinds of things. "Ten green bottles", Eagles, "She'll be coming round the mountain", that sort of thing.' They gazed at him blankly. 'Just a way of passing the time on long journeys.'

The two boys stared at him, polite but blank. *Jesus Christ* thought Bruno, *I'm an uncle, I'm old!*

'Mum's stuff is really boring,' said Noah, not critically, just sharing information. 'And she makes funny faces.'

'Well,' said Bruno, deciding that for the time being uncle-hood was in his job description and he'd better embrace it, 'I'm looking forward to it.'

For the concert the choral group had been asked to wear any combination of 'Christmassy' colours. It was neither raining nor too cold so Felicity had opted for a red dress with a black fur jacket, black suede boots and an emerald scarf with a gold pin. She'd put her hair up in a soft twist (her Danish pastry as Robin called it) and added a discreet red silk rose. When she saw the other members of the group she couldn't help wondering if they'd all had the same brief and if she'd overdone it, but one of the tenors made a point of telling her how 'wonderfully festive' she looked, which she took as a compliment.

A big crowd was assembling in the garden in the gathering dusk. Where possible patients were moved so they could see out. A buffet of mince pies, sausage rolls and cake, with tea or mulled wine, was set out in the big day room which could be accessed from outside. This was manned by a team of volunteers including Dorothy from reception. Felicity bumped into her beforehand and she was quite shiny-eyed.

'I'm so pleased to be part of this. We always used to come as visitors, it's so exciting to see it from the other side.'

Felicity realized she knew almost nothing about Dorothy. Who, for instance, was 'we', and why was that in the past? Dorothy on the other hand often asked about her family, and did so now.

'Will you have anyone here today?'

'Probably not – Robin's got an important business thing, he was going to bring the children if he got away in time, but I think it's unlikely.'

'Life's just so busy, isn't it?' agreed Dorothy sympathetically. 'Especially at this time of year.'

By the time the concert started there must have been two hundred people down on the lawn, centred on the huge Christmas tree donated by the local Round Table. The tree was covered in white and gold lights – more tasteful than the exuberantly multi-coloured ones indoors – and topped by a long-tailed silver star. The rooms of the building behind them glowed cosily, the lights dimmed for the occasion. Two free-standing spotlights illuminated the performers.

The hospice manager Caitlin welcomed everyone, including the mayor and the hospice's patron, an ennobled lady athlete, and referred them all to their programmes – people had brought small torches. There would be no breaks, the items would run continuously for about three quarters of an hour, after which there would be some carols for everyone to join in with, and a few words from the chaplain.

Felicity had already done her reading, and the choral group were just about to start their set, when she spotted Cissy. She was being carried at shoulder height quite near the front, so it was easy to see her funny Laplander hat with the tassels, and her blonde curls escaping from underneath. She was waving, vigorously, it was all Felicity could do not to wave back. Then, as they started to sing she saw the boys, too – people were kind, and made space for the children at the front. Noah and Rollo were straightfaced, paying attention, she hoped not too mortified. So Robin must have made it after all . . . She looked for him, and that was when she saw that the person carrying Cissy was Bruno.

Her voice wobbled slightly but she got through the songs, even 'The Apple Tree' without making a fool of herself. When it came to the joining-in carols the boys mumbled dutifully into their song sheets but Cissy was tiring, she flung an arm round Bruno's neck and turned her face into his shoulder. Felicity felt in her jacket pocket but her tissues were in her handbag indoors. Fortunately the kindly tenor offered her his hankie – she would rather he hadn't noticed at all, but it was better than having a runny nose and eyes in front of everyone.

The chaplain was a practised hand, and kept it short. Bruno lowered Cissy to the ground (he'd done well, Felicity knew how heavy she became after a while), and now he did wave, and nudged the boys to do the same. Felicity made a circling gesture to indicate she'd see them round at the front.

As they turned to go back in the tenor said, 'There's something about Christmas carols isn't there? Gets me every time.'

'I'm afraid so,' she agreed – useless to deny it after the hankie incident. 'And I suddenly saw my children down there.'

'Really? That's very nice. Here with their dad?'

'No, he couldn't come this time. They're with my younger brother.' She felt a certain pride in saying this, and the tenor picked up on it.

'Uncle to the rescue, splendid.'

The first person she saw in the covered walkway near the entrance was Robin. He came straight to her, very bright eyed and with a smile that was both rueful and warm, she could smell the post-lunch chasers on his breath. But there was no doubting the strength of his embrace.

'My darling . . . I just missed it. How did it go?'

She began to answer, but he kissed her, a vodka-flavoured kiss on the mouth, right there and then with all the visitors milling round them.

He released her. 'Sorry, couldn't help myself. So?'

'It went really well.'

'Do you know if Bruno got here, with the kids?'

'He did, yes. I saw them. They were near the front.'

'Good man!' He looked around. 'Where is he?'

'Bringing them round now.'

'You didn't mind my asking him? I just couldn't guarantee to be away in time, and Ellie was off meeting her cousin . . .'

She shook her head. 'He did really well. It was lovely to see them all together.'

Just then the rest of them came round the corner. 'Daddee!'

'Cissy! Come here . . . Boys – all three of you – what a pleasure . . .'

Felicity watched her family unite around her.

'There's tea and cake,' she said. 'Shall we—?'

Felicity's car was in the car park, but they couldn't all fit in that, so Bruno opted to go home separately. He still had the taxi money from Robin which Robin urged him to use.

In the event, he didn't. Once he'd waved them off – and given Cissy the kiss she demanded – he set off in the direction of the tube, with the pleasant and unusual sensation of spare cash in his pocket. He could get some weed off Sean, or at the very least go down to the pub with whoever was going later on.

In the end he hadn't minded taking the kids to Fliss's do. They hadn't given him any trouble and the concert hadn't been too embarrassing, he could tell they were glad to be there. For his part, he'd only gone as a favour to Robin, but it wasn't half as bad as he expected. There was something to be said for doing the right thing, at this time of year especially. Sitting on the tube, and even more on the walk back to the flat, he missed . . . he wasn't sure what. The kids? The feeling? Being part of something?

The other two weren't in, and the flat was dark as well as cheerless. He couldn't bring himself to sit down on the sofa where he'd have to spend all the hours between now and tomorrow. The TSs had asked if he'd like to go over on Sunday, but he'd said no, because then he'd have to go through this all over again. Christmas was on the horizon, and after that he hoped to be able to move to a better flat. It must be true that absence made the heart grow fonder, because he was looking forward to seeing his parents.

Rebuking himself for being pathetic, he left the flat and headed for the British Queen.

Fliss let the children watch TV when they got in – something suitable for Cissy, but which the boys tolerated well enough, Felicity suspected Rollo of rather enjoying the babyish programmes and Noah sat on the floor with a superior expression fiddling with a Rubik's Cube, only glancing up occasionally. Cissy, wearing the Santa hat Ellie had bought her, perched transfixed on the pouffe like a seasonal gnome.

Felicity and Robin opened a bottle of fizz and sat in the drawing room, looking out over the sparkling, endless expanse of London. Soon it would be the party, and then Christmas itself, with the parents arriving. There was a lot to do, but with the aid of excellent local shops and services Felicity had done most of it. The freezer was full, the tree had arrived, and the decorations would go up at the weekend.

She said, 'I've asked Bruno to spend a couple of nights when he comes. We don't want him tooling back across London.'

'Of course he must stay.' Robin sipped, smiled to himself. 'He rose to the occasion heroically today.'

'They're not that bad!'

'You know what I mean.'

A silence, not fraught but gently complicit, drifted between them. Felicity said, 'One of the patients died yesterday.'

'I'm sorry to hear that. Must be ghastly, I couldn't do it, but . . .'

'You're thinking it goes with the territory.'

'That is what I was thinking, yes.'

'You're right of course. And we get all the training and supervision and so on . . . I think what shocked me was that I bumped into his son not long afterwards and he was quite, sort of, bitter about his father.'

'Bitter?'

'I made some remark about how charming and funny he'd always been and the son pretty much told me he'd been a philanderer. He was divorced, so . . . I don't know, maybe their mother had been treated badly. They loved their father, you could tell, but they haven't forgiven him.'

'You don't know, my darling,' said Robin. 'And you never will.'

After they'd put the children to bed Felicity stood on the landing, the pale glow of Cissy's nightlight seeping round her feet and thought that in due course, in the new year, she might have a change of direction. Concentrate her efforts on the hospice, maybe do some additional training, but anyway order her life in such a way that she had a little more time at home.

By the time she reached the foot of the stairs this thought had been transferred to the back burner. Ellie had just come in, and was unzipping her Puffa jacket in the hall, her face pink and elated.

'Hi! How did it go?'

'Really well, thanks, Ellie.'

'Family make it?'

'Yes.'

'Great.' Ellie dragged off her scarf and headed for the stairs.

'How about you, did you have a good time with your cousin?'

'Oh, brilliant!' Her face lit up. 'It was so good to see him! We just laughed and laughed like drains, the way we always do, he's such a great guy!'

'Wonderful,' said Felicity. 'Have you eaten?'

'We did some damage to a doner kebab.'

'OK. Goodnight, Ellie.'

'Night. Kids asleep?'

'I should think Cissy is, the boys might still be awake.'

'I might pop in and say goodnight.'

'They'd like that.'

Felicity watched as Ellie trotted swiftly up the stairs, bag and scarf swinging.

This time of year pinned everyone down for a while, decisions were put on hold. But once the celebrations were over, decisions and resolutions would be waiting, demanding attention.

Later, when she came out of the bathroom, Robin was in bed, reading his current book, the autobiography of a wayward politician. Without looking up, he flicked the open page.

'Honestly, this guy is incorrigible. Completely without shame, but of course that's what makes him so readable.' She didn't answer and now he looked at her, closing the book but keeping his finger in his place. She wasn't wearing one of her beautiful nighties. She wasn't wearing anything.

'You look lovely.'

Felicity walked round to his side of the bed. She pulled back the corner of the duvet and sat down, leaning in to her husband.

'May I come in?'

'My darling . . .' Robin dropped the book and slid back to make room for her. 'Always.'

Eighteen

The campus bar was packed, the noise deafening, everyone seasonally sloshed on the staff bar's cheap booze. Charity told herself she'd stay twenty minutes and not a second longer. These quasi-obligatory end of term events were her idea of hell. She was solitary by nature and liked within reason to choose her own time, place and company. Here were shiny banners screaming *Season's greetings!* hung along the back of the bar and some half-hearted garlands strung around the walls. In one or

two places the desiccated Bluetack had given up and the garland
sagged like a drunk whose legs had given way. She'd parked herself
in a corner at one end of the long bar, standing with her back
to the wall. There had been a single seat at a table nearby when
she first arrived but she'd eschewed it in favour of this position
which would afford her a quicker getaway when the time came.

In spite of her Scrooge-like attitude, she wasn't without
company. She was like a cat who went to others on her own
terms, or simply let them come to her. A couple of nice female
colleagues chatted for a while and then fought their way back
into the melee, and her supervisor, a dull but dutiful man,
included her in his round of social obligations. Once she'd
finished her small scotch with its rapidly dissolving pellets of ice
she began the long struggle to the door, keeping her head down
to avoid further conversation.

Outside there was a scattering of smokers, but the cold was
refreshing, and she paused as she hauled on her coat. At night
this view of the modern campus was almost picturesque, with the
curving paths lit by round lights and the artificial lake surrounded
by benches beneath the trees, also softly lit. The admin block,
fiercely illuminated for security reasons, and the research building,
still with one or two lighted rooms, sat to either side. She could
hear the thud of music from the student bar. From tomorrow
the other people, students and staff, would start to ebb away and
she'd have a few days alone here but for the maintenance team.
She was looking forward to it.

'Want one?'

Someone was offering her a cigarette.

'No thanks,' she said, 'I don't.' And then, to be clear, she added,
'Just leaving.'

'Happy Christmas.'

'And you.'

'Got far to go?'

Whoever he was – clearly not a member of staff, most of
whom she knew at least by sight – he was in a chatty mood, but
it was such a relief to be out of the bar that she played along for
a moment, nodding towards the far side of the lake.

'No distance at all.'

'You live here?'

He was stocky and stubbly in a dilapidated leather jacket, but he had a lively, vivid face. Up for it, is what she thought, whatever it was.

'Live and work.' He nodded, no further questions. 'You?' she asked.

'Having a drink with friends. Best place for it, prices are a joke. In a good way,' he added.

She smiled agreement. 'I'm off, nice to have met you.'

'Me too. Hang on . . .' He dropped his cigarette end and trod on it. 'Just a thought, but fancy a curry?'

'Thanks but no.'

'Shame,' he said, with a thoroughly shameless grin, 'worth a try.'

Yes, thought Charity, *it was, you cheeky bastard.*

'Just in case' – he took a card from his back pocket – 'that's me. My credentials.'

She put it in her bag without looking at it. 'I can't reciprocate I'm afraid.'

'No worries, I'm going to go back in and get a bit more pissed.'

'Good plan.'

He laughed – they both did – and she headed off in the direction of the hall of residence. A glance over her shoulder showed that true to his word he'd returned to the bar.

She supposed she had been chatted up, which she wasn't used to because something about her repelled casual social advances. Well, not repelled exactly, but certainly deterred, which was how she liked it. Until now. Her sparse social life seemed to have taken on the character of the number twenty-seven bus – nothing for years, then suddenly two within months. She told herself she was amused, choosing to ignore that she was also rather flattered.

In her room she went to close the blind. From the window she could see the staff bar, a scattering of smokers silhouetted by the light from the door. She snapped the slats down and went to the kitchen to make herself some supper.

Now that term had ended and he was on his own, Mac had time to look forward to Christmas. It was years since he hadn't either a) gone to his married sister on the Wirral or b) stayed here on his own, of which he preferred the latter. This wasn't because he didn't appreciate Moira's hospitality, or like her husband, but because he had the sense that they felt they must ask him to save him from the perceived horrors of a lonely Christmas. The only times he wasn't invited was when they were going to their daughter's in Scotland, and they were always tremendously apologetic, commenting on his niece's busy life and the number of children she had. They didn't need to apologize. On these occasions he simply treated Christmas like any other day, with added scotch – he wasn't a heavy drinker, but he did treat himself to a half bottle of really top quality single malt and a side of Scottish smoked salmon, and was extremely content.

This year, though, he was excited by the prospect of having a guest. He had no qualms or reservations about having asked her after so short an acquaintance – Charity was nothing if not a modern young woman, and he'd soon intuited that she would favour a straightforward approach. At his time of life there was no point in faffing around. They had got on extremely well from the off (notwithstanding the disobliging circumstances of her brother's rustication), and he found her immensely attractive. Something about her air of austerity, her sagacious expression and slight, hard-won smile . . . Not to mention her slim straightness, he'd always liked that sapling quality in a woman.

No . . . He smiled to himself as he put away the last of his paperwork in the top drawer of the desk. In this as in so many things the Bard had it right.

What is love? 'Tis not hereafter . . . In delay there is no plenty . . .

He would be a good host, see to her comfort and happiness, and who knows what might happen?

Charity found the card when she was fishing out her car key the following morning, and dropped it on her work table. When she got back from her streamlined shopping expedition (she had a system for present-buying, mostly involving vouchers) she gave it a cursory glance as she was about to chuck it in the wastepaper basket.

> Luke Tanner
> Tanner and Bright's Travelling Top
> All the fun of the circus in your local venue!

There followed contact numbers and an address (including email, she noticed), and the reassuring words: *No animals.*

Good lord. Of all the scenarios she might have imagined to account for that man's chutzpah, this was the last. Circus? The parents had taken the three of them, long before Bruno's arrival, to a circus on the town green in Salting, and none of them had liked it. Honor had actually wept. Fortunately Marguerite had saved them from appearing ungrateful by getting her reservations in first.

'I hate to see animals being made to do silly things, and I always wonder what the travelling's like for them . . . and where they're kept.'

'And the clowns aren't funny,' Charity remembered saying, given leave to criticize.

'They're creepy,' agreed Felicity.

To comfort the sobbing Honor, Hugh had said, 'I bet those elephants would rather trot in circles and eat buns than be out chained to logs in some god-forsaken jungle,' but this turned out not to be helpful.

So the word 'circus' had unfortunate connotations. But something about the chirpy entrepreneurial confidence of both the man and his card – and the sensible 'No animals' – piqued her interest, and she tucked the card in the mirror.

Hugh's line on family life, and his role in the mix generally, was one of benign unflappability. The others would have been surprised to know how seriously he took this role, which often required some effort. Kipling, whom he admired and read, had recognized that to 'keep one's head while all about you' and so forth was one of the true manly virtues.

Marguerite had always worn her heart on her sleeve, her warmly emotional nature was one of the qualities that had first drawn him to her. That and her extraordinary beauty. She'd been a peach then and still was. As the babies had come along he'd coped pretty well with the lack of sleep and the general chaos (admittedly Daisy bore the brunt of it) but life got more complicated as the girls grew up.

They and their mother would have been astonished to know that he worried about them. He worried that his beautiful firstborn, Felicity, was too keen on how things looked, about what might be called her image, and that she might forfeit affection if she wasn't careful . . . That Charity frightened men off, possibly deliberately, and risked loneliness as a result . . . And that Honor, his little round one, his girl, had no real friends of her own age, she was just too tied up with her old people. He had no particular scenario in mind for any of his daughters, he simply wanted them to be happy. And the worst of it was there wasn't a thing you could do! Daisy sometimes tried to find solutions, to steer things, but it was a waste of time. He'd come to accept that parental love, once the bringing-up stage was over, was largely passive.

And then there was Bruno. Hugh had never been one of those men who yearned for a son to feel complete. By the time of Bruno's precipitate arrival he considered himself an old hand – his style of parenting didn't change because he now had a boy, and Bruno was so much younger than the others that he and Daisy had carried on as if things would pretty much take care of themselves. The system, such as it was, was in place, what could possibly go wrong?

And nothing had gone too wrong, until the incident at school. Not really. Bruno was inevitably a bit spoilt, but he was a sweet little boy and then a charming if rather idle teenager. He always had plenty of friends, so there wasn't that to worry about. The local comprehensive hadn't really suited, he'd been a bit wild, that was when they'd cast around and chosen Brushwood, one of the most famous of the 'free' schools. Free was a misnomer, it had cost a hell of a lot for a place that prided itself on not doing much. Still, things had gone pretty well. They liked the head a lot, and Bruno had been excluded only temporarily after that shocker with the maid (which they still hadn't got to the bottom of) and had done well enough in his A Levels to get into university, albeit one of those newly-designated ones.

But though his approach had been the same for all his children, Hugh had a nagging private sense of having failed his son. Or anyway failed to get close to him – and now it might be too late.

He had never mentioned this to Daisy, it would have sent her into a tailspin to know he was worried. *Hers* to worry, his to pour oil on troubled waters. He could hear her upstairs now, packing for their stay at the TS's. Or more accurately rifling through her wardrobe in order to decide what to take. Always a sensitive moment to approach, but uncharacteristic soul-searching made him reckless.

'How's it going?'

His wife stood with a dress over one arm, the hanger dangling drunkenly from the neck, several more items strewn over the bed and surrounded on the floor by a clutter of shoes.

'I know I'm making heavy weather of this,' she said. 'But I don't want to let the side down at Christmas.'

'You won't,' he said, 'you couldn't.' He was about to add *You always look marvellous* because it was both true and what he thought, but he knew that this simple blanket approval wouldn't cut it. *Be specific.*

'I've always liked that green one.'

'It's awfully old.'

'Timeless elegance.'

She dropped the one she was holding and picked up the green velvet, surveying it with a doubtful expression. 'Everyone will have seen it before . . .'

'No. And anyway only I will remember.'

'I wouldn't want Fliss to think I was just wearing any old thing when she goes to so much trouble.'

'Come on, she doesn't think like that,' said Hugh. Even as he said it he was by no means certain it was true. But there was no point going there.

Ellie chose the day of the party to deliver her bombshell. She'd just returned from taking Noah to a friend's house and the other two to the playground, and Fliss was putting finishing touches to the tree in the hall (the one by the picture window in the drawing room was done). Ellie chivvied the children as they took off their coats, helped Cissy with hers and then waited as they disappeared upstairs.

'That looks really really beautiful.'

'Good, do you think so? Not too much?'

'Not at all,' said Ellie. 'You've got such a talent for this sort of thing.'

Fliss was surprised, and gratified. Ellie was no gusher.

'Thanks, Ellie.'

'Would you call her an angel or a fairy at the top?'

They stood gazing up. Fliss said, 'I think in this house she's a fairy. At home, when we were growing up, she was an angel.'

'I reckon an angel. I'm not religious, but I was always an angel in the school nativity.'

Fliss laughed. 'You were?'

'Don't sound so surprised. I bet you were the Virgin Mary.'

'I was once,' admitted Fliss. 'But I did the odd angel too. And a star, there were always a few of those.'

'I bet.' Ellie chuckled, but didn't move to go. She still had Cissy's red quilted coat over her arm. 'Fliss, there's something I need to tell you.'

'Right.' Fliss leaned forward to tweak a glass icicle that was at an angle, but she felt an icy touch inside her, too.

'I wondered about leaving it till after Christmas but then I thought no, no time like the present.'

Damn, damn. It had to happen.

'You're leaving,' said Fliss, to get it over with. 'Is that it?'

'Handing in my notice, yes.'

Fliss continued to make minute adjustments. 'I'm sorry to hear that, Ellie.'

'I'm sorry too. Really sorry—'

'Was it something we said?'

This was a bitter little joke but Ellie seemed to take it to heart.

'No, no, far from it. I've loved it here. I love the kids, they're so great. I'm going to miss you all, but—'

'But you have to go.'

This time there was a pause, and Felicity looked round. She thought for a moment Ellie was crying, but then realized that the opposite was true – she was smiling, almost laughing.

'I'm getting married! Back home!'

'Ellie! Congratulations!' Swallowing her sickening disappointment Felicity went over to her and hid her own feelings with a brief hug. 'That's marvellous.'

'Thank you, yes – yes it is.'

'Come through, this calls for a glass of something.'

'Oh, I don't know . . .' Ellie glanced up the stairs.

'Don't worry about them for a moment, they know where we are.' She opened the fridge and took out a bottle of Pinot. 'Here we go. Tell me,' she asked as she poured, 'does this have anything to do with your trip into town the other afternoon?'

'Sort of. Al, my . . . I suppose—'

'Your fiancé!'

'I guess he is! Cheers! – my fiancé – he came all this way to get down on one knee.'

'He actually did that?'

'In the pub. Everyone cheered.'

Felicity leaned on the island, caught up now in the story.

'Wasn't that risky? You might have said no, in front of everyone.'

'Yeah, and then what?' Ellie laughed boisterously. 'Specially when I came to London to get away from him!'

'You did?'

'Yup – I couldn't handle it at all, I wasn't ready, so like the muttonhead I am I ran away from home.'

Felicity thought she'd never come across the expression 'muttonhead' anywhere except on the printed page. She was rapt, in spite of herself.

'And – what? The moment you saw him again you felt differently?'

'Pretty much. He's just, you know, such a great guy. The best. I feel *myself* with him – at home, you know?' Felicity nodded. She did know. 'I'd really like you to meet him, would that be alright?'

'More than alright. You must bring him round over Christmas. We'll have a houseful, but if he doesn't mind that.'

'No, really?' Ellie's delight was almost shaming. 'Are you sure?'

'Of course I'm sure. If you're going to go off and leave us the least we can do is take a look at the man who's stealing you.'

To Felicity's astonishment, Ellie lurched forward and enfolded her in another, more robust hug. 'Thank you! When shall we come?'

'What about Christmas dinner?' Felicity heard herself say. 'We're having it later this year, early evening?'

'You got it, we'll be there! That's amazing, he'll be made up to meet you, I've told him so much about you all.'

Of course Felicity had always known it was going to happen

sometime. Good nannies – especially really bright, nice ones – were in a seller's market. And these days they were young. No matter how good the pay or the relationship, they were going to take off eventually. There had been two nannies before, one English, one Scottish, neither of them as nice. Ellie had not been here as long as either of them, but in that time she had made a greater impression.

There were sixty people at the party, and Felicity wore her pale blue velvet off-the-shoulder dress, with the diamond teardrops Robin had given her on their first anniversary. Ellie was on hand to put Cissy to bed and spirit Rollo away when the time came, so there was a spurious air of normality. But amid the clink, sparkle and rising chatter and laughter of the party Felicity had to keep reminding herself that she was going to have to find someone else with all the nuisance and heartache that entailed. And something worse – she was going to miss her.

When they were in bed, exhausted and on the outside of too much Tattinger, Robin leaned over to kiss her goodnight and at once brushed her cheek with his fingers.

'Fliss . . . what's up?'

'Nothing.'

'I know that, but what?'

'I was going to tell you tomorrow.'

He leaned up on his elbow. 'Now I'm really scared.'

'Ellie's leaving.'

'Oh.' Robin lay down and eased her into his arms. 'Is that all?'

This wasn't good news, but he was still reeling from what Anton, their lovely French neighbour, had told him at the party. Couldn't wait to tell him actually, absolutely dying to unburden himself . . . And such a cliché, straying with the older lady from the residents' association . . . Even Anton had been nearly laughing at himself.

'So stupid, so easy, I can't believe I let it happen!'

'Let it happen?' Robin was appalled. 'What are you, a teenager?'

Anton popped a Gallic one-shouldered shrug. 'I went to her house to discuss . . . never mind what . . . She hit on me. She's not unattractive, she made it plain it would be only that and no more—'

'Idiot!' hissed Robin. Anton had wanted a cigarette, they were out on the patio. 'There's always more! What about Lilian?'

'She will never know.'

'Not just that!' Robin couldn't believe how angry he was, he wanted to hit his friend. 'She doesn't deserve this – don't you know how lucky you are?'

At this, Anton had hung his head. 'What can I say? My resistance was low.'

At this point Fliss had come out, and that was that. But the exchange had ruined not just the party. For Robin, something had been irreversibly spoiled.

He held Fliss close – she wasn't asleep.

'We'll be fine,' he said. 'You and me.'

The words were for him as much as for his wife. They were a prayer.

Nineteen

December the twenty-second was an auspicious date in the Blyth calendar. It had been Hugh's father's birthday and coincidentally the date of his death, too. He had been old, and Hugh, an only child, only fifteen when he died so none of the Blyth offspring remembered their paternal grandfather. And their grandmother had died with the first crocuses, of what some said was a broken heart but also an inability to manage without the man she had always called her 'dearest Bod'. The origin of this nickname was lost to memory – Hugh's father's name was Dennis, so maybe, their descendants speculated, their marriage had been a more passionate one than anyone knew.

Hugh had only the fondest memories of his father. A liberal with both large and small 'l', and a gentle parent who even when he couldn't understand some behaviour of his son's, was slow to blame and quick to forgive. Hugh remembered the long letters he received at boarding school. His mother sent parcels, but it was his father who wrote, and would often enclose a newspaper cutting or a cartoon as well. The family home had been in

Belsize Park, not so very far from where Felicity and Robin lived now, and Hugh was still susceptible to a strong, nostalgic yearning when he was in the vicinity. He could never have brought himself to walk down Calcutta Road, in case he found that the house had been turned into flats or, worse still, demolished, along with his past. A past which certainly informed his own family life, but which had been so completely different – urban, more ordered, solitary.

This December twenty-second he and Marguerite were on the train to London, travelling first-class courtesy of Robin and Fliss. They had window seats facing one another. He gazed lovingly at his wife, deep in the latest psycho-drama, her preferred festive reading. For someone whose emotions were so near the surface, she read these carefully imagined horrors with great calm, her expression one of repose, her fingers resting at the base of the page, ready to turn to the next atrocity.

Feeling his eyes on her, she glanced up and smiled. 'What?'

He shook his head. 'Nothing.'

'You're wondering how I can read this stuff.'

'No,' he said, 'I wasn't.'

Comfortably, she returned to her book. He looked out of the window, smiling to himself. It was their way of saying they loved each other.

The TS's party had been a huge success. The house looked beautiful, the caterers had excelled themselves, the children were adorable and well-behaved. All the guests, whether close friends or more recent acquaintances had risen to the occasion, feeling themselves to be part of the theatre of a TS occasion – the women glamorous, the men dashing, everyone warm and witty and fun. But the usual pleasant after-glow of satisfaction eluded Felicity. She was going to miss Ellie and dreaded the inevitable round of interviews and the tricky running-in period. And she dreaded telling the children that they were going to lose far and away the nicest nanny they'd ever had.

Also, now the party was over there was the different and more complex phase of the family Christmas to be negotiated. At a party, everyone had their best face on and their best foot forward. Everyone – anyone – could manage that for a few hours. And not many of them had history or hinterland in common. They were social friends, some of them no more than acquaintances. There was no agenda. But with family, there *always* was. Her mother's determination to be appreciative and agreeable . . . her father's jokey astonishment at how organized she was . . . and then of course there was Bruno in the mix. His extended stay with them had been without incident, he had made himself quite useful, but this would be different because the parents would be there, with their mother dying to know about where he was living and what he was doing. Felicity remembered Robin saying how horrible the street had looked, she didn't want there to be a drama. With a bit of luck Hugh would calm things down, he was so good at that. Felicity loved her father more than he knew. And in the time-honoured manner she had married a man who was rather like him, if not in looks then in manner – easygoing, imperturbable, not given to overreaction, nor disposed to argue. She had learned how fortunate she was, and was increasingly alive to the possibility of taking him for granted.

Today, for instance, he was going to meet her parents at Paddington. They could have got a taxi, but he'd insisted – it was the proper, hospitable thing to do. There were no preparations left to make, or not till Christmas Eve anyway. The stage was set – the main guest bedroom fresh and fragrant, with silky-smooth many-threaded Egyptian cotton sheets and furnished with white roses, a selection of books (some of them old and treasured), bottles of Evian and tumblers, and a casket of Fortnums' tiny violet-flavoured cookies to ward off night starvation. She'd even remembered the Christmas edition of *Private Eye,* a favourite of Hugh's. The smaller spare room was less lavishly equipped for Bruno, but spotless and with a small TV and a copy of *Viz.* Felicity had a genius for the practical side of hospitality and was famous for her eye for detail.

Cissy and Rollo were in the playroom with Ellie making paper angels to hold place cards. Noah was on his bed with his Playstation. Felicity felt she should have lured him away from that, but on the other hand peace would be in short supply for the next week so she might as well take advantage of it. She was at her computer when the phone rang.

'Hi there.'

She didn't at once recognize the voice. 'Sorry – who is this?'

'Give you a guess.'

It was the tone that did it. 'Oh, Charity, I'm sorry – how are you?' A wary, reflexive impulse prompted her to add, '*Where* are you?'

'Not outside your door, you can relax.'

'I wasn't—'

'I know you've got a lot on your plate. Are the Ps there yet?'

'Rob's gone to meet them.'

'I just called to pass on the compliments of the season in a sisterly fashion.'

'How nice.' Felicity didn't believe this, but let it pass. 'Thank you. Remind me what your plans are?' She must have been told, but couldn't remember.

'My plan was to spend a couple of days with a friend.'

Charity wasn't usually coy, but apparently details would have to be coaxed out of her. Ready to listen, Felicity went to sit by the picture window. 'But there's been a change?'

'Not yet.'

'Charity, is there something you want to tell me? If so, spit it out. The Ps are probably on their way as we speak.'

After a short, tense pause, Charity said, 'The truth is, I don't know. I'm in unfamiliar territory.'

'Go on.'

There was another silence which made Felicity think her sister might be smoking – which would be a pity, because she'd given it up a while ago. 'Charity?'

'You know what? I don't think I want to go through it all right now.' She made it sound as if Felicity had made the call, and had been interrogating her.

'All what?'

'Nothing. Nothing I can't sort out without boring the pants off you first.'

'You're not boring me, but I'm not a mind-reader.'

Charity gave a short laugh. 'Probably just as well. Look – have a wonderful Christmas, pass on my love to everyone, maybe we'll speak some time while the Ps are with you . . .'

'Of course we will – on Christmas Day. What time would be good? How about midday?'

'I'm sure that will be fine. I don't know . . . Tell you what, I'll call you.'

'OK, but don't forget.'

'I won't.'

Felicity sat with the silent phone in her hand, gazing at the sparkling black sea of the city. *Something's going on,* she thought. *Everything changes.*

A day later, at about the same time, Charity was thinking, *This isn't me.*

But if you were doing a thing voluntarily and without awkwardness, then presumably it *was* you, but a different version. One you hadn't met before.

Whatever the answer, she was elated. Standing there in the public bar of The Jockey with a Jack Daniels in her hand, waiting for a man she barely knew and with whom she had nothing in common – this was weirdly exhilarating.

She'd never have been there if she hadn't accidentally bumped into him a second time. She'd been in an unfamiliar part of town to pick up a picture she was having framed (a clever shot she'd taken of a site in Orkney). After she'd collected the picture from the framer's studio on the industrial estate she'd stopped at a little Cypriot supermarket to buy milk, only to bump into Luke Tanner by the cold cabinet. It was a small shop and there was no chance of pretending she hadn't seen him – they were no more than two feet away from one another, and he didn't bother to conceal his delight.

'Hang on, it's you, isn't it?'

'Who?' she'd asked dryly. 'Me?'

'Go on.'

She looked to either side. 'I suppose it must be.'

His smile was untarnished. 'I don't know your name.'

'And I'm afraid I've forgotten yours.'

'Luke – Luke Tanner. I bummed a fag off you up at the campus bar.'

'If you say so.' She wasn't usually so abrasive, but his perky, laddish confidence seemed almost to invite it.

'Do you live round here?' he asked.

'No.'

'Only we're putting on the show just up the road.'

'The circus?' Too late she realized she had given herself away but he showed no sign of noticing that, either.

'That's right. You should come along.'

'I haven't been to a circus since I was ten. And to be honest, I hated it.'

'Don't blame you,' he said equably, 'but ours is different. No animals, no not-funny clowns. Acrobats, juggling, magic – you'd like it.'

'I don't think so.'

'We could walk there now, it's on your way. Give you the idea.'

'No thanks.'

'OK.'

His unshakeable good humour implied that he had Charity's number and didn't believe she was half as frosty as she made out. She found this completely infuriating, and turned to go. She'd reached the till before realising she hadn't bought what she came in for, but no power on earth, let alone a pint of milk, would have made her go back, so she left empty-handed.

In her irritation she drove a touch too quickly. But stopping at a red light, she saw it – Tanner and Bright's Travelling Circus, luridly advertised outside the old British Legion Hall. You literally couldn't miss it. Curious in spite of herself, and because there was a pay-and-display space just beyond the junction, she pulled over. There was no way Luke Tanner, on foot, would be here in the next few minutes.

'Hello there! Are you here for this afternoon's show?'

The young woman in the foyer was in an electric blue sequined leotard and silver stilettos, a cockade of blue and silver feathers attached to her gold hair. Her upfront manner matched her outfit.

'No,' said Charity firmly. 'Just taking a look.'

'Feel free!' The young woman gestured in the direction of the door, which was heavily disguised with blue velvet drapes and gold cord.

'I don't necessarily want to watch.'

'No worries, take a seat and I'll be in later to see if you'd like to pay for it, how's that?'

Jesus, thought Charity, business must be bad if they were letting passers-by like her in on spec. But the hall, though admittedly not large, was three-quarters full. There was music playing, and curtains had been swept up to the centre of the ceiling to give the effect of a tent. A scaffolding frame supported a trapeze, some rings, and a bunched-up net. Colourful wooden blocks had been arranged in a horseshoe shape around the performance area, and behind these was a row of tiny chairs, the sort Charity remembered from primary school, most of them occupied by children. A man dressed as a large black and white dog was juggling. The juggling wasn't perfect, but it wasn't meant to be – it was comical. The children were laughing.

Charity stood at the back. A teenage girl walked on rather sheepishly, then proceeded to perform astonishing feats on the trapeze, followed by a couple of guys who could only be called tumblers, like the juggler not perfect, but that only added to the thrilling sense of jeopardy. Then another woman released the net like a suspended cat's cradle, and swung and rolled without ever getting tangled. Everything was, if not tacky, then low-rent and simple, but the children's faces were lifted, turning this way and that like sunflowers. There were exhalations of amazement, gasps of anxiety, sighs of relief. Engaged in spite of herself, Charity perched sideways on the edge of the nearest free chair.

Half an hour later the interval was announced. The girl in the blue sequins was waiting by the door.

'You enjoying the show?'

'Yes – I owe you.'

'That's alright, you can pay at the end.'

'No, I'm leaving now, but I'll definitely pay.' Charity added without meeting the girl's eye. 'It's impressive what you've done in that small space.'

'Thank you. Here's the boss, you should say it to him.'

'Hello there! Changed your mind?'

She was caught bang to rights, it would have been churlish not to admit to her enjoyment. 'I caught the first half, it was pretty good.'

'We aim to please. Look' – he cocked his head – 'I need to get back there, but fancy a drink later on? Or tomorrow?'

Having watched his show, suddenly she couldn't be bothered to fence with him. The girl had disappeared with a tray of ices. After all, what did it matter? None of this was important.

'Go on then. Name your time and place.'

They'd arranged this meet at the The Jockey, and then he'd picked up a container (it looked like a swing bin) covered in Christmas paper, and held it out to her with a shake.

'Here, help yourself.'

'What's this?'

'Present. Everyone gets one. It's on the ticket.'

'I haven't bought one yet.'

'Never mind.' He gave the container another shake. 'Go on. Lucky dip.'

Mac rang at the time she had suggested, but there was no reply. He didn't worry, it was a time of year when people were busy, having drinks with colleagues, doing last minute shopping, preparing to have people round or, of course, to go away. He didn't mind that she was doing any of these things. His own preparations were made and he was in a state of happy anticipation. He decided against leaving a message. He'd be seeing her soon.

Charity wasn't a great drinker, but she knew that she was getting slightly pissed. They'd moved on from The Jockey, where they'd talked about his job and hers, to a rather more salubrious cocktail bar, tricked out like a yuppy winter wonderland in silver, gold and ice-blue. The fresh air in between had highlighted her tipsiness, and along with it a change in conversational gear.

'No show today then?' she asked.

'I bunked off.'

'You're the boss.'

'That's right.'

She was perched on a bar stool, he was at her side, eye to eye.

'What am I doing here?'

The question was largely rhetorical. She leaned back slightly to gain some perspective, and he placed a restraining hand on her shoulder, smiling past her at the woman behind. 'You tell me.'

'This isn't my scene really.'

'No? I'd never have guessed.'

She quite liked to be teased by him, it made her feel frivolous – flirtatious, even.

'No.'

'What is it then – "your scene"?'

She could hear the inverted commas round the last words.

'I like my work.'

'Oh' – he spread a hand – 'me too.'

'But your work is different,' she pointed out, and then stalled. *Well that was stating the blindingly bloody obvious.*

'Drink up,' he said. 'You need that curry.'

She got back to halls in a horribly expensive taxi, still worse for wear, but with at least some of the alcohol soaked up by dhansak and naan bread. She felt pleased with herself as she pulled off her boots and clothes, cleaned her teeth and collapsed on the bed. When she closed her eyes she had a bad attack of the whirls, something she had only suffered once before in her life and sworn never to repeat. It was some time in the small hours as she stood in the bathroom gazing at her rumpled reflection, a pint glass of water in her hand, that some distant bell in her brain reminded her that there was something she should have done. But accessing the actual information was beyond her and she went back to bed.

Twenty

The thing about Christmas Day, Marguerite privately considered (she would never have said so aloud) was that it was anti-climactic. By the time the turkey was being basted, the bread sauce made and the festive board laid in all its glory, the actual *feeling* of Christmas was largely over. That potent, poignant mix of antici-pation and nostalgia was past for another year. Now there were only the ritualized practicalities to be gone through, differing only slightly according to host and location. There was the fraught giving and receiving of presents, those which might be considered too extravagant, a tad stingy, not quite right in a variety of ways, but the thought behind them was always duly honored. The feasting which left the adults bloated and soporific and the children hyperactive. The queen (though not so often these days), the obligatory short, dyspeptic walk and the games requiring more energy than most people had left. Until finally some nice family film could be turned on so the children could calm down and the adults subside comatose into the soft furnishings.

But this year Felicity had thrown a curved ball by announcing that Christmas dinner would be at six! It had traditionally been earlier, because of the children, but she decreed that it was time for a change.

'We'll have a walk in the morning, those who want to go to church can go, all have brunch at twelve, presents, and champagne from five.'

'What about the children?' Marguerite had asked, before she'd had time to consider if the question was wise. Her daughter's shining smile turned on her like a searchlight.

'What about them?'

'No, sorry darling, I was only thinking about Cissy – won't that be awfully late for her?'

'No, Ma,' said Felicity. 'It won't. Because it's only once a year and when it gets late one of us will take her up to bed And we have a couple of other people coming tomorrow. I've checked, and early-evening dinner will suit them better.'

If Marguerite could have turned the clock back forty-five seconds she would have done so. She could feel Hugh busy not looking at her. When in doubt, leave well alone.

She soon had something else to think about. Bruno arrived early evening on Christmas Eve and looked awful. He had put on weight, but looked far from healthy, his face pale and puffy, his eyes dull and his hair unkempt. His clothes were clean, but creased and greyish – the unmistakable look of garments that had been stuffed into the machine with too many other things and dried in haste. Heaven knows what his sheets were like . . . Apart from that, his mother told herself, he seemed his usual self, and it was nice to see how the children rushed to greet him. *Uncle Bruno!* That made silly seasonal tears sting her eyes. Mercifully, Hugh did his not looking or noticing thing again.

She wondered too who the other people were who were coming, but buttoned her lip – she'd find out soon enough.

★   ★   ★

Bruno knew it was only a matter of time before his mother made her move. He accepted that concern for offspring was in the job description, and his were the least interventionist of parents. But he still didn't look forward to fending off the enquiries, which eventually came on Christmas Eve.

'How is everything, love?'

'Fine.'

'Are you comfortable in the flat?'

'Sure.'

'Come on, Daisy,' put in Hugh, passing her Buck's Fizz, 'it's a student flat, remember those?'

Seeing his mother's expression Bruno thought it best to take pre-emptive action. 'I am actually looking for somewhere else, perhaps a bit nearer college?'

'Good idea.' That was it, Marguerite told herself, he had a long walk every day to college and back. 'Do the college have contacts?'

'Yes, no problem.'

With a bit of luck that would have put her off the scent. Nosy parkering aside it was good to see them, and to be here in Fliss and Rob's luxurious house and see the kids again. Rob had told him about Ellie leaving, that was a real downer. She and the lucky bloke were coming tomorrow which would be a bit weird.

The trouble with people who were reliably punctual was that you started to worry the very second after the appointed hour. Mac and Charity had agreed that she would be there between six and seven (a little leeway was permissible, even advisable, on Christmas Eve), so as the seventh chime of the long case clock in the hall faded, he became concerned. Was there some hideous delay on the motorway? Or worse, had she herself been the cause of a delay, involved in an accident from which the red tail lights trailed back as the hectic flashing blue converged?

Get a grip, man!

No news was good news. She would be here in her own good time with, of course, explanation, which he would brush aside – what did it matter? she was here now. The anticipated relief, the bliss, of that moment carried him through till about eight thirty when another possibility wormed his way into his thoughts and began to make its presence felt. He did his best to dismiss it. He prided himself on being the least neurotic of men, it was practically a qualification for his job, and he knew Charity to be the most truthful and dependable of women. Her directness was one of the qualities that had drawn him to her. It was simply beyond credence that she would have – no, it would not happen – she was not capable of simply changing her mind . . .

But there was no call, no message, nothing. Against his better judgement he rang the number of her mobile phone, recently acquired for contingencies like these, but an alien voice parroted back at him. Of course if she was driving she wouldn't answer. He wouldn't want her to.

By ten p.m. his preparations, such as they were, began to take on a pathetic, mocking appearance. *Silly old man. Deluded, vain. Stupid.* He packed up the makings of a light supper and put them away in the fridge, but fiddling about with clingfilm and tinfoil made him feel like a fusspot, so he retrieved the smoked salmon and egg mayonnaise and ate some of it though he wasn't in the least hungry. He'd left the curtains open in the drawing room so he could see her car arrive, but that too now seemed pathetic, and he half-drew them and turned off one of the lights so if she did show up he wouldn't be caught out watching and waiting.

Almost the worst thing was the not knowing. The pointless imagining. He tried to fight it to no avail. Everything about this silent, desolating absence was *wrong*. Either something appalling had happened, or she had behaved in a heartless and cruel way. Either way it didn't bear thinking about. He was in torment.

At one point he went out, simply because he could no longer bear to be inside, surrounded by the evidence of his idiotic, hopeful fantasy. He dragged on boots and Barbour, picked up his large torch and told himself he was going to get some air, stretch his legs . . . Perhaps just a look round the empty school to see that all was well.

There was an almost-full moon, and the further he went from the lights of the house, the better he could see, so he turned off the torch. Everything was calm, and bleached-looking. One read of scenes 'silvered' by moonlight, but it was more a kind of luminous grey, pewter at best. Monochrome but clear, like an old black and white film of the sort he had pictured himself perhaps watching with Charity, one of those witty romantic comedies with Hepburn and Tracy, whom he had allowed himself to think they slightly resembled . . . *Damn, damn!*

He walked right round the school building. The original house hadn't been large, but had been somewhat randomly extended and adapted over the years, so there were bays and promontories to be negotiated. As he passed one of the dark corners quite a large animal scuttled across, low to the ground – it might have been a cat, a fox, or an extremely large rat. He turned on the torch, but it had already disappeared into the night or more worryingly its hole. He reminded himself to come back and check in the morning – if it had been a rat he needed to know. While the kind of parents who sent their children here were by definition liberal, something told him their open-mindedness wouldn't extend to tolerating vermin.

At the far side of the school were the outhouses – the chicken run, the garage, the goat pen, the greenhouse and sheds for fuel and tools. During term-times these were checked every evening by him or whoever was on duty, because they were a prime spot for hiding out, to smoke dope or test the efficacy of French letters. More from habit than anything else he shone the torch into each of them in turn. The goats just stared back with their blank, dazzled eyes, the poor old chickens were a bit flustered, clucking and rustling like maiden ladies discombobulated to be rudely disturbed this late.

It was as he set out across the yard, back towards the driveway that he became aware that he was not alone. There the soft crunch of a footstep in the lane to his right, and a suggestion of movement. Without hesitation he swung the beam of the torch in that direction.

'Who's that? Someone there?'

'For God's sake put the gun down, it's me!'

He was always to remember how clear and strong her voice came back. Not the voice of a startled intruder, even less that of a shamefaced stop-out – just plain exasperated.

'Charity?' In the relief of saying her name, a warm tide of joy flooded through him.

'Who else were you expecting?' Her arm was raised in front

of her face, and now she put down the bag she was carrying and pushed back the hood of her quilted coat. 'Can you please stop with the interrogation technique!'

Obediently he switched off the torch. Round here there was just enough light from between the curtains of his living room for them to make one another out. He stopped a few feet from the front door, and she came across the gravel towards him, carrying what he could now see was a supermarket bag. Her rucksack was over the other shoulder, she was loaded down. When she reached him, she dumped the bag again, wriggled out of the rucksack and put up a hand, palm outwards.

'Don't ask.'

'Very well,' he said, 'I shan't. Come in.'

He picked up the bag and the rucksack – they weighed nothing, nothing! – and she followed him into the house, closing the door behind them.

Charity didn't tell him everything. She considered there was no need. She had made her decision, which was irrevocable, and with which she was entirely happy. To think of how close she'd come to making the wrong one brought on a kind of vertigo. She regretted the collateral damage, but something told her that Luke would bounce back almost at once. He always had less invested than her, because he took himself less seriously. He'd have her marked down as a cool customer and a tease, or perhaps more accurately as a woman who in spite of appearances to the contrary didn't know her own mind. She liked Luke, and was sorry that the circumstances meant they were unlikely to see each other again, let alone be friends.

She had needed him too, she could see that now. The encounter with him had been messy but instructive. It was a pity that inevitably he would think the less of her, but already any feelings of remorse were fading.

She was starving. Upstairs in Mac's kitchen she had wolfed smoked salmon and rye bread, washed down with a large scotch. He had joined her with the scotch, but not the food, feasting his eyes on her. He'd asked no questions, but once she was a little restored she'd told him the whole sorry saga of the car running out of petrol two miles up the road. She'd managed to freewheel on to the verge and left it locked, and he said that was fine, they'd go up tomorrow and check, and he'd get Charlie from the local garage to give it a tow, or provide a can of unleaded, for a seasonal consideration. She realized that this information didn't account for how late she was, only why she'd arrived on foot, but one of Mac's most admirable qualities was his lack of fuss. He would take her at face value.

With the plates in the sink and the second scotch in their hands they went through to the living room. He drew the curtains fully. The fire had almost gone out but he revived the embers and threw on a shovelful of coal. It was well after midnight. They sat down at either end of the sofa.

'I'm sorry I was rude,' she said. 'Feeling stupid doesn't bring out the best in me.'

He hated that ugly word, especially associated with her. 'You weren't stupid,' he said. 'It was late at night, you were tired, you made a mistake. It could happen to anyone.'

She sent him one of her sharp sideways smiles. 'I don't deserve that, but thank you.'

'The main thing is,' he said, 'that you're here. And I can't begin to tell you how delighted I am that you are.'

What had she said to Luke? *This isn't who I am.* For God's sake.

To his credit he hadn't called her a pretentious bitch. In spite of disappointment and injured pride he had confined himself to a little justifiable sarcasm. There had been a hardening in his expression, and he'd stepped back, removing his hands from her in an exaggerated gesture of surrender.

'We can't have that . . .!'

'I'm sorry.'

'Me too. You have no idea.'

'I'm supposed to be somewhere else . . . with someone else . . .' she floundered.

'Jesus!' He flung his hands in the air and brought them down on top of his head, closing his eyes as if to shut her out. 'Now she tells me.' Hands still on his head he opened his eyes and fixed her with a flinty look. 'Don't let me stop you being true to yourself, whoever the fuck that is.'

That – the gesture, the tone – had made her less sorry and

more angry. All she was doing was turning down what was probably destined to be a one-night stand with a man who was surely
the king of one-night stands. She could feel her resolve stiffening
along with her backbone. He wanted to trade sarcasm? He'd
picked the wrong woman, she was a past master.

'I'm so glad you understand,' she said.

That did it, as she knew it would. She didn't have to tell him
to go, or resort to cliché by opening the door. He walked out
of her room, his shoulder bumping hers as he went, barking a
brisk, 'Fuck the hell off!'

Charity hadn't always lived up to her name. There were people
out there who thought it was a downright misnomer. She didn't
suffer fools gladly and she cut ditherers no slack. But this experience changed her a little. Just enough. As she set out on the
long drive to Mac's a delayed reaction set in, and she found she
was shaking. She had to pull over to recover herself. She pulled
down the visor and stared at her gaunt, wild-eyed reflection in
the mirror.

You did a bad thing she told herself. *You showed poor judgement
and did damage. But now you are doing the right thing, so get your
skinny arse in gear and get on with it.*

Some time after one she heard Mac say, 'Come on, you're asleep,'
and she realized she had been. One moment her eyelids had
been heavy, the next he was taking the almost-empty glass from
her hand.

'Bed,' he said.

She was woozy with tiredness and scotch, and he put a hand
beneath her arm and helped her up. They stood close to one
another. His proximity was like that of a tall, sheltering tree.

'Happy Christmas,' he said. He put a hand behind her head,
cupping it, and kissed her on the forehead. She was almost
weaving, incapable of decision but the sweet comfort of that kiss
told her all was well.

He escorted her to the spare bedroom, spartan but comfortable with its single bed and washbasin, rather like her room in
halls. Her rucksack was on the chair.

'The bathroom's on the right down there, you have first dibs
at all times. The usual offices are next door, or there's one at the

bottom of the stairs, but it's rather more rugged, so emergencies only.'

'Thanks.'

He must have caught something in her expression, because he added, 'Sleep well and see you later' – he checked his watch – 'today. No rush.' He took her hand in both of his and pressed it. 'In our case, unlike the poet and his coy girlfriend, we have both world enough and time. Goodnight, Charity.'

Just before sinking into one of the best night's sleep she'd had in weeks, she thought how wonderful it was to be with someone who, without much help from her, seemed simply to know who she was.

Perhaps, she thought, with a sense of surprise, *this is what it means to find a soulmate.*

Twenty-One

Honor had been expecting to take her guests home at the end of the day. That had been the arrangement on which her invitation was based.

'And of course,' she said, 'I shall collect you and take you home afterwards.'

But when the time came, at around five (after some gentle wrangling about tidying up), she found she had been outmanoeuvred. Everything had gone better than she hoped. Archie had behaved impeccably, and been made much of. Lunch, if not up to Marguerite's or Felicity's standard, had been hot, tasty and plentiful and presented no health hazards. Her vegetables in particular had attracted compliments, and everyone had seconds. Presents had been exchanged, and she was enchanted by what nice, well-chosen things they had given her. She was deeply touched to think of Mr Dawson in Mason's of Salting (how had he got there, had Graham taken him?) looking for the beautiful red leather gloves. And Avis had been too extravagant with a gift box of Royal Jelly bath oil and body lotion, purchased through the agency of a friend. Honor's eyes got a bit shiny, which made Avis chuckle.

'It's no more than you deserve – you need a bit of spoiling, doesn't she, Alec?'

It was only today that Honor had found out that Mr Dawson was Alec – she wasn't going to use it herself unless invited.

'Yes, definitely,' he agreed. 'Speaking for myself I don't know what I should do without you.'

Just to make him feel better she nearly said that Graham would soon find someone else, but that would have been to undervalue both sides of the relationship.

'I can't thank you both enough,' she said. The presents were still on her lap as she looked up at both of them. 'This is a lovely Christmas.'

'One of the best,' said Avis.

'You've looked after us beautifully,' said Mr Dawson, gently stroking Archie's head.

Suddenly it became vital that they understood her exact meaning – that this was not an extension of her job.

'You're my dearest friends,' she said. 'Having you here has meant so much to me.'

Avis had chuckled again and blown her a kiss. Mr Dawson's eyes were a little too bright as he nodded, and then asked if he might possibly have more cake. She had bought it from the baker in town, and iced it herself. The pipe-cleaner robin on top was hers, she had learnt to make those at infant school.

The only other moment of slight awkwardness had been when her mother rang. She could hear cheerful family noise in the background, the slight difficulty this caused was a good reason not to extend the conversation beyond a very few minutes. Her father was put on and, briefly, Bruno.

'Alright, sis?'

'More than alright – it sounds as if all of you are, too!'

'Rob has a free hand with the fizz, what can I say?'

'I'm so glad. Have a great rest of the day, and look after yourself, Bruno.'

She had been talking on the phone in the hall. When she returned to the drawing room Alec and Avis were busily chatting, and looked up almost too obviously, to show they hadn't been listening.

'Talking to the family?' asked Avis.

'Yes, they're all having a wonderful time at my sister's in London.'

'Do they know you've got a rough crowd in?'

'They certainly do.' Avis's attitude was what she needed to keep emotion at bay. 'They told me to lock up the spoons.'

So everything had exceeded expectation, most of all how well Avis and Mr Dawson had got on. A case, she supposed, of opposites agreeing, because no two people could on the face of it have been more different. Avis had clearly been charmed by Mr Dawson's old-fashioned gallantry, and her natural bonhomie had rubbed off on him – he had laughed more than ever before, Honor had seen another side of him, one capable of having fun and being almost flirtatious in a quiet way.

When he struggled to his feet and announced that they should be going she was genuinely sorry.

'Oh, must you?'

'I think we must.'

Avis agreed, levering herself upright. Honor saw how Mr Dawson watched, ready to help if needed, but careful not to fuss. When she dropped her bag Honor let him pick it up, in spite of the agonising slowness, using the moment to go and fetch her coat and car key, the excited Archie in attendance. When she came back in her guests were standing side by side like a couple of school children caught in a conspiracy.

'Oh we should have said, there'll be no need for those,' said Mr Dawson.

Honor stood with her coat on, still undone. 'How do you mean?'

'I've ordered us a taxi.'

Avis saw her jaw drop. 'He would do it, and he won't even let me chip in. But we both want to save you the trouble after giving us such a lovely day.'

'But you don't need to,' protested Honor. 'I'm only too happy to run you back.'

'I know, I know . . .' Mr Dawson drew back his immaculate cuff and peered. 'But we decided to override you, and he'll be here any minute.'

And in fact Terry's trusty minicab drew up at that moment. There was no arguing with them, they would have had to pay now anyway, so she had to let them go. She kept her coat on and went out into the drive with them, carrying Archie who would otherwise jump aboard. Terry, in expectation of a generous seasonal tip, had both the passenger doors ready open, and was wearing his chauffeur's hat, reserved for special occasions. He knew his old people, who were an excellent source of income.

'Good evening all, Happy Christmas!'

They chorused back and he saw Avis and Mr Dawson into the back, closing the doors with a flourish and addressing Honor as the founder of the feast.

'Don't worry, I'll see everyone safe in at their doors.'

'Please do, Terry. I was going to run them home myself and, you know, make sure they were alright.'

'I know. I'll keep an eye on them.' He glanced back at his passengers. 'They look pretty good to me, what do you think?'

Still carrying the dog she went ahead of the car to the gate, to close it behind them and wave them off. As she leaned forward to mouth, 'Goodbye' she saw Mr Dawson's hand touch Avis's. Only briefly – checking that she was comfortable, perhaps? But there was something more than courtesy, or friendship, in the gesture. A remembered tenderness, perhaps? As the car lights fanned across the arch of trees at the start of the beacon walk, and disappeared into the dark gulley of the lane, Honor felt a squeeze of the heart at a job well done.

She spent a perfectly contented hour to the accompaniment of Radio Four getting things straight in the drawing room – not an arduous task compared with the usual Blyths' Christmas – and washing up. Even with only three people she was glad that her parents had finally invested in a dishwasher. All the dishes and cutlery went in there and the more heavy-duty cooking pots and pans she left to soak in the butler's sink. Her last task as hostess was to call Mr Dawson and Avis to check they were home safe and let them know what time she would be in the next day – there was agency cover at bedtime. They were both in fine spirits, and full of praise for her hospitality, she could tell from the timbre of their voices and not just what they said, that they were exhilarated.

After that she left Archie, exhausted by socialising, on the sofa, and went upstairs. She ran herself a bath, using Avis's wonderful golden products that filled the chilly family bathroom with richly scented steam. She was not usually a great one for indulgent baths – not one for self-indulgence at all – but this time she revelled in the limitless hot water and the silky texture of the soap, and turned the radio to cheerful music, quite loud. It occurred to her that this was a particularly good way to end Christmas Day – alone in a tidy house, with just enough leftovers downstairs and the sofa and television all to herself. She thought fondly, but only fleetingly, of her family, and not at all of the vicar.

The presence of Ellie and her fiancé lent an extra benign dimension to the TS's Christmas dinner. Non-family members made the whole thing feel more like a party, and the family, seeing themselves through their eyes, upped their game, and acquired an added lustre. It was impossible not to like Ellie, whom most of them knew anyway, and Brian – 'Bri' – was a charming, bearded joiner, the sort of man who could have got on with anyone. Bruno thought, *She's marrying Jesus!* But couldn't think of who to say it to, until he ran into Rob in the kitchen, and Rob leaned his head in with a man-to-man air.

'Is it just me who thinks there's something appropriate about Ellie marrying that agreeable hirsute carpenter?'

After that, whenever Bri was being especially likeable they caught one another's eye. But Bri's Christlike qualities didn't stop Bruno feeling slightly jealous. From the start he'd had a bit of a crush on Ellie, and felt that they shared a certain semi-detached position in the household. It wasn't just the TSs that were going to miss her. She even noticed when Cissy was about to fall asleep, and scooped her up. Fliss had leapt to her feet.

'Ellie, you mustn't, you're our guest this evening.'

'Don't say that,' said Ellie, 'from now on I can be one of the family.' And she took Cissy up to bed.

Marguerite glanced at her daughter – that had been a kind gesture, but had it hurt her feelings? She decided on balance not. Fliss was dishing up chocolate yule log and morello cherries. But as they all began eating and exclaiming, she rose and could be heard going upstairs.

Cissy was already asleep when Fliss came in. Ellie had put her underwear and tights over the back of the chair and was hanging up her blue velvet party dress. Fliss bent to kiss her daughter and was rewarded by a mumbled, 'Night, Mummy . . .'

The two women came out into the wide, windowed corridor, Fliss drawing the door to behind them.

'Thank you for that, Ellie.'

'It's OK.' Ellie's expression was quizzical, a little rueful. 'I'm sorry if I was out of line.'

'You weren't, not at all,' said Fliss truthfully. 'But I can't tell you how much we're going to miss you.'

'You already have.'

'Bri's such a nice man.'

'That's what I think. We're a good fit.'

They began to walk, but at the top of the stairs Fliss touched Ellie's arm to detain her.

'What you said – about being one of the family.'

'I've had a few bevvies . . .'

'But I hope it's true. It would be so nice to think we'd still see you even if you're not working here. Especially if you're not.'

'Thanks, Fliss,' said Ellie, 'that's sweet. But we'll be back in New Zealand, remember?'

On Boxing Day most of the family went to a drinks party, then home for turkey sandwiches and then to the pantomime. During the drinks party phase Bruno stayed home with the children, which he was more than happy to do. In fact it was almost a definition of comfort to have acres of empty space and luxurious seating, a kitchen furnished with delicious leftovers and cold beer, and the kids content with all their new stuff.

The whole situation was an inducement to indolence, but Bruno wasn't entirely idle. After half an hour or so he got off the sofa and wandered about. He liked to admire his surroundings. Fliss and Rob, he'd decided, had just the right level of richness. Not absolutely stinking, but enough so that everything was as nice as it could be, and they never had to think about it. Money was like sex, if you were getting plenty it wasn't an issue. Only the lack of either (or in Bruno's case both) kept it at the front of your mind. He'd never thought of himself as materialistic, but exposure to the TS's lifestyle had changed all that.

Standing in the drawing room overlooking the elegant wintry

garden and the stupendous view beyond he realized that he wanted
to be exactly as well-off as this. He wasn't a fool, he realized that
the gap between his current situation and their enviable one was
bloody enormous. But it was bridgeable, and he was determined
to bridge it.

Conscious suddenly of not being alone he turned to find
Cissy sitting in one of the big leather chairs with her hands
resting queenlike on the arms. She was watching him with the
unselfconscious wide stare of the very young.

'Hello,' said Bruno. Not so long ago he'd have felt awkward
with his niece, but he'd learned there was no trick to it. You
simply had to be straightforward.

'What are you doing?'

'Looking out of the window. You can see a long way.'

She slid down from the chair. 'How far?'

'This far.' He picked her up. Her arm went round his neck,
her fine hair tickled his cheek. She was a sweetie. 'See?'

Faces together, they gazed. Cissy said, 'What is that?'

'London.' He gave her a gentle prod. 'Where you live.'

'But . . .' She wriggled and he put her down. 'We live here.'

'That's right, this is part of London.'

She gave this due consideration before shaking her head. 'No.
We live in Hampstead.'

Bruno was an experienced enough hand these days to know
when he'd reached a sticking point.

'Correct. You do.'

There was the tiniest furrow between her brows, her expression
was stern. He wasn't going to get off that easily.

'We *all* live here,' she declared, spreading her arms. 'Mummy
and Daddy, Noah, Rollo, Ellie, Bruno—'

'Not me. I don't live here.'

'Yes, you do!'

'I'm staying here at the moment, just for Christmas.'

There was another scowling pause, during which Rollo
wandered in. 'I wondered where everybody was.'

Bruno said, 'We were discussing who lives here.'

'Bruno . . .' Rollo approached and sat down on the broad, low
windowsill, his back to the garden. 'Are you coming to the panto?'

'I believe so.'

'Cool,' said Rollo. 'It's Aladdin.'

Bruno forbore to say that it didn't matter what it was, they were all the same. 'That's a good one.'

'I'm coming,' Cissy informed him.

'Have you been before?' asked Bruno.

'Yes.' She nodded vigorously.

'No, she hasn't,' said Rollo the worldly wise, 'and she's too young. Mum will have to take her out.'

'I'll take her out if she needs to go,' said Bruno. 'I'm not bothered about missing bits.' He looked down at Cissy. 'We'll be alright, won't we?'

'Yes,' said Cissy, clearly satisfied. 'We will.'

After that, Noah tore himself away from his Playstation and the three chaps, with Cissy orbiting them, emptied the dishwasher, made sandwiches and put everything out for lunch on the kitchen table. It was a sort of game, but one which carried the added bonus of knowing they would be in everyone's good books when the time came.

'They'll be pleased we've done this,' said Noah, 'because they'll be drunk.'

He may have been right, but once again noticed that in the area of drunkenness, as in that of wealth, there were different flavours. The hosts on this occasion lived in what Robin cheerfully described as 'a seriously fuck-off piece of real estate' within walking distance, so no-one's imbibing had been affected by the need to drive. All four of them were probably on the outside of several glasses of Tattinger but any comparison with Sean after a hard night at the British Queen didn't compute. The Blyths and the TSs were merely gracefully convivial, pink-cheeked, tactile, full of jokes and general good humour. Vomiting and violence just didn't qualify. But after the sandwiches had gone down both Robin and Hugh fell sound asleep in front of the racing, and Marguerite withdrew to 'put her feet up for a bit' before the cab arrived to take them to the panto. Fliss, a woman of iron, cleared the kitchen with his assistance.

'How were the kids while we were out?'

'Great,' he said. 'No trouble at all.'

She cut herself a thin slice of Brie from the cheese board, the only sign that she was slightly pissed. Before putting it in her mouth, she said, 'Thanks, Bruno.'

'No prob. Pleasure.'

'No, I mean it,' she insisted. 'They like you.'

'I like them.'

'So sad about Ellie . . .' Fliss sighed, munched, swallowed. 'I hope I can find someone half as nice.'

'Yeah,' he agreed. 'Tough call.'

Rollo was right, the panto, and especially Abanazar, was too much for Cissy, and Bruno spent much of the time in the foyer area behind the dress circle watching her run about, high on sweets and over-excitement. The show was also incredibly long, and he was quite relieved when in the interval Fliss told him to feel free to take Cissy home if he wanted to.

'Let's bring her back in for while, but do scoot off if it's not working – is that OK?'

It was more than OK. Cissy took flight at the first sign of Abanazar's pyrotechnics, and the two of them hailed a black cab and set off home. He handed over Robin's thirty pounds (Boxing Day to Hampstead was at a premium) and they walked hand in hand up the drive. The front door with its magnificent evergreen garland, the window with the first of three Christmas trees in pink and silver, the soft light in the hall shining through the leaded fanlight, all reminded Bruno how much he was dreading leaving tomorrow.

He made buttered toast and they sat together companionably on the sofa in the family room, munching and watching *Mary Poppins*. Bruno considered Julie Andrews quite sexy. Perhaps nannies with their combination of discipline and kindness were sexy by definition. Jesus, if Ellie had had to wear a uniform . . .! He squirmed, and with some difficulty banished the image.

By his calculation, given the length of the first half, the others wouldn't be back till at least seven. When the film ended he sat Cissy in the kitchen and gave her a bowl of ice-cream (her second of the day but hell, it was Christmas), and then he suggested she have her bath.

'Will you do my bath?' She was round-eyed, severely enquiring. *This could go either way.*

'Would you like me to?'

'Yes.' Imperiously.

He may have taken the initiative, but there was no doubt who was calling the shots. Cissy micro-managed the entire exercise – showing him everything from how to turn the taps on and which bubble bath to use, to how her pyjamas should be laid out and which two stories she would like (also to be laid on the bed in readiness). Bruno did as he was told. He hoped this was the right thing and not out of order, but Cissy was so independent that his role was limited to helping her get dry and putting toothpaste on her toothbrush.

'I can do it,' she explained, 'but it sometimes comes out in a sploosh.'

He was just finishing the second story, about a dog who lived in a library, when he heard the clunk of a cab door, and voices outside. Cissy leapt out of bed and was along the passage and down the stairs like greased lightning. He followed somewhat sheepishly, book in hand.

The family were fanning out from the hall, removing coats, seeking refreshment, discussing the show. Robin stood in the hall holding Cissy in his arms.

'Golly, so what's this? Did Bruno get you ready for bed?'

'Yes.'

'Was he any good at it?'

'I told him what to do.'

Bruno stopped at the foot of the stairs. 'I hope that was OK – she was pretty bushed.'

'It's more than OK, it's above and beyond the call of duty. I see you've got *The Book Hound* there, want me to take over?'

'Sure, that's probably a good idea . . .' Bruno held out the book, but Cissy squirmed violently.

'No, I want Bruno to read it, Bruno!'

Robin, least touchy of men, laughed and put her down. 'Looks like you're the victim of your own success. When you've finished we'll come up and say goodnight.'

As they went back up the stairs, Cissy slipped her hand into Bruno's. The small gesture, confident and confiding, made him feel ridiculously privileged.

Hugh and Marguerite were in the drawing room with the

boys. Robin joined Felicity in the kitchen, where she was unwrapping a defrosted fish pie for the oven.

'That was a good show, but it was rather a marathon,' she remarked. 'I think we could all use a drink.'

'I'm your man. I'll go and take orders.'

'Oh – what about Cissy?'

'All ready for bed, and my reading was rejected in favour of Bruno's.'

'Really?' She pulled a smiling, incredulous face. 'I'm amazed.'

'He's a popular chap,' said Robin. 'Let's see . . . I think I'll offer fizz.'

Twenty-Two

Charity was due to return that afternoon. At her request, Mac was giving her a tour of the school before she left. They had reached the gym, a large prefab which doubled as an assembly hall.

Mac walked into the middle and stood there with his arms folded, slowly turning on the spot.

'Doesn't look much, does it?'

'As long as it does the job.' She dragged a hand along the wall bars. 'God, these things . . . Proustian in their horrible way. I hated gym.'

'We don't make anyone suffer, I promise. But we do favour physical exertion, it keeps them out of trouble.'

'You mean they're too knackered.'

'Not how I'd have put it, but yes.'

There was a pommel horse in the corner, and she leaned back, her arms stretched on either side. 'You obviously didn't knacker Bruno enough.'

'There's often one who's sufficiently determined to get up to no good.'

Now she looked at him. 'What did you think of my brother? I mean, really?'

'Charity, I'd rather not say.'

'You can be frank.'

'It wouldn't be appropriate.'

Charity had to laugh, the prim word sounded so odd in his mouth. She went and wrapped her arms around his big, rugby-player's chest, her head tilted up to look at him.

'It's a bit late to worry about being appropriate.'

She felt his small jolt of suppressed amusement. 'Be that as it may.'

Actually she was glad he wouldn't give his opinion of Bruno. That iron discretion, and the security that went with it, was such an integral part of him, and what she loved about him.

'Is there anything else you want to show me?' she asked.

'The kitchen,' he said. 'I've saved the best till last.'

She thought that was a joke, but in fact the kitchen was new, the product of fund-raising, a council grant, and a handful of individual donations including one from his own pocket.

'My oh my, this is swish.'

'And unexpected, something tells me.'

'Honestly? I pictured something a bit grim and institutional.'

He smoothed the work surface, his hand big and gnarly against the gleaming white Formica. 'The modern parent has firm views about catering. And I was advised, correctly as it turned out, that you can't attract a decent cook without a halfway decent kitchen.'

As he opened cupboards, turned lights on and off and demonstrated the hob and dishwasher with evident pride, she reminded herself that this place was not only his mission, but his business. At an age when most men would have been moving into a more leisured phase in which to engage in hobbies, long-deferred personal projects, agreeable travel and undemanding good works, Mac was running this highly individual, if not downright quixotic, enterprise which probably sailed quite close to the wind. And she suspected the only thing that would take him away from it would be his coffin.

This was food for thought as they returned to the warmth of Mac's house. She went to 'her' room, in which she had only spent the first night, ostensibly to pack her things. Instead she closed the door quietly and sat down on the edge of the bed. She put her hands over her face, blotting out her surroundings so she could think clearly.

For now, among all the delights and enchantment of a new love affair, it wasn't hard to be in the moment, and not to look too far ahead. The age gap between them had never been an issue, and now that they were close it meant even less. This – this warmth, pleasure, intimacy, excitement, everything! – was all that mattered.

Still, the phrase 'there's no future in it' had taken on a brutal new relevance. Accidents apart, Mac's future was likely to be shorter than hers. She forced herself to contemplate not just the ending that would come too soon, but what might come before – illness, mental decline, incapacity, the awful indignities of extreme old age. On any normal calculation Mac was lucky not to be already suffering any of these. She could not imagine him giving up any of what he currently did here – the sports, the property maintenance, the endless patrolling and surveying, the labour on the smallholding. These activities didn't only keep him fit and healthy, they kept him going. But not for ever.

He knocked on the door, and put his head round. 'All well?'

'Absolutely.'

'I'm going to heat soup. Do you like mulligatawny?'

'Fine.'

'Oh, Charity . . .' He walked across and dropped a kiss on her head. 'Come down when you're ready.'

She touched his hand, which was on her shoulder. 'I will.'

Because he had found the door closed, he closed it again behind him. He had a natural respect for her, and for people generally. That was what made him good at his job. But oh—! She closed her eyes and lifted her hands to her face again, this time to cover her mouth.

They already had a secret. What of when the secret was out? What were people going to say? She dreaded not the thoughtless, facetious comments about their relative ages but the inevitable *advice*. Oh god, the advice – from people who cared about her and had her best interests at heart. The content and delivery agonized over, the excruciating tact employed to broach this most delicate of subjects. When the years ahead were gently mentioned, with every allowance for her feelings, what was she going to say? She had to be ready, to have herself subjected the prospect to clear-eyed scrutiny, to know where she stood so she could stand firm.

And then, the secrecy would have to be maintained, for some time. Even today when they'd encountered Les, the school caretaker, she had felt the slight shift in body language and atmosphere, the need to present a formal facade. And this was a place that for three-quarters of the year teemed with hormonal teenagers who would like nothing better than a juicy lump of gossip about the headmaster . . . And they would tell their parents, all those muesli-nazis who whatever their liberal credentials might take a dim view of their kids' septuagenarian headmaster carrying on with a woman forty years younger . . . Try as she might Charity could not envisage a 'Mr Chips' scenario (she had once watched the film with her parents) with her in the Petula Clarke role and Mac . . . No. Secrecy it must be.

She carried her rucksack downstairs and into the kitchen. Her lover was stirring a saucepan.

'There you are. Sit yourself down.'

She dumped the rucksack just inside the door and sat at the table, shocked to discover that she was on the verge of tears.

'What's the matter?' He turned off the gas and pulled another chair close to hers. 'Darling girl. What's up?'

The gentle words did it, of course, unlocked the floodgate and now she was crying properly. He put his arm round her. 'Everything, eh?'

'I suppose . . . No – I don't know.' She nodded, then shook her head. Pulled away from him and fetched herself a square of kitchen towel.

When she'd blown her nose and was seated again, he said, 'I failed the test, didn't I?'

She stared damply at him. 'What test?'

'In the films I like the hero always has a large, pristine hankie he can give to the lady to wipe away her tears.'

'That's true,' she said, laughing feebly in spite of herself. 'You're rubbish.'

'Out of practice. Come on.' He stood up. 'Let me take you away from all this.'

'What?'

'I mean let's go and sit in the other room for a while.'

She followed him, and they sat down on the sofa. Or at least he sat – the old-fashioned sofa was constructed along heroic lines, suitable for a man of Mac's size. She had to curl up, bolstered by a cushion.

'I don't want to go,' she said.

'And I don't want you to. As a matter of fact I dread it. But as from tomorrow this place will start creaking back into life, and a week from now the pupils will be back. So we shall have to seek our opportunities elsewhere.'

'I know,' she said. 'I've been thinking about that.'

He folded his arms. 'Generally speaking I'm a big fan of thinking. Thinking calms things down and postpones hasty action. But in this situation I suspect it's the enemy.' He paused, watching her, and then when she didn't speak went on. 'I've been doing a bit myself, but I'm no further forward. Here we are, and speaking for myself, this is the happiest I've been in years. I can scarcely believe this is happening to a crusty old codger like me.' His eyes were fierce, piercing – a look that was in his head's armoury. 'I absolutely adore you, Charity. I fell for you, I pursued you after my fashion, I invited you to share my bachelor Christmas – and when I believed you'd changed your mind I was distraught, mainly because I had been such a thickhead to imagine you were going to come. I'd forgotten what an honourable person you are. That whatever your feelings about me one way or the other I should never have doubted your word.'

Her face grew hot. 'I'm not particularly—'

'You don't have to say anything, and I don't want to know.'

'I'm not particularly honorable.'

'Well, I believe you are. We both are – which is why we suit each other.' He continued quickly before she could demur. 'Let's enjoy this for as long as it lasts, on the understanding that the moment it's not enjoyable, for any reason at all, either of us is entitled without rancour or hard feelings to leave.'

At this moment both the leaving and the feelings that would accompany it were unimaginable. The sturdy resolve she'd summoned up in the bedroom had deserted her entirely. Something told her that in spite of his earlier remarks Mac had done just as much thinking and realized, like her, that there was no easy solution.

He carried her rucksack out to the car and put it on the passenger seat as instructed, giving it a rueful pat.

'I wish that were me.'

'Me too.'

'It's a good thing we both have work we like doing.'

The car was parked in the angle of the outbuildings. Apart from the chickens creeping and clucking, they had privacy. Standing close to the wall, they kissed. When she got into the driver's seat she felt thin and small, stripped of something. Mac walked ahead of her to the gate that led into that long lane – the lane she'd tramped down late on Christmas Eve, into a different life. He opened the gate, and positioned himself on the far side of the lane, one hand held up, palm outwards, to keep her there as he looked both ways. There was scarcely ever any traffic here, but she loved his care of her. When he beckoned her forward she rolled down the window, but he seemed not to notice as he tapped the roof of the car. Her last sight was of him closing the gate and moving off with long, heavy, purposeful strides towards the house.

Back on the main road she picked up speed. Once on the motorway she drove fast. She began to think about what lay ahead – her other life, her study, her pleasant colleagues. What had he said? *It's a good thing we both have work that we like.* Being apart, for them, was not going to be a problem. There would be no dragging co-dependence. Absence would make their hearts fonder.

Charity put her foot down and zoomed into the overtaking lane, past a container lorry. In front was an Audi, cruising at eighty, and she went past him too. The driver flashed his lights, in annoyance or admiration. Maybe just to say he could take her and her well-worn Micra any time.

She felt like one of those birds of prey, released from the hand that fed it, soaring, free as air. But like the bird, she'd be back. She could do no other.

Twenty-Three

Fliss had promised her mother she would take Bruno back to his flat personally. Hugh expressed mild reservations.

'Why is that necessary?'

'She's doing it for me,' said Marguerite. 'For reassurance.'

'Darling Daisy,' said Hugh, 'have you considered that she may not be reassured?'

'Don't worry,' said Felicity, 'I'll lie if I have to.'

The whole family – except Bruno, who'd slept late and said goodbye in his T-shirt and boxers – was seeing them off at Paddington. Felicity had wanted to, and was also aware that the Blyths and the TSs made a charming group on the platform – the dashing couple with their delightful children, the mop-headed boys rugged in Gap, Cissy in her little double-breasted coat, the handsome grandparents bidding fond farewells. Along with the scene on the beach this was the sort of occasion she had pictured as a girl all those years ago.

As Robin helped Hugh stow the bag in the first-class carriage, mother and daughter embraced. For the second time Felicity said, 'Don't worry, Ma.' But this time she meant it, and added, 'We're fond of Bruno too, you know.'

'You've been very good to him, Fliss.'

'Well, he's been pretty good to us as it happens. For a boy who used to be such an atrocious little scut he's improved out of all recognition.'

'And you will – you know – see how he's living?'

'Yes,' said Felicity, 'I promise.'

In the event she was unable to keep her promise, because when they got back to Hampstead, Bruno had left. On the kitchen table was a small pot of primroses with a note.

> Thanks for the great Christmas. Sorry for shooting off, but didn't fancy all the goodbyes. See you again soon, I hope. Bx

Felicity was touched, especially by the primroses. 'The greengrocer has these, I've seen them. He must have gone all the way down and back to get them.'

'Heroic,' agreed Robin dryly. 'But it's nice of him, yes.'

The boys had wandered off, but Cissy asked, 'Where's Bruno?'

'He's gone home,' said Felicity.

'But he lives here.'

Robin picked her up. 'Some of the time. He'll come back and see us, you bet. Why don't we draw him a picture?'

That turned out to be a good idea, and Felicity left them to it and went upstairs. Bruno's room was tidy, the bed stripped and the window, she noticed with amusement, wide open. She made a cursory check of the wardrobe and chest of drawers, but they were all clear. It was only as she turned back from closing the window that she noticed the wriggle of black wire under the bed – his precious headphones. As she wound the flex neatly round the headband she reflected that this was a sign. She would return them in person.

Robin had given her directions. 'You're in the right road when you start to see the three-legged cats chewing on ancient spliffs.'

Though fastidious, Felicity was less shockable than her husband imagined. She found somewhere to park, but was a little worried about leaving the Audi where its gleaming paint-work might attract vandalism. She drove round the block and found a space outside a respectable-looking Asian shop. She went into the shop and bought a packet of mints, asking casually, 'I hope it's alright if I leave my car there – you're not expecting a delivery or anything?'

The proprietor understood her. 'That's a very nice car if I may say so – we shall keep an eye on it for you never you mind.'

'That's really kind. I shan't be long.'

She walked back the way she'd come and found the house. The tiled area in front was lopsided as if about to disappear beneath the winter weeds. The overflowing metal dustbin had taken on the air of just another static feature in this dismal environment, surrounded as it was by bags of garbage including an enormous number of bottles.

There were two doorbells. Neither of the faded labels had Bruno's name on, so she rang both. After only a few seconds the door was opened by a fat middle-aged man in a tropical shirt.

'Hello, yes?'

Felicity bestowed on him her most dazzling smile. 'I'm so sorry to disturb you, I was looking for Bruno Blyth.'

'No idea, mate,' said the man. Felicity wasn't accustomed to being called 'mate' but she sensed that the smile had worked.

'I wonder if he could be in the other flat.'

'Might be. They come and go up there if you know what I mean.'

Sweetly imploring, she asked, 'Do you think I could go up and knock on the door?'

Tropical Shirt considered this. He had a Zapata moustache, as well. Then he seemed to reach a decision.

'Hang on!' He leaned past her and pressed the top bell again before bellowing up the stairs, 'Sean!' An impatient pause. 'Sean! You deaf?'

A door opened on the landing and a figure, Sean presumably, stumbled out.

'What the fuck?'

'Steady! Lady here's looking for someone called . . .?' Tropical Shirt looked at her for assistance.

'Bruno Blyth.'

'He's out,' said Sean. He came to the top of the stairs, a ferrety young man, barefoot, in a T-shirt and sweatpants. Seeing Felicity he said, a squeak more emolliently, 'Can I give him a message?'

Beaming, Felicity started up towards him. 'I've got something for him, that he left behind – I'm his sister? He's been staying with us over Christmas.'

Tropical Shirt muttered something about leaving them to it and went back into his own lair. Sean gave way a little in the face of Felicity's fragrant advance, but held his ground in the doorway.

'It's alright, I'll give it to him.'

'I'd like to leave them in his room – it's his headphones, he'll be lost without them.'

'That's OK, I'll take them—'

'Just show me where.' She brushed past him into what seemed to be a living area. 'Oh, and Sean, you wouldn't be an angel and put the kettle on, I've had a pig of a day and it took forever to park . . .' She pushed back a frond of hair and gave a little sigh. 'Would you?'

It was the only way she could think of to keep the impetus going, to shamelessly use her sexual capital on this unprepossessing young man. 'So' – she gazed around in pretty bafflement – 'where?'

He nodded. 'There. Milk and sugar?'

'Just a little milk – sorry, where?'

'Sofa, for the moment. Just a temporary arrangement. Put them on there, he'll find them.'

Still holding firmly on to the headphones she sat down on the end of the sofa where there was some space next to an empty Jaffa cake box being used as an ashtray. Now she could see Bruno's rucksack tucked behind it. A tiny kitchenette opened off the room and she could see Sean examining mugs, presumably for alien life forms. She reminded herself to put the tea down and forget about it.

'So who else lives here,' she asked, her expert gaze raking the horrors of the room, 'just you?'

'Me and another lad. Bruno's a sub-let.'

Felicity considered this a pretty grand term for the lumpy, sagging lump of wadding and wood on which she was parked. Sean brought a mug of tea and handed it to her with his fingers around the rim.

'Mm, thank you.' She held it to her face and sniffed the steam with an expression of appreciation before placing it on the floor. Sean, himself without a cup of tea, sat on one of the chairs at a small gateleg table – Felicity could tell it was a table because she could see the legs, the top was invisible beneath dishes, cutlery and clothing, all of which appeared to have been used. She had the impression that everything in the room remained exactly where last left until there was a pressing need to re-use it, or someone needed to sit, or lie down. Hanging in the air was a gamey cocktail of odours, among which not the worst but the most identifiable was weed. She had once had a nanny who during her short stay was partial to a nocturnal puff in the garden, and had never forgotten the smell.

'I tell you what,' she said. 'I'll put the headphones in his rucksack, will you tell him that's where they are?'

'Sure.'

'Thanks.' She leaned behind the sofa and unzipped the top of the rucksack, pushing the headphones down on top of the jumble of unfolded clothes. There was the plaid shirt he'd worn on Christmas Day . . . She experienced a pang of sympathy. How could Bruno stand this, after their house? How could he stand it at all? And presumably he had work assignments from college – where did that happen? She decided against asking Sean this, but she did have one other question.

'You said this was only temporary – do you happen to know

where he's moving to? I think he may have mentioned something but what with Christmas, and a houseful . . .' Her smile invited sympathy with her domestic plight.

'No idea. It's not ideal,' he conceded, 'for anyone.'

'No.' She sighed. 'Oh well, I mustn't keep you.' Truth be told she was taking a mischievous pleasure in talking to Sean as if he were some hectically busy Hampstead housewife.

'No worries.' This had been one of Ellie's catchphrases, but whereas that had always been a comfort, in Sean's mouth it sounded more like 'Clear off'.

At the door, she said, 'What do you do, Sean – I mean when you're not entertaining uninvited visitors?'

Flattered, he bridled a tad. 'I'm in the music business.'

She managed to get out of the door, and out of the house, before exploding with laughter. But back in the car (the shop-keeper gave her a cheery thumbs-up so she bought a bar of chocolate in recognition of his efforts) her mood changed. She could feel her organisational muscle twitching. She was beginning to see that this could be sorted, and in a way that was beneficial to everyone.

'It all sounds a bit radical,' said Robin later that evening, when she'd outlined her plan for Bruno to take up residence in return for a modicum of childcare.

'It's not just the squalor,' said Felicity. 'He's sleeping on the sofa, he's got nowhere to work—'

'My darling, that may be of more importance to you than him.'

'I don't like to think of him being there.'

'Again, I have to say it, my love, but that has more to do with your feelings than his.'

'I realize that. I do.' Felicity pressed her palms together, fingers against her mouth, eyes closed for a moment. She was about to make an admission – a confession – and this was something new for her. 'The truth is . . .'

There followed such a long pause that Robin cocked his head and peered at her. 'What? Spit it out.'

'I feel bad about Bruno. No—' She raised a hand to silence Robin as he began to laugh. 'Do listen. Please. And he's not the only one.'

Because he sensed what was coming, Robin was suddenly desperate to stop her. He'd never loved her more, he didn't want her to eat humble pie. He wanted her to remain his shiny, confident, adored Fliss.

'I don't know what you mean.'

'Don't you?' She gave him a wry look, both amused and a little sorrowful. 'I know I'm neglectful—'

'Tell that to a hundred friends and acquaintances, and see how they react.'

'Oh I don't mean all this!' She spread her arms, and let them fall again. 'I don't mean running things. I'm good at that.'

'And that's not nothing,' he pointed out.

'No, it's not. But it's admin, the same as I do at the Water Foundation and the hospice and all the other things.'

'I hope you're not thinking of giving those up,' said Robin. 'You're a powerhouse, what would they do without you?'

'They'd manage perfectly well, but that's not the point. Cliché coming up, but charity begins at home. I hope . . .' She broke off, and Robin realized to his dismay that she was struggling, close to tears. 'I hope you all know how much I love you.'

'We do! My darling, we do!' He wanted more than anything to reassure her, now that he was himself reassured. 'And we're so proud of you.'

'I'm not fishing. The children aren't proud – they shouldn't be, either. I'm just their mother, they don't know any different.'

'They liked your singing.'

'Did they?' She herself looked childishly pleased, he was touched.

'Absolutely. They told me about it.'

'That's nice, how sweet . . . Well, anyway – let's just say I want to do better. Get my priorities right. And that starts with giving my little brother a leg up. I think he's in a muddle, Rob. It may be a muddle of his own making, but it's too easy just to say "Oh, that's Bruno". We've all been saying that for ever, ever since he arrived, me more than anyone.' She looked at him directly, her mouth set – he knew that look. 'So what do you think?'

'In principle I think it's worth suggesting, provided we're absolutely clear about the terms of the agreement.'

'Of course.'

'And if we're reasonably sure he won't take advantage.'

'In what sense?'

Robin shrugged pleasantly. 'Any sense you care to mention.'

'He's been an absolute diamond recently – before when he was here, and over Christmas. And the children would absolutely love it.'

'I agree. But you asked. And then, Fliss, if you're determined to go ahead with this, you have thought that even if it works perfectly you'll have far less time – for your work, and for yourself.'

'That's alright. Part of the deal would be me spending more time with my family.'

'As the misbehaving MPs continually do cry.'

She smiled, they laughed. It was agreed.

Sean was totally, gratifyingly, gobsmacked.

'You what?'

'I'm moving in with my sister for a bit.'

'What? That one who came round?'

'That's her.'

'Why?'

Bruno continued stuffing books and papers into supermarket carriers. 'A, she asked me, B, you haven't seen their place.'

His eyes never leaving Bruno, Sean scrabbled among the clutter for a fag packet, found one, and lit up. 'I mean why would she ask you?'

Bruno had been asking himself this, and was still thinking about it. 'She's not just being kind. I'm going to sing for my supper.'

'Oh right, how much coal you got to heave for champagne and caviar?'

'Funny man.'

'So?'

'I'm going to help out with the kids, when I'm around. For as long as I'm there.'

Sean removed his fag so he could gape without dropping it. 'Now *you're* being funny.'

'No.' Bruno shrugged on his coat. Suddenly he'd had enough of Sean. 'They're nice kids. Thanks for the sofa.'

Loaded down as he was, as Bruno set out he had never felt lighter. He was heading not just for the tube station but for the hills, the sunny uplands . . . He was on his way!

Twenty-Four

1996

The hounds of spring were definitely snuffling around, thought Honor as she drove in through the gate – there were big clumps of snowdrops in bloom in the grass outside the garden fence, and bravely massing green spears beneath the fuchsia hedge just inside. This was one of those soft late January days when spring seemed a distinct possibility. Even though there were probably weeks of harsh weather ahead, the solstice was behind them and the world was slowly and steadily turning back to the light.

There were no other cars in the drive. As she closed the front door behind her she could feel the edges of her presence breaking the stillness, sending out little ripples and eddies into the emptiness. This was when she was most conscious of the distinctive atmosphere of Heart's Ease, and its smell – comprising lemons, polish, boots, embers and a general woodiness. This was when she half expected to come across the brigadier and his young wife. Especially him. She pictured a tall, dignified figure walking quietly from room to room, winding the long-case clock, tapping the barometer, pouring himself a whisky . . . In the dusk of this winter's afternoon she could almost fancy she saw him sitting out in the loggia, a hat on his head – fedora, tweed cap, panama – enjoying the pleasing prospect of the sloping enclosed lawn with the Fort presiding over it. She had always suspected the house was haunted, but that any ghosts were entirely benign.

The truth was, she thought, as she went along to the kitchen to make herself a cup of tea, that she herself didn't belong here anymore. The brigadier was entitled to his peace, and had more claim to the house than any of them – it had been his parents' anyway, so he'd grown up here. There had been a square of ancient yellowish newspaper inside the big clock, on the floor beneath the pendulum. Honor could remember her mother taking it out, holding it carefully between fingers and thumbs because it was so fragile.

'Oh do look,' she'd said as if addressing a roomful of people though there had been only Honor there. 'It's about this house! "A gentleman's residence . . . five bedrooms including house-keeper's accommodation". Isn't that wonderful? "Three quarters of an acre with mature shrubs and trees and kitchen garden . . ."' She and Honor had sat down together on the uncomfortable not-really-for-sitting-on bench in the hall, on top of the slithering pile of coats that were always slung down there in spite of the row of hooks in the porch. Marguerite had gone through a few more details. '". . . All the usual offices" – love that – "kitchen wing . . . garage and stabling . . ."' Stabling – where was that, I wonder?'

Honor used to love those afternoons with her mother, when she was at nursery school in the morning only and the others didn't get back till later. They'd gone out into the garden to try and work out where the stabling had been. Marguerite quickly decided it must have been where what was now known as 'The Sheds' stood – Honor always imagined them with capital letters. The garage, a more recent addition, stood between The Sheds and The Yard, and *now* they could readily picture a horse being led out and saddled up before being ridden if not by the brigadier then certainly by his father. Honor had asked whether there would have been a carriage, and her mother had said, 'Good *point* . . .', which had been very nice, and broached the subject with Hugh that night when he came in.

'Honor was asking if long ago the people here would have had a carriage?'

'I wouldn't have thought they'd be rich enough for that,' he said. 'It's not that big a house, not for that time – just a nice middle-sized one.'

'So did they ride everywhere?' asked Honor, to some not unkind eye-rolling from her sisters.

'I doubt it. Perhaps they had a pony and trap. And bicycles, cycling was a big thing. The ladies in those rather fetching bloomers . . .' He began to sing, '"Daisy, Daisy, give me your answer do . . .'" until quelled by the others. 'Outnumbered by females' as it amused him to say.

Honor had loved the house then, and still did. But since Christmas she'd felt indefinably different about it. This was a special house, no doubt about it. A place that had acquired a patina over time. But entertaining Avis and Mr Dawson here had reminded her that she was only playing house. There was a sense in which Heart's Ease belonged to no one, people simply passed through it leaving, perhaps, a trace of their essence behind to linger in that special atmosphere, redolent of the past.

She carried her mug through the loggia and stepped outside. There was no wind but the garden seemed to breathe softly around her. She wondered if the old soldier's young wife had loved it here, or had she always been longing for something, or someone, else?

From the far side of the lawn she stood and looked back at the house. She had only turned on one light, in the kitchen, and that was at the back, and the curtains were not yet drawn, so the windows looked dark and mysterious. She'd always thought that houses, like cars, had faces. Some were snappy and sharp, some grinning, others frowning, or supercilious – Heart's Ease was always welcoming. And perhaps a little wry, tolerant of the goings-on of its various occupants.

She walked up on to the Fort from where she could see the lights of Salting beginning to appear. Beyond it the buttress of red cliff between this bay and the next, topped by a fringe of scotch pines, distant companions of those that stood sentinel around the Fort. The tide must be low because she could make out the broken black line of rocks that marked the mouth of the river. She heard the secretive rustle of an animal in the shrubbery by the drive. And – what? Her peripheral vision was caught by a movement in one of the upstairs windows, the window of her parents' bedroom. Honor stood with breath held, a faint ringing in her ears. Someone was looking out, then raised an arm, as if about to draw the curtain – then gone. Though transfixed, she wasn't frightened. And she was equally sure she hadn't imagined it. If that had been a ghost, it was the spirit of Heart's Ease.

Back inside the house she went upstairs. As always the door of her parents' bedroom stood open, and she went in. The curtains were open, everything undisturbed – or at least not by any myste-rious outside agency; Marguerite and Hugh were untidy. Honor caught sight of her reflection in the dressing table mirror. For the first time she formulated the thought clearly, and resolutely. *I need a place of my own. It's time.*

Next time she encountered the dreaded Graham at his father's, he made an elaborate dumbshow of beckoning her out into the kitchen 'for a word'. But it was nothing ominous, far from it.

'Thank you for entertaining Dad on Christmas Day – we never expected that.'

'Of course not, but I was going to be on my own and it seemed like a good idea.'

'Well, it certainly was. Perked the old chap up no end.' Graham was smiling, but his rather pebbly eyes were tracking over her face as he spoke. 'And you had another guest too, I hear.'

'Yes,' said Honor, 'three's more of a party, so I thought why not?'

'How very kind.' She knew exactly what he was doing, he was determined to make her lovely hospitable day seem like voluntary work.

'I wasn't being kind,' she said firmly.

'Have it your own way.' Graham's smile grew more fixed, and he lowered his voice another notch. 'And a lady, I hear.'

'Avis, she's a great friend.' After a second's thought she added, 'Like your father.'

Graham nodded. 'Another of your charges?'

'I do help her out.'

'You know' – he tilted his head almost flirtatiously – 'you won't mind my saying this' – (she was sure she would) – 'but an attrac-tive young woman like you shouldn't have to spend Christmas with a couple of oldies that she works for.'

The cheek of this almost took her breath away, but she collected herself. Swiftly, casually, *clearly* on her way out of the kitchen, she said, 'I can't think of anyone I'd rather have spent the day with – excuse me.'

She was off to look at a flat. She had learned very quickly that in the rental market there was a straight trade-off between location and value for money. She now knew that for the same rent she could get a two-bedroom flat in a Victorian terrace near the former railway station (long since fallen under Beeching's axe), or one half the size in the town. Or something usually referred to as a 'studio', more accurately a bedsit, overlooking the sea.

The estate agent was good about forwarding details – the one she was going to see had only come on to the market that day. It was over the old-fashioned draper's in the High Street, the door was next to the shop window with its corsets and plimsolls and Chilprufe vests. She knew for a fact that Graham got his father's socks and underwear from here – she'd been delegated to get them on more than one occasion – but still the entrance didn't inspire much hope. The young man from the agent's unlocked the main door and went ahead of her up a narrow staircase.

'It's a compact little place,' he said over his shoulder. 'So once I've let you in I'll leave you to it and wait outside.'

Honor had learnt the lingo – 'compact' meant a shoe box with plumbing. She nearly told him not to go, because her decision would take only seconds . . . But wait a minute . . .

. . . *Oh!*

The door closed and she heard him trot briskly down the stairs. Yes, it was a shoe box, but painted a bright white, with a tiny kitchenette ranged along one side, and a shower and loo in a neat cubbyhole on the other. She calculated that there would just be room for a bed with storage beneath it, that could also be used for sitting, and a small round table with chairs – but none of that mattered, because *look!*

In two quick strides she was at the window opposite. The flat was a full block and a road's width away from the beach, but in this part of town the high street was on a gentle upward slope, and her window – it was already hers – was positioned so that it looked between the roofs of the houses behind, and over the strip of formal public garden beyond, to the sea! She could make out the white horses on the steely winter surface, and the gulls wheeling above – there was even a gull sitting on a chimney pot! The window had an old-fashioned catch, and opened like double doors, the catch was stiff, but she managed it and stood there entranced and exhilarated with the smell of the beach and the fresh, salty air.

She didn't even bother to close the window, or the door, but scampered down the stairs and out into the street, where the young man was leaning on the wall next to the corsets, consulting his mobile.

'I'll take it! Definitely! Is it still free? I'll take it!'

'Sure . . .! Really? That's great. I think you're the first to view . . . Yes, yes . . . Looks like it's yours if you want it.'

He was new to the job and had only had a few clients. If it was always going to be like this, he told himself, he was going to enjoy himself!

Honor told Avis when she saw her later in the day. Her delight was gratifying.

'I must say that's smashing news! I know just where that is, over Grover's, but who'd have thought it had a sea view?'

'Well, sea view might be a bit of an overstatement . . . but you can see the sea. And walk to the beach in a couple of minutes, I could go for a swim every morning!'

'And they're not charging silly rent?'

'I can afford it.'

'I think that's wonderful, I really do,' said Avis. 'Shall we break open the sherry?'

By this she meant the bottle of scotch in the sideboard. Honor never normally drank neat spirits, or anything at all, but at Avis's they had a nip together when there was something to celebrate. She poured them a glass each, Avis's a solid measure in a tumbler, hers in a liqueur glass, and they clinked.

'Bottoms up!'

'To my new flat!'

Marguerite and Hugh professed themselves equally pleased, but there was no avoiding the implications.

'We'll be all on our own here,' said Hugh in a pleased voice, 'for the first time in how long?'

'God, don't count!' Marguerite was putting on her nightie, the one Hugh referred to as her 'pioneer's wincyette'. Her head popped out and she wriggled her arms into the sleeves. 'Too long, witness this thing.'

'I wasn't going to say anything.'

'My darling, you don't have to.'

'Anyway . . .' Hugh, who preferred to be naked in bed except in the coldest conditions when he wore a nightshirt 'for easy access', fell into bed and pulled the duvet over his legs. 'Much as we love our girl, this is a good thing all round. Soon we shall be what I believe are called empty-nesters.'

Marguerite followed suit more decorously, arranging the pillows for her preferred reading position. She picked up her reading glasses, but not her book. Instead she clasped her hands on her lap.

'That's a horrible phrase.'

'Oh I don't know . . .' Hugh nudged her leg with his. 'Remember it symbolizes a whole new chapter of license and riotous living.'

She laughed but drew her legs up primly. 'Don't be ridiculous. This is a family house, it's going to seem big without anyone else here.'

'In that case,' said Hugh, 'we shall downsize.'

'Another horrible phrase, and that's even more ridiculous.'

Hugh turned off his bedside light, and removed the glasses from his wife's hand. 'You look beautiful without these, Mrs Blyth.'

A little while later he was sleeping like a baby. But Marguerite lay awake, the snail's trail of a tear running down her temple and into her hair.

Twenty-Five

Mac was halfway there and in the middle lane of the northbound motorway when he realized this wasn't a good idea. The previous night, after he'd spoken to Charity, it had come to him suddenly, and seemed brilliant in its simplicity. He wasn't a sender of flowers or fulsome messages, but by gum he would show her that he could be a romantic. He would simply turn up on the evening of February the fourteenth, with the sole object of telling her that he loved her.

The element of surprise appealed to him though God knows,

there was no chance of them becoming stale. What with the need for discretion, and pressure of work for both of them, they managed to meet about twice a month and that after exhaustive planning. There was an excitement to all this, but sooner or later they were going to have to – well, regularize things a bit. Even as he thought it, he realized that the phrase was generally a euphemism for marriage – God, no! That would never do. He couldn't put her in that position, it simply wouldn't be fair on either of them. But for all his brave, reassuring talk at Christmas there was no doubt that this way of life was a strain.

Unfortunately that hadn't stopped him embarking on this foolish, wrongheaded enterprise. And now here he was, having to pull over on to the hard shoulder, hazard lights flashing, to catch his breath, sweating and trembling. He felt bloody awful, as if he might pass out. And enraged, humiliated, to be this silly old man. Charity was such a sensible, intelligent young woman, clearsighted beyond her years, she would take a dim view of his foolhardiness. *Romantic?* He could hear her voice, ringing with censure. *Romantic? Setting off to drive over a hundred miles in the dead of winter, without telling anyone, let alone me, what you were doing? And you were intending to drive all the way back the same night? What madness is this?*

What indeed. He wiped his forehead with his cuff. Suddenly he could taste bile, and pushed the door open, conscious of the traffic zooming past, loud and close as he threw up. There followed a few seconds of relief, tempered by the shame of what those whizzing passers-by had seen, a disgusting sight. Then came the predictable second bout, equally violent but with less volume. The whole horrible business took him back to his childhood – his mother's calm hand on his forehead, her voice, the enamel bowl specially reserved for the purpose, the smell . . .

He waited another few seconds in case there should be a third spasm, then closed the door and fished a packet of tissues from the glove compartment. As he did so he became aware of a blinking blue light, and saw a police car pulled in about twenty metres ahead of him. An officer in a high-vis jacket was walking back. To make matters worse, he saw that this was a woman.

Wearily, his humiliation complete, he rolled down the window.
'I'm sorry, officer.'

'Everything alright, sir?'

'I'm afraid I was taken ill.'

She frowned sympathetically, a practised, automatic glance flitting round the inside of the car. Satisfied, she asked, 'How are
you now, sir? Should we call an ambulance?'

'Oh good God no. Just an upset stomach, probably something
I ate . . .' She was still looking at him, making her own seasoned
assessment. 'I'll be fine, but I did have to pull over for a moment.'

'Of course. Do you need to get out and walk around for a
minute?'

This might not have been a bad idea, but the thought of
being out there with all the racket and the freezing temperature
accompanied by a police officer, was too ghastly. 'No, no thanks.
I'll be fine.'

'Right you are.' She pursed her lips. Did they learn this repertoire of expressions in training college? 'The thing is, sir, you
can't just sit here on the hard shoulder.'

'Of course not. I'll be on my way.'

'Here's a suggestion,' she said – she could only have been in
her twenties but her tone was both neutral and authoritative.
'There's a service station less than five miles along. Why don't
you follow us as far as there, and you can go in and get yourself
a hot drink and rest up a bit?'

'Very well,' he said, 'how kind. Thank you.'

At the services he bade farewell to his escort in the car park. As
he walked to the entrance they drove very slowly past him and
the driver, a young man he hadn't seen till now, addressed him
through the rolled-down window.

'You OK from here on in, sir?'

'Yes, perfectly. Thanks for your help.'

'Safe journey then.'

Mac grunted. If he had to thank them one more time he swore
he might explode. His fists were clenched, and it was an effort
to unclench them, but the cold air dried his clammy palms.

The inside of the services – what they were pleased to call the
'food court' – was teeming. There didn't seem to be anywhere

without a queue, but he did spot a free payphone, one of four clustered round a central pillar. Still lightheaded, his face damp and chill, he laid claim to the phone and dialled.

'I'm sorry,' she said – 'you're *where?*'

'At a motorway service station.'

Charity pulled a face, as if he could see her. 'This may sound odd, but why?'

'This is going to sound even odder. I was on my way to see you.'

'What?'

'I wanted to give you a surprise.'

She looked round at her untidy, cosy room – her desk with the anglepoise bent over a slew of papers. 'It would have been!' There followed a silence, during which she could hear his breathing. 'Mac – Mac, are you alright?'

'Not really. No crisis, if that's what you mean. But I'm not going to make it. No, no' – a short laugh – 'I mean I'm not going to get to you.'

'I should hope not.'

'I had to pull over but the boys in blue were extremely helpful. Look, Charity, actually I need to sit down as a matter of urgency.'

'Do! Go and sit down. Which services are you at?'

'I've no idea . . .' There was a pause, and she heard another voice. 'Kind chap tells me it's Longmere. Look—'

'Go,' she barked. 'Sit down. I'm coming.'

They sat facing one another in a booth at the side of the food court's central corral. On the table between them was Charity's cappuccino and the remains of her chicken tikka sandwich, and Mac's pot of tea. He would have liked a scotch, but that was out of the question here.

Charity's first thought on putting the phone down had been, *This is the test. I need to think hard about this.* But as soon as she'd seen Mac, rising carefully from his seat to greet her, thanking her, asking what she'd like – as soon as all of that happened any chance of objectivity went out of the window. And then, when she got back to the table he explained what he had been doing.

'But we agreed!' Even as she protested she had to laugh. 'Valentine's nonsense not for us – didn't we?'

'Correct.'

'And you were honestly going to drive back tonight?'

He tried, not very successfully, to suppress a certain pride. 'Or very early tomorrow.'

'Mac! Darling – what were you thinking of?'

'You,' he said simply. 'Just you.'

Two women sat at the table on the other side of the aisle. One of them put her hand up discreetly beside her mouth as she cut her eyes to the side.

'What do you reckon?'

'Who? Oh.'

'Sweet or sleazy?'

Her friend glanced briefly. The handsome elderly man and the rather schoolmistressy young woman were holding hands across the table. There was no pretence. Neither of them was trying to conceal their feelings. As she looked the man lifted the girl's hand and kissed it.

The woman picked up her cup and, making round eyes over it, said, 'Sweet, definitely.'

In the end they arranged to have the car brought back, for an eye-watering sum, and Charity drove him home. She spent the night, leaving while it was still dark next day. There was no particular rush for her, but they were both mindful of the need for discretion. In the hall they embraced tightly, Charity folded in his arms, her own wrapped around his back, her ear to his chest, eyes closed, as if listening to his heart.

'Please,' she whispered fiercely, '*please* look after yourself.'

'I will,' he said. 'I do.'

Though neither had mentioned it, they both realized that the events of the previous night had very slightly altered the balance of their relationship. It had been the wake-up call they needed. Their Valentine's night at Longmere Services may not have been romantic in the conventional sense, but it had certainly been memorable – a turning point which had given them both food for thought.

★   ★   ★

It was a mercy that half-term was only forty-eight hours away, because Mac still didn't feel right. The whole of that day he was weak and tired, his joints ached and he had no appetite. Almost uniquely he asked a couple of the older pupils to stand in for him on garden fatigues because he couldn't trust himself not to fall over. When Charity rang at eight p.m. he didn't disguise matters.

'I'm in bed.'

'That sounds a good idea.'

'Necessary, I think. Hoping for better things tomorrow.'

'If,' she said, and he could tell how careful she was being, '*if* they're not, you might consider going to the doc.'

They both knew (it was a source of pride to him) that he hated the doctor and had only been about three times in the last twenty years.

'Don't worry,' he said, 'I'll consult the medics if I have to.'

That was as far as he'd go, and she'd have to be content with it.

After the call ended, Charity knew concessions had been made. Mac had admitted the need to look after himself, and she mustn't push it. She wished she was going down there for this weekend, the first of the half-term holiday, but she'd arranged to visit the parents for the first time in months, and had a site visit, a busy teaching timetable and a chapter to finish before then.

She arrived late Friday afternoon to find Honor and Hugh out in the drive, stowing boxes in the boot of Honor's car. More stuff lay on the ground nearby – a couple of stuffed black bin bags with the tops tied, a box of books and another with pictures. The front door was open and as she switched off the engine Marguerite came out. She wore a wide smile but Charity knew the signs – the water table was high. Hugh hailed her first.

'Hello! You find us bang in media res!'

'What's going on?' She and Marguerite exchanged a glancing kiss.

'I'm moving to my new flat,' said Honor. 'Down in the town.'

'Looks as if you could do with another vehicle,' said Charity, determined not to show surprise. 'Want to load me up as well, save you a trip?'

'I was going,' said Hugh, 'but mine's in the garage. If you're offering . . .'

'Darling, you've only just arrived . . .' began Marguerite, but it was Honor who closed the subject.

'Fantastic. I'm coming back here for the night anyway, in your honor.' She smiled at her sister's raised eyebrows. 'Are you sure?'

'There's nothing too heavy here,' said Hugh. 'We got a man with a van last weekend for the big stuff. But be warned, the stairs are a swine.'

It took an hour to unload it all. Parking in the high street was a problem – the only place to leave the car on a permanent basis was round the back, in the road that ran between the buildings and the public gardens. Charity's heart sunk somewhat as they carted the first load up the narrow stairs from the street and faffed around at the top while Honor struggled with the key. She'd never been all that close to her younger sister – she wasn't close to any of her siblings really – but she did hope this wasn't going to be a dingy, pokey hole . . . She dreaded feeling sorry for Honor and not being able to say so, or why.

Instead: 'Wow!' she exclaimed, 'this is terrific.'

'I think so. And I'm really glad you do.'

'I really do. It's a little gem, and the sea view makes it.'

They dumped their loads on the floor and Honor opened the long window. 'I could have a window box.'

'You definitely could – you must.'

Honor laughed, and Charity laughed too, not because anything was funny but because Honor's laughter was a rare thing and her lightheartedness made her look prettier. *I hardly know her,* she thought. *My little sister is an independent woman with a demanding job, a job not many people could do, and she has chosen this nice flat – but we're no more than familiar strangers.*

This train of thought made her gruff. 'You won't be doing much cat-swinging – where are you going to put everything?'

'There's storage under the bed, and this dresser Ma and Pa bought for me.'

'I suppose . . .' Charity thought of the two cars, their boots still full of stuff.

'Anyway,' said Honor, 'I'll get rid of stuff if I need to, this is where I want to be.'

When everything was in they did, in fact, manage to stow about two-thirds of it, and the rest they piled against the wall just inside the door.

'You need bookshelves,' said Charity. 'Maybe I could give you some of those — housewarming present. I bet there are perfectly decent ones to be had in Barley's yard.' She mentioned the secondhand dealer so Honor would understand there would be no extravagance.

'Maybe I could come with you,' said Honor. 'He has some good stuff.'

They went the following morning and spent half an hour poking around happily. Ken Barley was a trusting soul who made a good enough living not to bother supervising when people were out in the yard. What were they going to do, scale the wall with a chest of drawers? And these were two of the nicest girls one could hope to meet. He hadn't bargained with the haggling power of the taller one, who beat him down to forty quid on a good white wood bookcase. There again they hadn't thought about whether it would fit in the car, he offered to drop it round that evening, and they were too well brought up not to offer something for that, so it all worked out in the end.

The morning was nice enough that they sat by the open window. Honor had officially moved in now, this would be her first night here. The bookcase when it arrived would just fit to the right of the window, so although that half of the window wouldn't be able to go right back, one of the shelves could double up as a bedside table.

The sea glinted in the cold spring sunshine. The sentinel gull (Honor was sure it was always the same one) sat on his chimney pot. It was a moment of harmony between the sisters, so Charity saw no reason not to ask the question that was uppermost in her mind.

'One drawback, you couldn't have anyone to stay here.'

'I shan't mind that,' said Honor. 'I like my own company.'

Charity kept her eyes on the gull. 'How's the social life?'

'Quiet.' Honor contained a smile. 'Just as I like it.'

'What about your Christmas guests?'

'We had a good time.'

Now Charity sent her sister a half-teasing, half-challenging look.

'If you wanted to have them round again, they'd never make it up these stairs, would they?'

'No. But I'll see plenty of them.'

Honor had in fact considered this, but the charm of the little flat had outweighed the inconvenience of the stairs. She loved her work and the special friends she'd made, but even she knew it would be unwise to run her life for their benefit. She took a quiet pride in that thanks to her, Mr Dawson and Avis had formed a friendship. She would go to them, as she always had, to see to their comfort and enjoy their company, but there were other things she wanted to do, things for herself. St Peter's Salting was only a couple of hundred yards away, she would go there too, perhaps become involved. The little museum with its cafe, the bookshop, the masonic hall boasting shows and concerts – all were now within walking distance and she intended to make the most of them. She had taken charge of her future, and it opened out in front of her, busy and bright.

'You're sorted then. I'm pleased for you,' said Charity. She was suddenly impelled to make this a fair exchange of information. 'You know I was with a friend at Christmas too.'

'I did hear something.' Honor's expression was sweet, attentive. 'How did that go?'

Charity cut to the chase. 'He's not much younger than your clients. Probably older than some of them.'

'I bet that's not the most important thing about him though,' said Honor. 'Is it?'

The relief, and pleasure, of talking about Mac was so intense that Charity found it quite hard to stop, and had been going for about half an hour when she finally ran out of steam.

'Sorry to bang on. Not like me.'

'Not like you usually are,' conceded Honor, 'a different side of you, but this is all so wonderful! He sounds so lovely.'

Charity wasn't going to quibble about words. 'He is.'

'Are you what they call, you know, an item?' Honor's cheeks were a little pink, she thought she might have overstepped the mark, but Charity was past being coy.

'We are, yes.' She hadn't mentioned what Mac did, his provenance – that could wait. But Honor was enraptured now.

'If he's not retired, what does he do?'

She opted for the truth but not the whole truth. 'He teaches.'

Impulsively, Honor got up and leaned over her sister, putting her arms round her. The gentle hug was like the sunshine that poured through the window – natural, cheering, uplifting. Charity returned it cautiously.

'Thanks . . . I ought to be going, and leave you to settle in.'

'When do you go?'

'Monday morning.'

'Drop in if you want to, any time.'

Driving back to Heart's Ease, Charity considered that she might very well do that. And that in any case it was going to be nice to have Honor here to visit on future occasions. Not always to exchange confidences – she might have done too much of that already – but just to relax with. Charity was not good at relaxing, and hadn't realized till now how easy her younger sister was to be with, what pleasant and undemanding company. Here there was no agenda. In her mind the little flat was already beginning to take on the aspect of a bolthole, a sanctuary.

In the afternoon, after the roast which Marguerite cooked whenever there were more than just her and Hugh in the house, Charity walked with her father and Archie up to the Beacon. They walked in a companionable silence, their steps quiet on the pine needles and leaf mould. Once at the clifftop they sat down on the bench while the dog pottered and sniffed perilously close to the edge.

'So,' said Charity, 'you and Ma are on your own at last.'

'That's how I see it,' he said. 'I'm not so sure about your mother.'

'She'll get used to it.'

'Well of course she will, one gets used to anything in time. But she feels pretty bereft at the moment.'

For the second time that day Charity thought what a blessing it was to have the sea in one's sights – it gave you something to gaze at when broaching sensitive subjects.

'What will you do?'

'We're coming round to the idea' – she felt her father huddle inside his coat, collecting himself – 'that we'll move.'

She'd been half expecting this, had even perhaps provoked it, but it still came as a shock to hear the words. A shock that she stifled.

'Have you discussed it? Covered all the angles?'

'Pretty much. Your mother's in favour in principle . . . She thinks it may be too soon.'

'She may be right.'

'I accept that, but the thing is' – his tone became firmer – 'we need to start moving in that direction, because rather like the blue whale Daisy and I need plenty of time and space in which to turn ourselves round.' He leaned forward and rose, catching Archie and clipping his lead.

'I reckon by this time next year we'll be somewhere else.'

Twenty-Six

One Saturday in late summer Bruno was with Sean in a wine bar in the Docklands. The wine bar was wittily named the Vino Veritas and was an improvement on their usual watering holes, if a touch poncey. They were sitting outside but under the awning, because the sun, unusually for a bank holiday weekend, was beating down. The place was buzzing, the decking walkways full of people, the Thames a-dazzle and alive with river traffic.

Life was good for Bruno, and every swig of cold beer increased his sense of wellbeing. His friendship with Sean, put under strain by the living conditions last winter, had revived. Sean was a good bloke. Nobody made him give up his sofa, shit though it was, and now that he was out of there Bruno was properly grateful. They were able once again to have a few beers and some laughs.

Fliss and Rob had been nothing short of epic. For the past seven months he'd been part of their household, and never a cross word. Sure, he'd been kept busy. The first thing Fliss had done was sit him down in the study so they could work out a schedule, taking into account his college timetable and study

time. In between were his childminding duties. There was a
moment back then when he thought it was all going to be too
much, but he soon discovered that having his time strictly appor-
tioned, combined with great living conditions, meant he was
more effective. He decided to stop whingeing about the course
and just get on with it. He kept up with the assignments, and
was surprised how much he enjoyed his time with the kids.
He didn't drive, which might have been a drawback, but Fliss had
taken that into consideration and joined the mums' car pool,
and he'd got used to the bus service between the schools and
home. She told him she would be doing less of her charity work,
so it was all pretty much of a shared operation. Rob had confessed
himself over the moon about the whole thing, and confided as
much one night at the pub.

'Don't take this the wrong way, nothing to do with you,
but I was a bit worried. And I needn't have been – I reckon she's
happier, much.'

'She seems it,' said Bruno, always mindful of overstepping
the mark. His brother-in-law treated him as a mate, but one didn't
want to go too far.

'My wife is a perfectionist . . .' Rob was the tiniest bit pissed.
'Everything has to be just so, you know? . . . and it usually is,
you'll have noticed. I thought she might break out in hives under
this new regime, but well . . .'

'It was her idea,' Bruno reminded him.

'Indeed!' Robin slapped his shoulder. 'Indeed it was . . .
Another half?'

The situation had changed, inevitably. Fliss had given up a
little too much of the work, and if she wanted to take back even
some of it she was going to need another full-time nanny. And
with summer and the sap rising Bruno felt the need of a place
of his own. He'd got a room in halls for September, so he'd
be well placed to find something else local. For the time being he
was still in Hampstead, showing the ropes to the new nanny
Kirsten, a Scottish girl with a soft voice and firm views, less
jolly than Ellie but perfect for the job. The children, especially
Cissy, had made no bones about not wanting him to go, but Kirsten
had taken all that in her stride and not been touchy.

'We'll shake down in no time, I'm no bad at football and I

know more card games than you lot have had hot dinners. Do
you like cooking, Cissy, have you ever made shortbread?'

The idea of becoming cardsharps went some way towards
mollifying the boys and although Cissy continued to follow
Bruno around with spaniel eyes something told him she'd have
no trouble transferring loyalties once he was gone. He'd hooked
up with a girl called Isabella and a month later they still had
plenty in common outside of the usual, so he was optimistic on
all fronts. They were going to go Interrailing in the spring. He'd
even mentioned her to Sean.

He saw her now, swinging along towards them in her long skirt
and biker boots, her pinkish-red hair in a bobbing cloud around
her head.

'Here she comes,' he said. 'That's Izzie.'

'That her?' asked Sean. 'Fuck me, you're punching above your
weight there, mate.'

Felicity and Robin were having supper with the Lachelles.
Unusually it was only Robin who'd known about the bit of
local difficulty, he'd never mentioned it to Felicity and wasn't
even sure if Lilian had found out. Since then Anton had assured
him it was over, forgotten, of no consequence! Well, maybe . . .
He was glad if that was the case, because he'd been badly shaken.
This evening a considerable amount of wine had been taken, so
he and Fliss would be walking home, and the mood among the
four friends was mellow. Anton leaned in to Robin.

'Am I allowed to say that your wife is looking especially
beautiful this evening?'

'You already did. And no. Feel free.'

Fliss exchanged a 'what are they like?' look with Lilian. They
were at ease with each other and this was late in the evening.

'Thank you. I'll take that, especially today.'

'Why's that?' said Lilian.

'Because I feel like a bag of spanners,' said Fliss. She'd heard the
expression on the radio, and liked it, but it sounded so strange in
her mouth that the others burst into fits of laughter.

'What?' She was baffled in the face of their hoots and snorts
and gasps.

'Oh Fliss . . .' Lilian rose from her chair and swooped down to put her arms round her friend. 'You can try all you like, you'll never be one of the hoi polloi!'

'What's oyploy when it's at home?' asked Anton, and that started them all off again. When, after a further hour and another bottle, Fliss and Rob got out of the door and were strolling gently along, bumping against one another every other step, Rob said, 'Anton was right, though.' He began to sing, or rather to warble, 'Darling, you look wonderful tonight . . .'

'Well good. I just can't imagine why.'

Rob stopped, and when she stopped too, took both her hands. 'I can.'

'Go on then.'

He studied her ardently, his lips pressed together like a child concentrating. Lifted her hands and lowered them again while she smiled back at him. The trouble was, she was always the most beautiful woman in any given company, but it was true that there *was* something – an added lustre, an inner glow, a sweet disorder . . . something along those lines . . .

'Actually,' he said, 'scrub that. Words fail me.'

They both began to laugh again, so that he found it quite difficult to kiss her, but succeeded in the end.

Sex that night wasn't a complete success, they were both a little too tired and a little too drunk. Rob came much too soon and Fliss not at all. But how sweet it was to fall asleep cosily spooned, snug as the petals of an artichoke. Each of them snored slightly, but the other didn't notice. Kirsten heard as she went to get water from the bathroom, and noticed their door was wide open. Tutting pleasantly under her breath, she pulled the door to, discreetly, before going back to bed.

The church fête was always on August bank holiday Monday, and the weather was traditionally bad. But this year the sun had beamed down from a cloudless blue sky all day long and it seemed as though everyone in the town was there. Honor had helped set up yesterday evening and early this morning, and manned the children's tombola all afternoon. Her final contribution had been to act as Ken Barley's 'lovely assistant' in the auction of produce for church funds.

But she had loved every minute! Since living here in the town she had got to know so many people, and most of them had been here on the green today, so friendly and disposed to chat. Several of her clients were there, including Mr Dawson, pushed by Graham, and Avis on her walker, with a nice woman she described as 'my oppo from the Essex days'. Honor was pleased to see that the four of them sat together in the tea tent, and that Graham appeared quite smiley and not at all obnoxious – perhaps he was improving, or at least making an effort. Or it may have been Avis's friend who in spite of being elderly herself was quite an eyeful, with spun-sugar hair and a twinkle in her eye.

Honor's life had opened up exponentially. These last months she had felt herself becoming a part of the lively Salting community. She'd joined things, gone to things, volunteered for things, and the various organisations were delighted to have someone young, energetic and personable on their team. The young man who ran the interactive events at the library had even asked her out for a drink, and she had gone! They were due to have a pub supper during the week, date to be decided – she supposed that this *was* in fact a date! But the thought didn't fill her with anxiety as it might have done before. She had too much going on to be worried, fish and chips with Gerry just took its place in her busy calendar. Of course she had no idea how this new chapter affected her looks – how bright and pretty she appeared, as if she'd just shed a rather drab outer skin. She just knew she felt full of energy and enthusiasm and optimism.

She didn't get back to her flat until nearly eight o'clock. There was a message winking at her from the landline. Just for once she did hope it wasn't a client needing her tonight at short notice, but just in case she didn't (as she longed to) kick off her shoes before pressing the button. It was Charity.

'Sis? Knowing the size of your flat, I imagine you'd have picked up if you were there. I just rang to tell you, we've done it. For further details phone back.'

Once Charity and Mac had decided, they'd done it at once. It was frightening how quick and easy it was to get married. Afterwards they went to a pub opposite the register office. Mac said, 'I don't imagine we're the first couple to sit here with this look on our faces.'

'What look?' she said, giving him his cue.

'Shell-shocked.'

But the thing was that now they *knew*. Whatever anyone said, whatever the world thought, whatever the future held, they had said the words that bound them together in the eyes of the law.

'At last,' he said dryly, 'the respectability we craved!'

'I never craved—'

'A very lame joke.'

'One thing we must do. We *must* tell my family.'

'Indeed we must,' he agreed. 'Your parents in particular.'

He could not for the life of him imagine this meeting, or the exchange that would take place. For him and for Charity, getting married was an entirely personal choice, a statement of intent. It removed uncertainty and, for him, ensured the future for the wife who would probably live the entire second half of her natural term without him. He had rewritten his will. But her parents were going to have to accept that she had tied herself to a man at least ten years older than them, without warning or discussion. Since leaving the army, Mac had spent his entire adult life running a school which espoused, and celebrated, liberal, democratic values. But the thought of telling the Blyths made him sweat tacks. The phrase 'dirty old man' lurked threateningly in the back of his mind — is that what they would think?

Knowing her parents as she did, Charity was less anxious. One thing was certain, there would be no scene. Their natural openness and good manners would prevail. Afterwards, they'd have to process it, and after *that* was when her mother would want to talk. She would make it plain that she was 'on her side', always, and that's what would make it difficult — that decisive moment of separation, of gently but non-negotiably aligning herself with Mac. That, Charity told herself, would take some handling.

'Shall we go down tomorrow?' she asked. 'While we can?' They had both taken a couple of days off before the start of term. This was generally a busy time for Mac, preparing for the start of the academic year and the new intake, but under these special circumstances he had left the maths master to deputise for forty-eight hours. All these people, he reminded himself, would have to be informed if he and Charity were to conduct any sort of normal life at the school, however intermittent. He was not a draconian head – part of Brushwood's ethos was that he should lead by example – but a marked churning in his stomach reminded him that this was how pupils must feel when asked to come and see him.

'I think we should,' he said. 'Grasp the nettle.'

Charity rang three times and received no reply, before calling Honor, who told her they were away.

'They've gone on a cruise to celebrate the house sale. Or get over it.'

'A cruise?'

'I know, they always said they wouldn't, but they liked the idea of the Eastern Med – they're going to some incredible places—'

'How long for?'

'A fortnight. They'll be back in a week, and straight into the rented house till the one on Cliff Parade's ready.'

Honor could hear her passing this information on to Mac.

'Have you told them yet?' she asked. 'Is that why you wanted to come down?'

'You guessed it.'

'It'll be fine, you know that,' said Honor.

'You haven't said anything have you?'

'Of course not! Not to anyone. But I'm just sure it will be. Moving from Heart's Ease was such a huge decision, especially for Ma, it's given them a whole new perspective. They don't expect everything to stay the same any more.'

Hugh put his arm around his wife's shoulders.

'Look at us,' he said. 'Like a couple in an advertisement.'

He felt her laugh. 'Sanatogen?'

'I was thinking more Campari.'

'They were in a balloon, weren't they?'

'That was Martini.'

'Picky.'

'All too long ago.'

They were leaning on the rail of the *Princess Marina*, the black shot silk of the sea all around. Band music floated on the warm air. Tomorrow they'd be putting in at Heraklion, whose lights were visible on the far side of the ship, but from here there was just the shimmering sea, and a sky fizzing with stars.

'We did the right thing,' said Hugh. 'Coming away, doing this.'

'Of course,' said Marguerite. 'It's good to gain some perspective on everything . . . the house, the family . . . I get so tangled up.'

'That's what I think.'

'I know I worry too much.' She touched her head briefly against his shoulder. 'It must be quite wearing to live with.'

'Ye gods! I'm worn out!'

She smiled. 'Stop it. I'm trying to be more self aware.'

'I knew what I was getting into.'

They relapsed into silence. It was late in the evening and the band had moved into a slower phase. Hugh swayed gently to the tune of an old Nat King Cole number.

'Listen.' He joined in softly. ' ". . . it will be forever, Or I'll never fall in love . . . in a restless world like this is . . ." '

'Care to dance, Daisy?'

She didn't answer, but stepped inside his waiting arm. Together they moved gently, from light to shadow and back again, in time to the distant music.

Twenty-Seven

The young man from the estate agent's was fifteen minutes early, so he let himself in. Truth be told he'd got here early on purpose. He really liked this house, Heart's Ease. The office had wanted to take out the apostrophe, which was nothing but a nuisance, but the vendors had insisted it be left in.

Nice people, the vendors. He could tell it was a wrench for them selling up, and he could see why. The house wasn't the biggest or grandest they'd had on their books but in his humble opinion it was the nicest. The all-important location was second to none (he always mentioned, though never needed to point it out again – people gasped), but it wasn't only that. The place had a good atmosphere, the lovely garden with its view over the bay and especially the interior.

He left the door open and went for a wander. Even empty, the rooms had a soft, sweet smell that breathed welcome. The

kitchen could do with a re-furb and the decorative order wasn't
great – the gloss on the skirting boards was chipped, and you
could tell how long it was since the walls had a lick of paint
because there were ghosts where the pictures had been. Lots of
pictures. And books! When he'd first come to do the valuation
he couldn't believe how many there had been, not just on shelves
and in cases, but piled on tables here there and everywhere, how
could people have so many books? He didn't have the heart to
tell them that this number of books could actually put people off
– that these days potential purchasers liked to see a bare, pared-
down house so they could project their own ideas . . . In the
end it hadn't made any difference. Out of the six lots he'd
shown round two had fallen in love with the place instantly, and
one couple – the one he knew would be stretched on the price
– had hung in there as if their lives depended on it, and the
woman was coming for a final look-round before completion.

There were a lot of keys and he didn't bother to undo the
door into the 'loggia' (they'd had to look that word up, a conservatory in normal language). He went upstairs and into the master
bedroom. There was a little single bedroom leading off it, a
dressing room. He'd pointed out that if the two were knocked
through you'd have a magnificent double-aspect bedroom into
which an ensuite could be incorporated, or a glitzy walk-in
wardrobe . . . but for once his heart hadn't been in this selling
point. He liked the place as it was.

He stood for a moment in the bay window overlooking the
garden. In September the rhododendrons formed a rampart of
glossy green, one or two of them so big that through the gaps
in their branches you could see the dark cave inside. And there
was the hill with its crown of scotch firs, known as the Fort,
what a garden for kids to play in, and this was only about a third
of it! He was just turning away when a movement caught his
eye. He paused, eyes narrowed, peering. He thought he'd seen
a figure, someone looking back up at him from among the leaves
. . . but there was nothing there now.

As he started back down the stairs he heard tyres on the
drive, and glanced out of the window on the half-landing.
The purchaser's battered Volvo was just drawing up. He ran
down the last flight and went out into the porch to greet her.

She was a lovely, rather scatty lady, all the prettier for not knowing how pretty she was. She sent him a wave and a 'Hi, hang on—!' and bent to undo a child seat in the back. After a brief struggle she hauled out the baby – going by his sister's he reckoned it was about a year – and came over with it sitting on her hip.

'Hello! Sorry if I kept you waiting, the others are at school, and I was hoping to come unencumbered but my arrangement fell through, so here we are . . .' She bustled past him, her mane of hair swinging merrily. 'You know, I can't believe this is ours, that we're actually going to live here!'

She turned to him, a massive smile on her face.

'I may have to hand him to you for a moment while I wield my tape measure, is that alright?' She was already passing the baby as she spoke, and he took it from her.

'All part of the service.'

'He's used to being passed round, he won't give you any grief.' She felt around energetically in her bag for tape measure and notebook. 'He'd probably like the garden if you could be bothered.'

'OK – sure.'

He went out of the front door and carried the baby – heavy, soft and warm, no trouble at all – round the side of the house and out on to the lawn. For no particular reason except that he'd not done so before, he climbed the three tussocky steps on to the Fort. He could see the mother, busy busy, reaching up to measure the hall window; she gave them another quick wave.

The baby was studying him calmly at close quarters.

'Hey, look over there . . .' He pointed, and to his surprise the baby did, also stretching his arm, copying. 'That's yours, that is. Not bad, eh?'